Shadow with N

C000217371

Mark Laming

First Published in 2018 by Blossom Spring Publishing
Shadow with Nowhere to Fall Copyright
© 2018 Mark Laming
ISBN 978-1-9996490-6-7
E: admin@blossomspringpublishing.com
W: www.blossomspringpublishing.com
Published in the United Kingdom. All rights reserved
under International Copyright Law. Contents and/or
cover may not be reproduced in whole or in part without
the express written consent of the publisher.

For Michael, my father, for being an
inspiration to me.

Chapter 1

There was a palpable feeling of unease in the air as the woman, clutching her handbag to her chest, hung back in the doorway of the chapel of rest. Funeral director, William, a large man with overlapping front teeth and bulging cheeks, spoke kindly telling her to take her time. She was aware he was short of breath and noticed the beads of sweat that ran down his forehead. Before he shuffled out of the room, she detected the smell of his expensive aftershave that reminded her of her late partner, John, and this really upset her.

On hearing the door click shut, she shuddered as her eyes focused on the large brown coffin and regretted having chosen such a dark colour. John would have hated the imitation oak as well as the enormous silver handles. Then again, at the time she was in deep shock, and the process of arranging the funeral was all a blur.

Standing totally still, the silence was unbearable. She took in the room with the white sterile walls devoid of any pictures. The only furniture was the heavy wooden coffin stand and hardback white chair with a floral cushion. She gazed at the wooden casket lid and long silver screws that lay in a box on the carpet and shuddered. Aware of the sweet scent of roses that wafted into her face, she was unable to see where it was coming from and wondered if it was being pumped through the wall into this cold and awful place.

Her eyes strayed to the window with partly raised blinds that afforded a view of a small but manicured garden. A rusty metal archway with pink climbing roses stood next to a path leading to a garden shed. An array of colourful perennial flowers came into view, many competing for space in the crowded beds. Her gaze was drawn to the oblong lawn covered in daisies that bordered onto a tangle of woodland from the neighbouring industrial unit.

A moment of terror filled her mind. It was the prospect of seeing her partner lying motionless in that horrible box. Yes, she'd been with him when he died after being rushed to hospital following the car crash, but being here today in the chapel of rest brought home that she would be on her own from now on. At the time, with all the mayhem that accompanies an intensive care unit, she held his limp hand and kept whispering she loved him. Her tortured head kept playing over a new scenario. She would not have insisted he collect her cleaning from town leaving him to enjoy his well-deserved day off work. There was to be no turning back off the clock. Twenty-three minutes was all it took for him to slip away from her, no longer than the short journey to reach their home in South London.

Today she felt nervous about crossing the room to be with him. Her thoughts harboured on his cold lifeless form. A few days previously she'd brought in his favourite blue-striped shirt and wondered if they had done up all the buttons or just a few. Crazy macabre thoughts raced through her mind like the cremation process and whether the ashes would truly be those of John. Some time ago, she'd assured him that if anything happened to him, he would definitely not be buried. John hated the thought of being left in a hole to rot and had given specific instructions in his will to be cremated.

She read somewhere that during the embalming process they drain all of the blood to preserve the body. Also, the corpse's mouth was padded with cotton wool to convey a happier appearance. She hoped the mortician hadn't left John with a smile on his face. He had been a happy man but rarely smiled; death shouldn't be the catalyst for him to start looking pleased with his lot. She had insisted they left him wearing his glasses and not cut him when they shaved his handsome face.

Taking small steps, her breathing increased and her heartbeat started to race. On reaching the coffin she glanced down at the body that was nestled in a cream silk interior with a cushion supporting his head.

She stepped back and gasped. Her scream was heard by everyone in the offices.

'That's not my John!'

Within seconds, William, the owner of the business was at her side as were a number of staff who were shocked to hear her cry out that the man in the coffin was not her partner. The funeral director was panting for breath having run from the front desk. Struggling to control the shaking of his arms, he managed to grasp the distressed woman's hand before ushering her to his office.

Her loud sobbing continued for some considerable time.

* * * *

William Jones organised for Beth his secretary, to sit with their client whilst he went off to make her a drink. Before doing this, he went to the adjoining office and anxiously selected file number 3732 John Johnson. He read the death certificate before gazing at the photograph of the dead man's face. They always took a photograph, as it was their way of checking the correct corpse was in the coffin prior to transferal to the hearse. The brass nameplate on the casket lid was included in their checks.

Then, there was the paperwork, computer backup with the unique numbering and of course the tag tied to the toe. The chance of getting the wrong body was highly unlikely.

As he carried the documents along the corridor to the chapel of rest, he glanced momentarily at the delivery of formaldehyde that his son had not stored away in the embalming room. How many times had he spoken to him on the subject of health and safety? Just recently Steven seemed to have his head in the clouds and been making quite a few mistakes. He would have to speak to him again.

Glancing at the brass plate on the coffin lid, his worst fears came true.

The inscription read: John Jonson and not John Johnson. With just one letter missing from the mostly identical names, the worst of nightmares was unfolding and about to shake his family business to the roots.

He pulled away the sheet covering the corpse to grasp the foot, revealing the plastic identity label. They definitely had the wrong body on display. The poor woman had been subjected to a terrifying ordeal all because of their mistake. And worse still, only days before they had buried the wrong person. Her partner now lay six feet down in St Michael's graveyard.

Chapter 2

William Jones' son, Steven, sat uncomfortably in the leather chair in the side office waiting for the berating he was about to receive. The twenty-six-year-old man, with the tidy haircut and immaculately trimmed beard, hung his head down low as his father's voice rose to shouting point.

The owner of the funeral company smoothed down the fabric of his black waistcoat covering a somewhat rotund belly. 'The police will soon be involved, as will both sets of lawyers. I can't believe you got the final sign off so wrong.'

With his hand on his forehead Steven muttered, 'I'm sorry, Dad.'

'For God's sake Steven, sorry is not enough. This is a bloody disaster. Wheeling out the wrong body would have been bad enough, but burying this woman's loved one is unforgivable. The heartache we've brought to these two families is unreal. There will have to be an exhumation!'

Steven looked shocked at the idea and fidgeted with the lid of a blue felt-tipped pen that he had been clutching since entering the office.

William paused for a moment to straighten some files on his desk. He gazed at the antique brown furniture, then at his grandfather's American wall clock that was running slow. His recent attempts to adjust the old clock had failed. He had refused Steven's offer of help and continued to push the clock hands forward to set the correct time. He acknowledged his office needed a fresh coat of paint, something lighter on the walls than the historical brown that had been repainted so many times. It was a depressingly dark place to work. The rusty metal-framed window with red, velvet curtains had seen better days. The view was over an industrial site and at times the noise from the engineering company was excessive. His office was definitely gloomy with bookshelves crammed full of catalogues of coffins, linings and handles. How he now wished he hadn't ignored Steven's advice to buy iPads to show grieving relatives' images of the various woods and accessories that were available for the caskets.

In essence, the company had not moved with the times, mainly because of his insistence on holding onto the past. One office that had been transformed was his son's and long gone was the old-fashioned furniture and hideous floral curtains. Steven's modern light, grey desk with matching filing cabinet was complimented by a blue deep-pile carpet that was soft to walk on. His space was welcoming and hanging on the cream walls were paintings of magnificent steam trains. Steven had always been a railway enthusiast; his favourite locomotive was the Flying Scotsman and a model train set could be found in his small terraced house close by.

William switched his thoughts back to the current problem. He positioned both hands together in a pinnacle shape before addressing his son. 'Our reputation is at stake here – nobody will ever trust us with their loved ones after this. We will be sued, and our company may even fold.'

Steven was now ruffling his hair and furiously scraping at his scalp. He was looking anywhere but at his father. His eyes strayed to the various silver-framed, sepia photographs that held the history of the family business that was over a hundred years old. Magnificent jet-black horses with plumes of feathers pulled a glass-sided hearse. One of the images pictured his great-grandfather in front of the funeral procession. His hair was parted in the middle with long sideburns and a moustache that portrayed a serious gentleman going about his duty. With his magnificent black top hat held at chest height, he was standing totally erect in his long, tailored, dark coat. The founder of the company looked so proud. Steven's father coughed loudly. 'I'm still waiting for an explanation.'

When Steven replied, it was in a nervous voice. 'I was having a really bad day. Both clients had similar names and were called John. If only the surnames had been different I may have spotted my mistake. Also, with the lack of staff and you not here, the security checks failed.' Feebly he added, 'But we are insured, aren't we Dad?'

'Not for breakdown of working practices,' came the stern reply.

William stared at his son before reaching into the drawer of his desk for a tissue to wipe his damp forehead and sighed. Earlier in the week he had been aware of the two bookings with similar names. Why hadn't this rung a warning bell? Probably because they had so many checks in place, nothing like this could possibly happen. He had also been confident his son, who had clocked up nine years in the family business, was on top form. William hoped he would eventually take over from him but, after this colossal mistake, now he wasn't so sure.

On the day of the mix up, it was William who had headed up the funeral whilst his son stayed behind saying he didn't feel well. He'd commiserated with the relatives, but still interred the wrong corpse. Unaware of his company's blunder, he had felt proud of the service they offered, but as proprietor of the business, he should have seen this one coming. He now regretted not reminding Steven and the staff to be fastidious with their checking of this particular client. He had too many other things on his mind.

Continuing to vent his anger, he raised his voice not caring if the staff in the adjacent room heard him. 'I accept this was an incredibly rare case of similar names, but how many times have I told you to double check everything.'

Steven took off his glasses and nervously bent the arms back and forth. 'I reckon it happened when I dropped the two client files on the floor. I stuffed the papers and photos back in the folders and the tags must have gone back in the wrong place.'

William shook his head and muttered, 'Shit.'

Steven gazed up at the antique clock on his father's office wall. Twelve painfully slow strikes of the bell followed with the return to the noisy and foreboding tick-tock.

'I must have tied the wrong identification markers to the feet of both men. I did one in the morning and the other at lunchtime. When I pulled out the body from the store in preparation for the burial, I ignored the spelling and glanced at the name on the foot. I thought I had the right corpse in the coffin.'

'Bloody hell Son! You are usually so professional.'

Nervously tapping his fingers on the desk William whispered, 'And I bet you didn't carry out the photo check of the face, did you?'

Steven shook his head. 'I was under pressure waiting for you to come in to help me. It all got too much for me. Earlier we had the delivery of coffins from the new supplier. The special arrangements for the linings and handles had been ignored, so I ended up having a right go at them. When you finally arrived, you weren't interested when I told you about my morning. I really needed your support, but you weren't there for me!'

William shook his head, 'For God's sake, just listen to yourself. I was late coming in. It's not the first time you have been left on your own. I remember when I was trying to get changed for that burial, you were flapping around like the business was about to go under. I thought you said you had a handle on things and wanted to take the reins.'

In a whisper of a voice that took a few moments to grow, Steven said, 'I left two messages on your phone, but you didn't ring back.'

This time William thumped the desk in frustration. 'Give me strength, I told you I was held up! What more do you want me to say? We all have bad days – you just needed to man up! You know it is our golden rule that we always use a second member of staff to witness the release document. You must have done this hundreds of times. Who assisted you on the checks?'

Steven stood up and loosened the thin black tie around his neck. Unsteady on his feet, he held onto the desk for support. His father was now concerned for his son's wellbeing and urged him to sit down again.

Holding a hand on his forehead Steven muttered, 'It was Peter. He was having trouble with one of the cars and when he finally came back in, I rushed things.'

'What do you mean rushed things?' William replied, emphasising the last two words.

'As Peter went through the form, I lied saying I had already checked everything thoroughly.'

'You ruddy idiot! You do realise this is gross negligence. You also put our employee in an awkward situation.'

'Look Dad, it's crystal clear I am to blame. I even screwed the lid on the coffin. I'll make a statement to the police. One other thing, Beth picked that morning not to come in, I thought you told me you'd spoken to her about her time-keeping.'

William ignored the remark. 'Don't make excuses – even if Peter hadn't been able to help, you could have called on driver Harry to assist. I know he's not trained for this but, as manager, you could have worked together and prevented this mess.'

William gave his son short shrift as he insisted he left

him in peace. With his large hairy hands covering his face, his eyes peered through fat fingers to the picture of his wife. He lent forward in his chair to turn the silver frame face down. Recently, he'd taken his eye off the ball too many times. If only he'd been in the office and not mucking about with his fancy woman, he may have saved the day.

* * * *

With all the bedlam that accompanied a crisis, there followed a protracted investigation with much exposure in the local press and TV. The days that followed saw irreparable damage to the reputation of William's company, resulting in a slow-down of business. As the lawyers got stuck in, this left William and his son unsure of their future.

New instructions from the family's solicitor for the corpse they should have buried were put in place. It must have been heart-rending for the unfortunate family who believed they had already buried a relative and now had to go through a further interment. This time another firm would be trusted to look after the arrangements.

The build up to the exhumation was unbearable for all concerned; digging up a recent grave was the stuff of nightmares. The partner of the deceased must have wished it to be over as quickly as possible so as to make new arrangements. This time she would make sure it was a cremation. Her solicitor had mentioned there was likely to be a financial settlement. No amount of money or people saying sorry was going to undo her suffering, or for that matter erase the thought of another family having buried him.

* * * *

The removal of the body from the grave took place in the early hours on a rainy Tuesday morning, with policemen present to deter any press or onlookers. Even at that ungodly hour, the roar of the traffic on the Brighton Road shattered the peace of the graveyard.

A flimsy, white, mud-stained tent that stood over neighbouring gravestones was anchored down with large metal pegs. Industrial bright lights held high above the opened grave cast eerie shadows around the cemetery. The mostly Victorian gravestones held a fascination for people by daylight, but in the dead of night the graveyard was a scary place. Placed on the slippery grass was an oblong grey tarpaulin that was piled high with mud from the grave that was being emptied. The thud of the wet earth being stacked from the deep hole was an unsettling sound for those present.

Everyone was wearing wellington boots and the squelching sound of wet mud continued as the gravediggers dug deeper. The photographer who recorded the whole procedure kept being asked to stand back as the grim process of exhumation continued. The floral tributes from relatives and friends were dutifully stored in heavy plastic sacks. The sound of shovels continued for thirty minutes until the distinct sound of metal hitting the wooden coffin was heard. With care they started to uncover the box that held John's remains.

Heavy rain pounded on the exposed muddy casket as the gravediggers raised it from the deep abyss. Unfortunately, the lifting straps slipped several times resulting in it falling with a heavy thud as it hit the bottom. Eventually, it lay on the uneven ground with the red ropes still attached to the handles. Of course, as already established, the body they were retrieving bore no relation to the brass nameplate.

* * * *

The following day, Steven went back to his office to complete some paperwork. He slumped heavily down in the leather office chair and sighed. He nervously picked at the stitching on the seat and kept kicking the tips of his highly polished black lace-up shoes against the side of his desk.

He was soon joined by his father who refused to sit down and wandered over to the window to raise the net curtain. A white handkerchief was extracted from his suit pocket to wipe a mark off the glass, then used to dab beads of sweat that had formed on his forehead.

Breathlessly he said, 'Thank God that kind woman is not taking any action against us. I wish I could make it up to her.'

Steven held his head down low. 'There's not much chance of doing that Dad, is there? What worries me is although the customer we failed is not taking legal action, what about the other client? I've hardly slept for days and I feel really rough.'

'Me too,' replied the older man.

'Dad, if you don't take care of yourself you'll drop dead. You've been out of breath all morning. I keep asking you to go back to the doctor. Your heart scare last year should have been a wake-up call. How about I ring to get you an appointment?'

'Stop worrying about me… I'm fine.'

With his back to his son he stared out of the window. How he would have preferred to be out in the garden rather than having this conversation with Steven.

His thoughts were interrupted. 'I let you down badly. I think I ought to leave the business to find a job elsewhere, something different from this trade.' Steven laboured the point, 'What do you think?'

Still looking at the garden, William shook his head. 'No, you're not going anywhere. You have to stop blaming yourself. I'm as much at fault after all it's my name over the door. I should have been there on that morning. I told the police it was my fault and I don't want you contradicting my statement. Would you like me to make you a cup of tea?'

There was no response and then William heard the thud. He turned swiftly and to his horror saw Steven slumped over his desk.

William cried out for help, struggling to lift him back into an upright position.

'Steven, wake up, for God's sake, wake up! What's

wrong with you?'

He battled to free Steven's black tie and undo the top button of his shirt. As the main first-aider for the company his head was buzzing with what to do next. He was horrified not to find a pulse. He pressed his hand firmly against his son's chest and thought he felt the ribcage rise, but knew it was just wishful thinking. He screamed out for help again, all the time kept saying aloud, 'Please God, not Steven.'

Beth, the office secretary, ran into the room and was shocked to see William propping up his son. She burst into tears and remembering that the two of them were friends, William realised this scenario must have been very frightening for her.

She helped him drag the young man onto the deep-pile carpet then pulled out her smart phone to call for an ambulance. There was much noise in the room as the staff became aware of the owner of the company and his secretary who were desperately trying to save Steven's life.

Beth started to give mouth-to-mouth resuscitation followed by CPR. She suddenly stopped and with a look of helplessness on her face, she shook her head, but William begged her to continue.

When she moved away her waterfall of tears said it all.

Her boss screamed, 'Get out of the way! I'm not sure you were doing it properly; I'll have a go. You chase up the ambulance.'

He moved over to Steven and began to pump the

young man's chest. Not pausing even to wipe away the never ending stream of tears that clouded his eyes, he persisted relentlessly. 'He's not gone. I know they will save him when they get here.'

William struggled to pull the young man on to his side. When one of Steven's arms tumbled heavily onto the carpet everyone in the room gasped. Rocking him from side to side and ignoring Beth's suggestion to lay him down, William refused to give up.

The entire staff was now present and the realisation that Steven had died began to sink in. They were all used to death, but this was different. He was so popular with everyone and now he was gone.

The wait for the ambulance was unbearable. Beth placed an arm around William, but he pushed her away as he continued to stare down at Steven who looked like he was sleeping. He stroked his son's lifeless face. 'Come on don't give up on me. The ambulance is almost here.'

When the medics finally arrived, they had to prise William away from Steven's body. They went through the process of trying to revive him but quickly established there was nothing more they could do.

The police were involved, and statements were taken from William and Beth. The staff were sent home leaving the owner and his secretary to lock up. A notice was posted on the door that the business was closed until further notice. Fortunately, there were no other funerals to arrange; orders had dried up as the word had got around that this company was experiencing problems.

William made the rash decision to close the business.

Enough was enough; he was a broken man with no wish to continue in the trade. One hundred and three years of trading was about to come to end. Just before locking up the premises he went back to Steven's office to stare down at the floor where his son had passed away and wept loudly. Then he remembered Joan his wife would shortly be arriving at East Croydon station having returned from her shopping trip in the West End. How was he going to tell her that their son had died? He set off on foot to walk up the busy Cherry Orchard Road with vans and lorries pumping out fumes. It normally took fifteen minutes to reach the station, but today he did it in twelve. Caring little for his health, he kept punishing his body with every step he took.

He caught sight of Joan walking through the busy concourse. As he reached her she was concerned to see him looking so desperate. He steadied himself by a shop doorway. His breathing was hurting his chest and, unable to form his words, he continued to stare at his wife. Gasping for breath, he was dribbling and kept wiping his mouth with the back of his hand. In his confusion he knocked off his glasses, which fell onto the concrete floor. A young man picked them up and enquired if he needed help. Above the noise of the railway station Joan was frightened to see her husband in this state.

She shouted, 'Calm down, take deep breaths and tell me what's happened. There's nothing we can't sort.'

* * * *

17

The hospital later confirmed Steven had died of catastrophic heart failure and that a post-mortem would follow in a few days.

When William finally went to bed that night, he just knew there would be no escape from the nightmare that was to continue whether he was asleep or awake. He lay next to his wife who was still weeping and kept trying to comfort her. How could he tell her he'd let Steven down so badly? All he wanted to do was get up and go for a walk, but he could hardly leave his wife, could he?

His mind was doing somersaults conjuring up images of Steven lying so still but never waking. He tried to sum up his life and felt a deep shame; in in his mind there was one remaining option. He'd close the company down and sell to the property development company who'd been hounding him to agree to the sale. The one million pound sum he'd share with his wife allowing him to start all over again. First, they had to bury Steven and when the moment was right he'd tell Joan about his affair. Two long years of switching between lovers was unforgiveable. Joan deserved better than him. He knew that he had to confess and that his wife would insist on divorce. Four years ago she'd warned him that this was his last chance.

William's head was pounding with a voice that kept repeating the words – *If you hadn't been entertaining your secretary Beth in a hotel off the Sutton Road that morning, instead of supporting Steven, the poor lad wouldn't have been under so much stress.*

On that fateful morning of the mix-up of bodies, William was with his employee who was half his age. Just before midday in a budget hotel on the first floor overlooking a busy shopping complex, the couple kicked off their shoes and dropped their coats on the faded carpet.

William was anxious to kiss the young woman and held her against the wall running his hands all over her clothes feeling her sensuous body underneath the fabric. Her short tartan skirt rode high every time he pulled her close. Their gasps of excitement led to a frantic struggle as she ran a hand under his shirt then lower which made him cry out with excitement.

Carrying her to the gigantic bed he lowered her onto the floral duvet where he peeled off her skirt. He could see the outline of her small breasts and nipples through the flimsy shirt and became very excited. Stripping off, he launched his sixteen stone onto the sprung mattress to continue with their lovemaking that would go on for fifteen minutes. It had been an expensive treat paying for a hotel room and there was still the embarrassment of booking out after just one hour.

And now, with what later followed at his workplace, the whole episode of having a bit of fun seemed more like a dirty interlude that was going to bear consequences for him. The few moments of satisfaction with her were brief, and to be honest, nothing to write home about. What she saw in an overweight, sweaty, fifty-year-old man like him remained a mystery. Probably the rumours about her being free and easy were true, then again at the time he wasn't complaining.

His foolishness in playing away from home would haunt him for the rest of his life, but not as much as losing Steven; the lad he had failed. With only himself to blame, right now, it felt like his life had split at the seams. He felt like a *shadow with nowhere to fall.*

Chapter 3

Frustratingly for William, the man from the broadband company failed to show up. If he had known in advance he wouldn't have cancelled that game of golf with his friend Martin. Having wasted an entire morning, he decided to tackle some much-needed housework. Cleaning the apartment was never his favourite occupation, so first he settled down in a chair on the balcony to gaze at the wonderful view of the castle and the glistening sea beyond.

Today something was different on the headland. His eyes focused on bright orange flames and dirty black smoke billowing from one of the houses. Horrified, he moved swiftly onto the balcony to get a better look. The sound of sirens filled the air as he caught sight of a bright red fire truck with flashing lights making its way up the back road. A moment of panic filled his mind as he wondered if anyone had been hurt. He prayed it wasn't Martin's property. Martin was his saviour, the man who'd persuaded him to live here. He was the person who accepted him for who he was and hadn't asked too many awkward questions. He reached for his binoculars on a small table inside the balcony door and looking through them was relieved to see that it was not his friend's house on fire. If he wasn't mistaken it was a larger, white-fronted dwelling three doors further along the lane.

Back inside he glanced at the only birthday card that lay flat down on the smoked glass coffee table. One solitary '*best wishes*' from an old friend in Brighton was all that marked the day. But why should anyone else bother, or for that matter remember him? He was now paying the price for having distanced himself from everyone after

Steven's death and the divorce. Somewhere along the line he'd become a different person, someone who thought more about himself than others.

The events leading up to Steven's funeral had seen him fail to look out for his son. William had piled on far too much responsibility for running the company on his shoulders. There wasn't a day that passed that he didn't think of him and after the funeral he vowed to change his life. He had decided to tell Joan about the affair with Beth, but she insisted they dissolve the marriage. It wasn't the first time he'd strayed from home. He moved out of the family house in leafy Shirley and put the business up for sale. A property company snapped up the land for a housing development. Whilst Joan moved to a flat close by, he rented a room on the approach road to Norwood Junction station. It was at this point that he turned his back on his friends and relatives to start over again.

Over the period of a year William transformed his appearance by slimming down and losing an incredible five stone. He now looked much younger and the previous breathing problems had vastly improved. He'd even shaved his head bare. Gone were the large black-framed glasses, as had the suit and waistcoat. It was smart casual for him now, sporting jeans and pastel coloured shirts.

Whilst William knew he could never change the past he was convinced he could do something about his future. His arrogant manner and fixed opinions on most things had been swapped for a caring attitude that now saw him looking out for others. Nowadays, he was looking through clearer eyes at a beautiful world and a new life. Retrieving his mobile phone from his jeans pocket, he swiped the screen to call Martin. It seemed an age before his friend picked up and there was anxiety in his voice.

'Not a good time. One of my neighbour's homes is on fire. Can I call you back?'

* * * *

Pleased his friend was safe, William decided to have a late lunch down at the beach. He grabbed his sun hat and walked slowly down the narrow lanes past gift shops and busy bars. It was peak season in the sun-drenched medieval Spanish town of Tossa de Mar. The streets were hellishly busy with tourists visiting the Costa Brava and avoiding the holidaymakers was tricky as the place was practically bursting at the seams. Even at this time of day, many of the bars with enormous television screens were churning out football matches. Fortunately, despite all the chaos, the charms of this quaint seaside town were still there to be seen. But why had he chosen to live abroad and in such a busy place? Possibly because, even with all the mayhem that existed, there was a strange feeling of belonging, it was a place that instinctively felt like home.

He had come to love this quaint Catalan town situated just over one hundred kilometers north of Barcelona. In the old town, steep steps led down past small houses with hanging baskets of geraniums and front doors that always appeared to be open. Old men seated on the obligatory white plastic chair enjoyed the warmth of the sun as if they had all the time in the world.

Closer to the main square the road widened with a plethora of gift shops and many bars serving tapas. Everywhere you went, the incredible smell of food on barbeques was so tempting. Fantastic seafood restaurants lined the promenades affording a wonderful view of the sea and boats gliding into the bay.

In the early fifties, the likes of Ava Gardner, Frank

Sinatra and James Mason visited the area. A statue modelled on Ava existed behind the ancient castle walls in the Vila Vella where the restaurants and bars flanked the narrow streets. The bronze monument marked the making of the film *Pandora and the Flying Dutchman* that was shot in the town.

The picturesque bay with the mostly ruined twelfth-century castle was always the welcoming sight that William saw every morning from his balcony. He adored staring at the Mediterranean whitewashed houses with sandy coloured tiled roofs. Jacaranda trees with delicate fern-like purple leaves were plentiful, adding colour to the town. Lining the beach road that weaved its way past the castle, decorative streetlights accompanied tall pine trees that reached high into the sky. Today there wasn't a whisper of a cloud, just the sun belting out its warmth and the squawking seagulls riding the air currents. Brightly painted fishing boats were returning to the bay with their throbbing engines soon to be silenced. Worryingly, there was still the smell of smoke coming from the headland as the fire fighters attended to the burning villa.

Attempting to take his mind off the fire, William walked briskly through the town staring at the tacky gift shops selling towels, fluorescent green inflatable crocodiles and sunglasses, just a few of the cheap gifts to draw in the tourists. Restaurants were grilling calamari and fish on wood-burning stoves and the mouth-watering smell prompted him to increase his pace. He was very hungry and looking forward to his lunch. As he passed the promenade there were stark white hotels resembling office blocks still under construction. A tall yellow crane worked relentlessly in the unforgiving heat that bore down on the site.

There seemed no end to the package holiday companies' efforts to lure further tourists to this magical place.

Most days it was nigh on impossible to find a place to sit on the stony beach with hundreds of umbrellas and sun worshippers occupying every single inch. For those who wished to cool off in the emerald green sea, the stony beach afforded a painful hobble down to the water's edge. All along the beach vendors plied their trade selling watermelons, cold drinks, bikini tops and wraps. Two glass-bottomed boats lay anchored close to the edge of the beach where they bobbed up and down in the waves. Then there were always the speedboats that towed inflatable banana boats which thrilled the holidaymakers clinging on in their bright orange lifejackets.

The attraction for William living in this Spanish town was unquestionably the fact that when the summer holiday season ended, tranquillity returned to the area. During the winter months the tourists left and this resulted in a peaceful and less hectic environment.

Walking along the cliffs to look back at where he lived always reminded him how good life really was. Perched on the headland to the west of the town, a magnificent single story villa commanded one of the best views of the bay. How he longed to wake up every morning in that house with the sound of crashing waves on the rocks below and seagulls squawking overhead.

Martin was right, we never truly let go of the past but do learn to move on, and that's exactly what he was doing. He was learning Spanish, mixing with the locals as well as making friends with the many British people who lived here.

More recently William had started recording the details of his new life in notebooks with pencil sketches highlighting each new chapter. Living in Tossa was what his future was all about, and that's what most of his stories were based on. When asked about his past, he never lied but simply bent the truth. To many of his friends he remained the mystery man from London who rarely mentioned his earlier days back home.

It was meeting Martin in London that firmed up his plans to move overseas. They met in a club in Soho and Martin soon became concerned for his welfare. It was obvious he was stressed and he wanted to help. He kept telling him to keep looking for the sunshine and remain happy. Over a period of three months Martin helped William to get things in perspective and to move his life to the Mediterranean town he himself called home.

As William approached his chosen restaurant he observed a group of policemen, a number of whom looked bored and were playing with their mobile phones. He was aware of people looking up towards the fire; the smell of burning wood still laced the air. Whilst there were no longer any signs of flames, the occasional wisp of grey smoke formed dragons in the blue sky.

His thoughts went out to the owners of the damaged villa. William knew all about disasters. He'd lost his son, wife, home and business; in essence, without Martin's intervention, his life may well have been over some five years ago.

Just a stone's throw off Carrer Sant Ramon, the *Bar de Mar* restaurant came into sight. Housed in a relatively new building with a mostly chrome and marble frontage, this was the eating house that was the talk of the town. Owned by two charismatic men from Birmingham with impeccable manners, their signature remarks each time a drink or meal was served was, *'You are welcome.'*

Judging by its popularity with both tourists and the

Spanish locals, the restaurant was doing well. Local artists displayed their work that was impossibly large to transport home on a plane, but they still sold. Whilst waiting for his drink, William stared at pictures of the Alhambra and the neighbouring city of Granada. The horizontal red and orange stripes confused him, as did the enormous black dots with purple ones fading away. In his opinion the artist's interpretation of the glorious Moorish palace nestled on a hill had been lost.

Enjoying a leisurely lunch, he tucked into freshly grilled calamari and tomato salad accompanied by a glass of Rioja.

He was aware of many tourists outside the restaurant studying the menu board and hoped that one particularly noisy family would choose somewhere else to eat.

Startled by a voice behind him he was pleased to turn to see his friend. Martin, an older man in his mid-sixties who greeted him with a playful punch to the arm. He lowered his heavy body onto the cushioned seat and sighed. Dressed in knee length yellow shorts and a bright red tee shirt he was always in holiday mode. He was wearing a leather bracelet that was probably something he'd picked up from the Thursday hippy market. The heavily tattooed arms depicted male faces and William often speculated on the people these images represented. Today his hair was held back in a ponytail with a brown plastic clasp instead of hanging loosely around his shoulders.

Martin opened his mouth to speak exposing a set of teeth in various stages of deterioration. 'You old lay about, I thought I'd find you in here. You know that fire earlier, well it was quickly put out. It looked a lot worse than I first thought. I think it started in the kitchen.'

'Thank God it wasn't your place. Was anyone hurt?'

Smoothing the tablecloth with his huge hairy hand, Martin eyed up his friend's wine. 'I could murder a drink.'

'Tell me, was anyone hurt?'

Martin, a little out of breath and anxious to attract the attention of the owner, shook his head. 'No, the place was empty. I think the kitchen was destroyed. I imagine the police will contact the owner who is back in the UK. I've met him and his sister, a lady who can be rather annoying at times – I think she must be away at the moment.'

Sipping the last of his wine, William muttered, 'I don't know the owner, do I? What's he look like?'

'Oh, you know, a Londoner, about fifty years of age, tall guy with short frizzy red hair. He's got the annoying habit of finishing off people's sentences. Never brings over a wife or children so I assume he's single, but his sister Sarah permanently lives in the villa.'

'What did you mean about the sister being annoying?'

'I've been round for drinks with them. I suspect she likes her wine a little too much. She's full on and boasts about the books she's had published. Not sure if she's famous. First impressions she did nothing for me. I certainly won't be asking for her autograph or buying her book for that matter.'

William's ears pricked up at hearing the mention of an author and listened with growing fascination. He acknowledged his own solitary attempts at writing would no doubt measure low against this woman's achievements.

Martin pulled off his hideous green-framed glasses to wipe the lenses with a paper serviette. 'I understand she lived in Basingstoke before coming here. She runs a writing group every Friday, at least that's what it says on her advertisement.'

He became anxious to order and grasping the menu card called over to one of the restaurant owners who was admiring his reflection in a huge mirror. The wafer-thin, middle-aged man in tight red trousers and white tee shirt crossed over to their table. The smell of his expensive aftershave was overpowering as he leant over to lay a place for Martin. Holding his body taught as if not wishing to crease his clothes, the man waited patiently to take the order.

In an excitable manner Martin tapped his hand on the table almost knocking over William's drink. 'Neville, I'm parched. Bring me a cold lager and some tortilla and don't go easy on the chips.'

Without any trace of a Birmingham accent, the man with the silver, pointy rimmed glasses wasn't going to disappoint and promptly replied, 'You're welcome.'

'How's Jonathon?' enquired Martin.

The owner ran a hand through his thick, dyed blond hair before waving a dismissive hand at his partner who was clearing away dishes from a table. 'Sulking darling, he's in a huff again and we are not speaking.'

William felt embarrassed changing the subject to whether he'd seen the fire. Judging by the puzzled look on the man's face, he'd missed all the earlier activity. Martin was keen to fill him in and exaggerated on the extent of the damage. But then again at times his friend could be a bit of a drama queen.

'It's one of the villas practically next door to where I live. It's the chap with the sister who writes.'

'Oh her, I'm not sure I like her.'

So here was another person who didn't take a shine to this woman. William still felt sorry for these two siblings having to cope with the fire damage. Neville left them to welcome new diners and they heard the cursory greeting '*you're welcome.*'

William punched his friend's arm and whispered, 'You like him, don't you?

* * * *

Two days later the owner and his sister of the damaged property returned from the UK and were shocked to find every room in the entire villa had been doused down. The fire fighters had contained the blaze but managed to dampen every square inch of the place in the process. Everything was wet or damp and the business of emptying the house began. The back garden became the drying area for all their possessions. Fortunately, the community spirit was there to support the villa owner Tom and his sister Sarah. Teamwork soon saw the interior of the house aired and dried out. Although the kitchen was mostly destroyed where the fire had started, it was hoped that no structural damage to the rest of the property had occurred. An insurance assessor had inspected the damage and was to submit his report. William and Martin joined other British expats with the clear up and were grateful for the pizza and lager breaks that writing lady Sarah supplied.

William was pleasantly surprised by Sarah's friendly nature and hoped Martin's first impression of her was wrong. He gauged her age to be early-forties, possibly a bit younger. She had an attractive slim body and blonde hair tied back with a red ribbon. Dressed in a short yellow dress with a low-cut neckline that revealed a large bust, she looked gorgeous. When they shook hands, she held onto his fingers for a while and it felt good. He was warming to her and was pleased to hear that she soon hoped to be back living in the house. The kitchen, however, would be out of bounds for some time.

Martin's high-pitched voice rang out, 'William is a great writer.'

'Be quiet, you've never seen anything I've written.'

Sarah's eyes lit up at the mention of a new member for her classes. 'That's great what genre do you write in?'

With embarrassment building, William shrugged off the attention. 'Ignore him please. I am a complete novice.'

With a shake of her head she said, 'An author in the wings I suspect. Perhaps you are writing your life story.'

She went on to pat William on the arm which really annoyed him. He hated being patronised but shrugged of the remark.

Uncomfortable with the thought of recording his darkest secrets and revealing them to others, he knew it could never happen. Even Martin didn't know all the details of his past, just that he'd been through a divorce and his head was in a mess. He lied when he said he had always worked in an office. There was no mention of all those years running a funeral business.

Changing the subject back to the fire, he enquired where she was going to live while the villa dried out. She mentioned the name of a small hotel off the main square.

As he turned to leave, she tapped him on the shoulder.

'Why don't you come along to one of my classes? The first one is free.'

His face relaxed into a smile with the suggestion of attending.

Sarah's voice rose slightly, 'We meet this Friday at eleven. We won't be in the house though. It will be warm enough in the garden. I will guarantee the sunshine and will be buying cakes from that incredible bakery on the corner of Carrer Miramar. There will be no pressure to

31

read out your own work. We can talk more, and I can get an insight into your life back home. What did you say you did and where did you live?'

Looking anywhere but at Sarah's eyes, William snapped, 'I didn't!'

On the way back down the steps that led to the castle, William's thoughts dwelled on this woman. Okay, she was friendly enough, but he wasn't keen on all her questioning.

* * * *

Come at eleven the writing lady said. She emphatically guaranteed the weather would be the usual wonderful Spanish sunshine but it wasn't. Torrential rain with dirty dark clouds scudding across the sky gave way to the occasional loud crack of thunder. Any thoughts of attending her class in the garden were dismissed. Perhaps he'd go along some other time.

Chapter 4

The naked lady from Girona with the overpowering smell of body deodorant arched her back with every move as the man beneath her thrust deeper. Her large breasts swung like pendulums as their lovemaking reached its climax. In truth it was no more than a frantic tumble that never measured anywhere near to satisfying. There was no sign of pleasure on her face as her eyes focused on the older man who lay beneath her. When their hurried exchange concluded, she extracted herself from his sweaty body to roll onto the crumpled sheet beside him. He gently kissed her neck and she pulled away.

This was the third time William had shared Micaela's bed since he moved to Spain. It irked him the arrangement extended as far as her going through the motions and no further. What he really wanted was to feel his partner responding but paying for the experience he knew that this was not on the cards. It was an arrangement that cost him dearly and left him wanting. This lady barely spoke and seemed eager to complete her duty. He knew her as Micaela, but in reality, she could have been anyone.

He experienced a brief moment of relief followed by regret, he was determined not to visit her again. He longed to meet someone special to share his life and bed.

He thought briefly of the writing woman and her beautiful body wishing it had been her he had been making love to instead.

He momentarily gazed at the tired looking sixty-something woman as she buttoned up the much-creased white blouse. With rapid speed she secured the zip on the stained white skirt and slipped on her shoes. Without a further word, she waited for him to complete his dressing before leaving the room. This time he shuddered with the image ripping away in his mind of what he'd just done with her. He wondered how thoroughly she washed after each client and vowed to take at least two showers when he got home. Using the services of this lady of the night had to stop.

William quickly left the foul-smelling bedroom with the brass bedhead and dusty oil painting of a rural scene. He walked swiftly away from the building to catch the bus home.

Chapter 5

Late July saw Tossa de Mar celebrate the festival of St Peter that included the procession of the statue of the Virgin Mary. Holidaymakers from the neighbouring seaside town of Lloret de Mar made the short journey to enjoy the food market and various shows put on for the children. Much to William's delight, Catalan circle dancing known as the *sardana* took place on the promenade. The flamboyantly dressed dancers encouraged people to join in which often swelled the circle to fifty plus.

Much of the town turned out with many local elderly Spanish residents joining in with the fun. The bars and restaurants offered all-day refreshments that included tapas and churros with chocolate dipping sauce. Musicians in bright costumes entertained the crowds along with street artists who worked their magic securing money from the tourists. The grand finale was a firework display, scheduled for later in the evening. It was always a spectacular show with rockets illuminating the castle walls and the town below. Many small boats would traditionally be moored in the bay with much partying going on.

Martin arrived at William's apartment at exactly midday. They were going to see the festival before taking in lunch at a small bar on the outskirts of town.

In an anxious voice Martin quizzed him, 'I tried to call you last night, did you go out?'

William shifted from one foot to another and with clenched teeth muttered, 'We are not joined at the hips. I do go out sometimes on my own.'

'Keep your hair on.'

William frowned. 'I just went to Girona for an early

meal.'

'Girona, what did you want to go there for? Oh, I know to see that woman you told me about that was past her sell by date.'

'Don't be rude; she's just a bit older than I would really have liked. Last night was the last time; it's all too tacky and pointless visiting her. I'm finished with all that lark. It wasn't the main reason I went to Girona – I'm keen to buy a clock and...'

With a smile that lit up Martin's face he interrupted, 'You're giving up on the girls you say. Well, does that mean you'll be joining my camp rather than all that romantic stuff with the senoritas?'

'Behave, won't you. You know my feelings on that subject and I respect yours – I'm not interested, end of. I've told you I'm going to meet the right woman any time soon. Anyway, as I was saying, there is this clock shop on one of the bridges and I'm thinking of buying a weight-driven one.'

Martin yawned. 'I can't stand the sound of ticking. I didn't think you liked clocks.'

William was telling the truth, he had visited a horologist to view an antique farmhouse timepiece but it was too expensive to buy. He wasn't sure where Martin had got the idea he disliked the heavy thud of a well-balanced clock. He had always loved his grandfather's Vienna Regulator that hung in the office hallway, the one that his son Steven hated.

* * * *

Back down in the town the streets were already bustling. Saint Peter and the Virgin Mary had already returned from their outing and no doubt there would be a repeat performance later that evening.

It was late morning and most of the bars were packed, as the screening of a British football match happened to coincide with the festival. Many holidaymakers clasped beer glasses as they stood around watching the enormous screens. The two men dodged the families on the promenade heading for the less popular area of the town. Hopefully, it would be quieter in the district where a few of the smaller hotels were situated. Wedged between old colonial-style houses and a gift shop with toys in the window was a small bar that served a mean twelve-euro *menu del dia*.

Normally it was a peaceful place to spend a few hours but today the two men hesitated before entering. The sound of excessive laughter hung in the air. Martin's face turned to one of disappointment, but this did not stop him gazing into the premises to ascertain what was going on.

'Bloody hell, it's Sarah who runs the writing group and it looks like she's had a skinful. I really think she suffers with a drink problem; it's not the first time I've seen her like this.'

William shook his head; another piece of information on this woman was being added to his list. An alcoholic possibly... he hoped not. Martin was often exaggerating about things and hopefully was wrong on this occasion. Surely Sarah was just having a good time with her two friends.

Martin waved a dismissive hand at the window of the bar before turning to leave and that's when they heard Sarah's slurred voice as she called after them. It would have been rude not to talk to her, so they went inside to join the small party. It was obvious the women were well into their drinking session. Sarah raised a glass of wine in their direction spilling some of the contents on the table.

Dressed in shorts that rose high on her tanned thighs, William lifted his gaze to the ample bosom that always appeared to be in holiday mood and determined to be seen. Half of the buttons on the white blouse were undone exposing far too much flesh for his liking. It was at this point he wished he hadn't agreed to accompany Martin for lunch. Trying to avert his eyes from the sorry looking woman, he observed her two companions who were of similar age and equally drunk. Their table was littered with empty glasses and remnants of half eaten tapas.

Sarah's high-pitched quavering voice pierced the air as she addressed her friends. Fortunately, the bar was practically empty and the owner, who appeared to be ignoring the commotion, continued to read his newspaper.

'This is our new man from back home. Say hello to William, he's really sweet. I'm buying – what's your tipple?'

William accepted the outstretched hand and shook it briefly. 'No thanks. I'll get my own.'

Smiling at her friends her voice rang out, 'I'm hoping he will be joining our group.'

Both women smiled in unison, leaving him feeling rather uncomfortable. Listening to his inner voice that was telling him that attending this writing group might not be such a good idea, he frowned. He was quickly forming a picture of Sarah whom he suspected may well be an alcoholic and heavens know what else. One of the other ladies, who was dressed in a short dress and had a hairstyle with an enormous floppy fringe, kept staring at him. He wasn't sure he wanted to go anywhere near her. Her eyes seemed to be fixed below his waist level at the shorts he was wearing. He secretly questioned if all the members of the writing group looked and acted this way?

'William is writing about his life, an autobiography.'

Annoyed with the suggestion, he managed to remain calm. 'That's not what I'm doing; I'm more into short stories. I've just completed one about a farm back in the Spanish countryside.'

Martin tried to suppress his laughter and ended up snorting like a pig which in turn brought about a rendition of crude farmyard noises from the others. When the hilarity died down, Sarah in her drunken state pointed a wobbly hand in William's direction. 'Do say you will come along to the meeting. We are a friendly bunch of people and we'll make you welcome. Now, can I get you another drink?'

He saw the funny side of her comment, as he hadn't yet had a drink.

William tugged on his friend's arm to leave. 'No thanks, we have to be somewhere, maybe another time.'

Then embarrassingly, Sarah leant forward and even more of her bosom threatened to break loose. She stood up to shake his hand. This time she hung onto it for what seemed an age before he managed to gently ease it free.

Back in the street Martin was laughing. 'God, when she bent over like that it got me worried, she was practically falling out of her shirt. I think she has the hots for you, William.'

'Don't even go there. She's really very attractive but I'm not sure I could cope with being with her for too long.'

Martin stopped to stare at a restaurant menu board. 'I'm starving. I think we ought to get some lunch.'

'No, I'm not hungry any longer. Let's just go and get a beer down by the sea and forget about Sarah and her mates.'

Not wishing to miss the chance of winding William up further, Martin stopped in front of the window of the English library shop. 'Look there's her advertisement.'

The flimsy leaflet that was blue-tacked to the inside of the grubby glass window read: *New members always welcome. We are a warm and friendly group. One-to-one attention is always available.'*

As they walked down the street William joked, 'I think we have already seen enough of her one-to-one support. I've been thinking that there must be a less stressful hobby I can adopt.'

When William got back to the apartment, despite what he'd said to Martin, the first thing he did was write up his day. Today had certainly been an insight into a more than strange lady with her obvious baggage of life. It begged the question, just what had she been through to act so strangely?

Her character was ideal to be included in a short piece of fiction he'd call: *The Time it Takes.'* As for attending one of her classes, well he was intrigued to learn more about this woman so perhaps he should consider going along.

Chapter 6

William's choice of decoration and furnishing for the Spanish apartment was totally different to anything he had when he lived back in the UK. His home had been old fashioned with heavy, antique, brown furniture and anaglypta wallpaper that had been painted over many times. The few modern things in the living room were the large TV and his sound system.

Back then, William and his ex-wife's dress sense would be classed as dated. Her long green tartan skirts with enormous safety pin were accompanied by safe high-necked blouses. Casual for him was a pair of smart trousers and jumpers. They both looked much older than their years, possibly a mirror image of their parents. His barrel of a body and neatly combed hair with a parting in the middle set him apart from their friends who had moved with the times.

More recently, living on his own in Spain and achieving his incredible loss of weight, he wondered how many people would recognise him now. His choice of clothes included brightly coloured shirts with long shorts and trainers. He'd even bought an iPod and the wires from the earphones hung over one of his shoulders like escaping snakes.

Where he lived now, the two-bedroomed apartment was small but modern with a bright orange couch and a glass-topped dining table. The pictures on walls were photographs depicting the sights of Barcelona and Madrid, these being places he'd enjoyed visiting. The obligatory coloured floor tiles were wonderfully cool to the touch in hot weather. Set in the corner of the room his new smart television and all-round sound music system were his pride and joy. His latest acquisition was an iPad that he was forever tapping away on checking e-mails, Facetiming, searching the net or checking online banking. He had turned his life around and gone was the frumpy old British man of old.

The view of the bay from the lounge balcony never failed to thrill him. The steep drop down to the quaint Mediterranean town and beaches was an incredible sight to wake up to each morning. He liked observing holidaymakers as they paraded on the promenade. He often enjoyed his alfresco meals sitting at his yellow-tiled table and made notes on the people going about their business. His writing was solely for fun with no desire to get published, just a hobby that made him very happy. He did however have a desire to meet other writers to sample their work to give him a few pointers.

William had just switched on the coffee machine when the intercom rang. He was surprised to hear Martin's voice. His friend entered the apartment looking so despondent and broken with a face that was sallow and drawn. Today, he hadn't bothered to shave and it was obvious he was wearing the same clothes as the last time they last met. His expression was set in a frown suggesting he had the worries of the world on his shoulders. It took a while for William to wheedle out of him the reason for his glum mood.

'I may have to move back to the UK. I've got myself into a mess with my finances and can't afford to live here for much longer. Basically, I'm running out of dosh.'

William was taken aback by his revelation. Thoughts of his friend returning home worried him. 'Don't say that. I thought you were okay on the money front.'

'I suppose I misjudged the cost of living abroad and have gone over the top with buying the house, even though it is a really small one. Day-to-day living is more expensive than a few years back and with the exchange and interest rates being so low, my savings have dwindled.'

'You could always sell the house and move into a small one-bedroom apartment. Surely to remain living in Spain is worth making those changes. And what about your state pension that you are due, that will help, won't it? You will be sixty-six soon so you are entitled to it.'

Martin's face lit up. 'Oh, yeah.'

'Nine thousand pounds a year is not to be sniffed at.'

William smiled, 'I've still got a number of years until I can claim mine. I can help you apply online for it. This extra money and moving to a less expensive property will reduce your expenses.'

Martin suddenly looked much happier. 'Bless you William, I'd completely forgotten about the pension. You always have a solution, don't you? My other issue is my teeth. They are in such a mess the dentist says I need to have many of them extracted. I'm not going to wear ruddy dentures, so I need implants and they are costly.'

'How much?'

'Six thousand smackers for the worst ones in the front.'

'Bloody hell, that's a lot of money.'

'Perhaps I will just have a few done to keep the cost down. I look so ugly with these crooked teeth. It's not surprising I have trouble attracting a partner.'

He suddenly clapped his hands together making William jump. 'You're right – I've lived out here too long to give up and go home. I can downsize on the house; replacing the old nashers will just have to wait.'

William rushed his words. 'No, I'm going to give you four thousand towards them. I've got this ISA that has recently matured – you can have the funds from that.'

'Now hold on. That's really kind of you, but like me you need to save your money. I couldn't possibly accept it, not even as a loan.'

'That's what friendship is all about, you don't have to pay me back. If it means you look and feel better, then that's all that counts.'

Martin threw his arms around his friend and planted a kiss on his cheek. His warm lips momentarily remained on William's face that left him feeling uncomfortable.

Pulling away he said, 'You can cut that out or you keep the crooked teeth.'

'I'm just so lucky having you as my friend. You are the kindest person I have ever known. If I take any money from you it has to be as a loan.'

'Suits me.'

'Thanks, that means the world to me. I just remembered that couple from Coventry you helped last year with sorting out their finances. That was a great thing to do. There are some good guys out there and you certainly are the top man. I don't think you've probably ever hurt anyone in your life, let alone told a lie.'

William remained silent; he certainly didn't feel like one of the good guys. As for being blameless or hurting his family, his track record was far from being unblemished. Okay, since moving over here he'd tried to help others, but he still had a long way to go to redeem himself.

Suddenly Martin's attention switched to a small-framed picture on the wall of a unicorn with a spiral horn.

'That's new. Whatever made you buy that?'

'It just appealed to me. I bought it in that shop where the writing lady, Sarah, advertises her courses. I went back to look at her card in the window. I've been thinking about going along. It may help me to broaden my experience by meeting other writers.'

Martin laughed, 'You mean like those two drunk women who were propping up Sarah in the bar.'

Ignoring the remark, William stood up to study his picture of the unicorn and ran a finger over the surface of the crude oil painting. 'I only paid ten euros for it.'

'You were robbed; just don't leave it to me in your will. Anyway, I best be off as I've things to do.'

'Me too, I have some writing to catch up with.'

'What are you writing about?'

'What do you think? It's a tale about some old guy with dodgy teeth. Now leave me in peace.'

As Martin rose to leave he reiterated his earlier statement about not accepting the money for his dentistry unless it was a loan.

'Okay. I agree it can be a loan, but no more talk of moving. We'll get those teeth sorted and hopefully you can get your house on the market.'

Martin nodded vigorously with closed lips then moved over to hug his friend almost knocking his glasses off.

Extracting himself from the powerful hold William limply said, 'Why you have to do that every time we meet is a mystery. Please don't do it again.'

A thought suddenly came to him that he needed to remind Martin he was off to the UK the following week for four days.

Martin drew breath and lowered his heavy body onto a chair by the table. He rested a huge tattooed arm on the surface and glanced at his blue watch with the silver dial.

'Is it that time of year already when you go home to pay respects to your son? I don't think I've ever told you that I have a son. I haven't seen him for at least twenty

45

years.'

'Wow, that's awful. I assumed you didn't have any children.'

'Mine was a rocky marriage and I wasn't a good father to Billy when he was younger. When I came out he completely disowned me, but then he was in his late teens. He couldn't come to terms with me being gay. Always into trouble, one day our lad went missing and nobody in the family seems to know anything about him any longer. There isn't a day I don't think about him.'

William was shocked. He knew so little about this man's past. The one thing for sure was if his own son were still alive he would never lose touch. He wondered just what he meant about not being there for Billy.

'You never told me you had a son. I am so sorry things have worked out so badly.'

'Just like I don't know much about your past. We agreed never to enquire too much. I don't even know exactly what work you did.'

'I'm not going to bore you with all that now, but I'm going to tell you the whole sorry story sometime soon. No more secrets, I promise. More importantly, have you really tried to make contact with Billy? How about you have another go?'

'I don't even know where he lives or if he's even still alive.'

'There's nothing to lose trying to track him down though, is there?'

He simply replied saying he was frightened to go down that route again. Judging by the distressed look on his face, it was obvious an old wound had been opened. The man was crying and William's heart went out to him.

* * * *

Having said goodbye to Martin, William anxiously pulled out his iPad and signed on to his online banking. He sighed when he saw the balance that seemed to lower every time he looked. His outgoings had recently increased not helped by his purchase of a new bed and eating out so frequently with Martin. Giving that money to his friend felt the right thing to do, but he'd have to watch his own spending in future.

Earlier in the week he'd booked the flight to Gatwick and reserved a hotel room on the outskirts of Croydon. Going back each year never got any easier, but it was imperative to mark the anniversary of his son's death. Five years had passed and there wasn't a day he didn't think about him, or for that matter his ex-wife. It was always a sad event visiting the cemetery and seeing the stone with the inscription that read *'greatly missed and always in our thoughts'.*

On these trips he visited the location of his old work premises, where a development of three storey town houses now climbed into the Croydon skyline. Still the memories of his old undertaking firm rattled around in his head. The saga over the wrong body and the events that ensued were forever tattooed in his mind.

He was still in regular contact with Joan and as the years passed they were getting on better. He just hoped that when he saw her again this time she wouldn't go on about his friend Martin. She'd never met him but was always probing for details about him.

* * * *

Two days before William's trip back to the UK, he plucked up the courage to attend Sarah's class that was being held in the garden of her brother's villa. Not wanting to be the first to arrive, he took a leisurely stroll before arriving at the impeccability manicured garden that over looked the bay. A warm Mediterranean breeze rustled the rose bushes and he watched the gulls swoop over the garden and out of sight. The heat was stifling and many of the writers were sitting in the shade under two enormous green umbrellas taking sips from their water bottles. William felt nervous about joining them and glanced over in the direction of Sarah for reassurance. Unable to catch her eye he turned his attention to the hammering sound and builder's mess outside the villa walls. It was clear the repairs to the kitchen were still on-going.

A sea of grinning ladies' faces greeted him and he felt unsettled that he was the sole male attending. He stared at the selection of folders they carried before weighing up where to sit. The turnout was in the region of ten and William inwardly groaned as he spotted the two women from the bar. The tall woman with the floppy fringe was wearing a denim skirt that ventured high up her thigh. What did she think she looked like?

He turned his attention to Sarah who was now waving madly in his direction. Today she looked quite beautiful in her loose dress and there was something different about her hair. Patting the hard-backed seat next to her, she made it obvious where she wanted him to sit. He smiled wondering what was in store for him. He reminded himself that today was all about seeing if the group suited him.

Momentarily Sarah removed her sunglasses and he spotted her beautiful nut-brown eyes and tiny nose. She ran slender fingers through her fine hair and closed her eyes. William was thinking that perhaps she wasn't the wicked witch that Martin thought her to be. Time would tell.

'Good to see you,' she said smiling brightly.

'Thanks, it's just a taster session, if that's all right.'

Sarah excitedly introduced all of the other women, telling them he was a keen writer. There were nods from tanned faces as everyone stared at him. He was beginning to wish he hadn't worn his shorts rather than trousers. If he wasn't mistaken a number of the ladies' eyes were scanning his body and being the centre of attention left him feeling embarrassed. He quickly retrieved his writing folder from his bag and placed it firmly over his groin.

Then, much to William's relief, the leader of the pack clapped her hands loudly saying they'd better make a start. Amusingly, on the grass by her feet was a long transparent ruler that she reached down for and tapped forcefully on the side of her chair. The chattering came to an abrupt halt.

She glared at one of the women who was still talking. 'One conversation at a time if you don't mind, I'm trying to start the lesson.'

All went quiet as Sarah opened her folder and stared hard at her untidy handwriting. 'Oh yes, Berry sends her apologies for not coming.' She lowered her voice to address the group. 'Women's problems.'

William certainly felt uneasy, wishing there had been just one other man to share his corner. He prayed he wouldn't catch snatches of conversation about the new bras they'd bought or the not so exciting husband back home.

The sound of one of the writer's mobile phones ringing disturbed the meeting.

Sarah pointed a finger at an embarrassed woman in red shorts who was desperately trying to silence her phone.

'Make sure it's on standby or better still turned off,'

she said quite forcefully. 'Now, in last week's session I covered point of view. Whilst writing in third person try not to stray into more than one character's thoughts, unless there is a clear break in the story, so as not to confuse the reader.'

She then addressed one of the other writers and said, 'Mary, perhaps you'd like to read out your homework. I hope you have paid attention to what I've told you and haven't slipped up again like last week.'

William felt sorry for the pretty woman with the steely silver hair who was clearly embarrassed at being put on the spot. Sarah's insensitive manner was far from ideal. What if he read out one of his stories and her critique veered more along the lines of criticism, how was he going to feel?

Mary nervously coughed before pulling out her homework. Attempting to control her shaking hands she started to read. Her tiny voice was just about heard above the jet skis in the bay that were particularly noisy.

Frowning, Sarah interrupted the reading with more banging of her ruler. 'Stop please. You'll have to speak up Mary. Take a deep breath and start from the beginning.'

Just before the clearly embarrassed women continued, Sarah quickly turned to William and whispered in his ear. 'You have to encourage everyone, but honestly this one is hard work.'

Hearing this made him cross; it was a cruel thing to say. This woman was obviously a bully and he felt sorry for the reader who had stumbled with her words. He failed to understand why the leader of the group adopted this attitude, after all these people were paying good money to attend and should not to be humiliated. William muttered to Sarah that he felt sorry for this writer. Her perfunctory glance as she turned to talk to someone else infuriated him.

It was at this point he addressed Mary directly asking if she would like him to read out her work. Sarah shook her head at him, but he still reached forward and grasped the three sheets of typed paper with the generous layer of staples in one corner.

With an air of confidence in his voice he did the story justice. It was a well-balanced tale about a character with a problem but had a satisfying ending. Turning to the author who still looked to be in a nervous state, he said, 'I think that was really well written, well done.'

There was a round of applause; something William was to learn took place each time a writer's work was aired.

Everyone took a turn to read and it was clear there were different levels of ability showing through. Some stuck to prose with average reader appeal, whilst others shone with their incredible twists and turns.

Panic set in when it was his turn to read and reveal his work about a young English man who pretended he'd won the lottery and the lies that inevitably followed. When he finished he got his own satisfying round of applause. Several people said his story was very moving and that he should send it to a magazine to publish.

Sarah looked pleased. 'Well done, William. I would say it sounds more like a novel than a short story. It's obvious you are a very talented writer.'

Feeling proud of himself he joined the others as they took a break to have cold drinks and sample Sarah's cakes. Talking to a number of the women he quickly established that a few had been published back home in weekly women's magazines. The common thread was a number were in the process of writing novels. There were also people who just enjoyed writing and attending the class.

Being in this garden everyone seemed relaxed and there was much chatter as they enjoyed their refreshments. Back home in the UK it was probably raining, and he cast his mind back to his early days when the seeds were planted for his storytelling. Some years ago, he'd briefly attended a group that met in a retired man's house, but it lacked substance with poor leadership. Only the bravest chose to read out their work.

Here in Spain the sun was shining and the other ladies he'd just spoken to were friendly and praised him for helping their colleague. He was warming to the group, but still wary about their leader's manner. Humiliating that woman was unforgivable in his mind.

When the class resumed William witnessed a change in attitude from Sarah. This time she adopted a more professional approach by encouraging her students. She spoke for about twenty minutes going through the necessity to edit one's work before reading it out. There were tips for structuring a compelling story. Capturing the reader's attention for turning the pages was paramount. A satisfactory ending to either a short story or novel was expected. The most satisfying conclusion lay in a main character-achieving redemption.

William sat on the uncomfortable chair without any cushion and was pleased to be learning so much from this woman who obviously knew her stuff. He wondered if she'd written anything that had been published and decided to search the internet later for any evidence.

Sarah set the homework for the following week and closed her folder signifying the end of the lesson.

Turning to William she said, 'You will come again, won't you?'

'Yes, I think I will, but not for a week or so as I'm

going back home for a few days.'

Sarah excitedly grasped both of his hands and shook them a little too enthusiastically.

As he was about to leave he felt a tap on his shoulder. Turning around he was dismayed to see the woman with the crazy haircut. He observed her tight, sullen face. His eyes travelled down to the short skirt and back to the outline of an enormous black bra that was visible through her white shirt. Her lipstick was the colour of dark red blood and large earrings with silver balls swung into the hideous blue locks of hair.

'Oh, hello, it's you…'

'I just wanted to say it was good to see you again. That was kind of you reading out Mary's homework. Now William, a few of us go to a bar after the class, would you like to join us?'

'That's really kind of you, but I'm so busy I will give it a miss.'

Busy, what nonsense, he had all the time in the world. There was no way he was going with this woman to a bar or for that matter anywhere else. Brushing away the hair from her eyes she gave him a toothy smile. 'That's not a problem. There's always next time.'

* * * *

On reaching his apartment he pulled out his iPad and searched the web for evidence of Sarah's writing credentials. Sure enough, on the main book sites there were three of her novels with superb reviews. The most striking comment was from one of the main UK tabloid newspapers that praised her writing. It would appear that Sarah Barney was an author of some repute. Her most recently published book was set in Helsinki. It featured a Finnish office worker who guarded a secret but she was running out of time as the net closed in. Aptly called *Wrong Side of Sanity* the title resonated with William and the bumpy path he'd taken. He promptly downloaded an eBook version onto his device. He couldn't wait to start reading it.

Sarah was a strange woman but there was no denying he was intrigued to learn more about her. He disliked the way she spoke to her writers and wondered just what her past held. In a weird sort of a way he was beginning to feel like she was drawing him to her side. It was a strange sensation and he just knew he had to see more of her.

Chapter 7

The flight from Barcelona to Gatwick was on time with an estimated thirty minutes before touching down. Seated in the front row on the aisle with extra legroom, William relaxed listening to a new album he'd recently downloaded. He was suddenly aware of someone tapping him on the shoulder. It was a young airhostess in her smart green tunic and scarf.

'Sorry to disturb you, sir, but would you mind helping me?'

Unsure what was going to follow he limply replied, 'I'll try.'

'Further back in the plane we have a woman who is feeling poorly. She has an upset stomach and needs to be closer to the toilet at the front. As you are on the aisle, would you mind swapping seats?'

Without any hesitation he readily agreed and followed the wafer-thin girl up the fuselage to the seating directly over the starboard wing. He sat down again and briefly acknowledged two women next to him. William struggled to locate the seat belt straps.

The passenger by him looked familiar, leaving him pondering on just where he'd seen her before. Possibly in the terminal before boarding, or in the restaurant.

'You could be sitting on your belt,' she said.

William shuffled around in his seat and was relieved to retrieve the missing strap and buckle.

'Thanks for that. Tell me, did we meet in the departure lounge?'

The woman tried to stifle her excitement. 'Oh my God, is that you William? It's Beth your old secretary. You look so different being that slim and with no hair; it really suits you. I really didn't recognise you.'

William felt like his heart was about to stop. This was the woman he'd slept with all those years ago. Now here she was back in his life greeting him as a friend like nothing had ever happened.

Beth repeated her question, this time a little louder. 'It is you, isn't it?'

Before he had a chance to reply there was an announcement from the pilot stating that there was severe turbulence ahead and to ensure that seatbelts were securely fastened. Almost immediately the plane shook and momentarily there was the sensation of losing height. There was further shuddering and one of the overhead lockers fell open with an almighty creak. Two of the airhostesses were moving along the fuselage and slammed the lid shut. They were checking people's belts and when they finally reached William an assurance was given that the bumpy weather would soon settle down. He wasn't worried and felt quite safe. More frightening thoughts filled his head, like bumping into Beth again. The past came thundering back and however much he tried to stop his hands shaking, he couldn't. The last episode of this happening was on the day of his son's death. He'd had years of better health and now the involuntary movements of his hands had started all over again.

Beth leaned towards him. She was staring at his arm. 'I knew it was you. Are you okay? I remember you used to suffer with shaking.'

The turbulence had lessened, and William enquired if she had been on holiday.

'Barcelona for a week with my friend who's sitting two rows back. What about you, were you on a break too?'

He shook his head and muttered that he lived in

Spain. Not wanting to reveal the exact location, he simply told her it was a fair distance west of where she had been staying.'

'Wow, you actually live out there; how cool is that. I can't get over how much younger you look. It's like you've been totally transformed.'

'Yeah, I slimmed down and got rid of the suits. Since the divorce I have a new life. How about you?'

'Oh, I'm still in our old profession mainly as a secretary but I also assist more on the funerals which I really enjoy. Don't you miss your old work?'

Fortunately, the wobbling of his hand had settled into a calmer mode, not like his brain that was reliving the old days. In a quiet voice he replied, 'No, undertaking is something I don't want to even think about.'

He was suddenly aware of a man sitting in the opposite aisle listening to his every word and frowned at him. This seemed to do the trick as the passenger turned back to talk to his wife.

William stared at Beth. The reason he hadn't recognised her was the short vivid red hair with intermittent streaks of purple. Also, the glasses she wore; she never wore glasses back then. She was still remarkably thin; then again, she was relatively young in her mid-thirties. Thoughts of lying naked with her in that hotel room suddenly became real again. The excitement of being with a younger woman encouraged him to go that bit longer. Unlike his wife, this girl was happy to experiment in bed taking him to heights he had just dreamed of before. In truth, she must have been mad sleeping with him. He had been an overweight man who was living his life in a time warp. What could she possibly have found appealing about him? On the other hand, she was young and eager to satisfy her needs. She had made him feel great. It was a casual relationship that centred around sex which suited both parties.

Still in question mode Beth asked, 'So, what do you do now? You look too young to have retired.'

'Actually, I have retired really early to enjoy the sunshine and my writing.'

'Are you an author?'

William shook his head and decided he'd had enough of being interrogated. With just ten minutes to landing he lied when he said it had been great meeting her again.

Beth wasn't giving up. 'Are you on Facebook and Messenger? We can chat more.'

Determined not to keep in touch, he told her that he was not on any social media. This wasn't entirely true as he regularly spoke with his friends in Tossa via Facetime.'

'An e-mail address then?'

'No, let's just leave it there Beth, great seeing you and all that.'

Then she whispered in his ear and the bombshells of all bombshells was revealed. The nightmare was gathering speed again.

This time she touched his hand. 'I still miss Steven so much as I know you must do. We were an item for a while and I have something of his which I think you should have back.'

William's mouth dropped open. 'You and him! No, I don't believe you.'

Trying to keep his voice down, he was still aware others may hear him. 'Are you forgetting our time together?'

She now looked embarrassed and was possibly feeling disgusted at the thought of what occurred six years ago with this older man.

'It was complicated; Steven and I were more like

good friends. I have his watch that he left in the flat and I want you to have it.'

William was shocked to hear her say this. He had spent so much time searching for that watch prior to the funeral and it was in her possession. How could she have been carrying on with his son at the same time as him? Determined to get Steven's keepsake returned he pulled out a notepad from his bag. He scribbled down his mobile number and passed it to her. Beth's last words before she left the plane was she would call to arrange for the return of the watch. He pressed the point that he would be in the country for just three days.

Walking towards the baggage collection, William scanned the screens for the designated carousel. He prayed he wouldn't see Beth again. The revelation of her being with his son struck hard. Just what sort of a woman was she? He'd managed to mostly come to terms with the past and now with her turning up it was raking up all the agony again. Taking back the watch was imperative, so he would have to see her again. God, how he wished he'd picked a different airline to travel and none of this would have occurred.

* * * *

The ride in the taxi through Croydon included the usual slow crawl through the underpass. Seeing the high-rise offices lining the dual carriageway, it all seemed a long way from where he now lived. His friend, Martin, had been right when he said Croydon was just like Benidorm, but without the sea or sand. This concrete jungle bore no resemblance to their wonderful Spain. The mountainous sights here were the high council buildings and offices that soared into the dirty grey clouds. There was so much graffiti and litter along the roads that this reminded him just how tidy and clean his Catalan town looked. He felt

59

cold in the back of the taxi and should have asked the driver to shut his window but didn't wish to enter into conversation.

* * * *

The Surrey Brooker Hotel off Moorland Road was a welcome sight. This was the place he always stayed, having consistently enjoyed the accommodation and locality to the shops. The lavishly decorated rooms boasted a sunken bath that you could fully stretch out in. The sumptuous king-size bed was always comfortable after traveling. He enjoyed dining in the hotel as it offered good English cuisine along with a bar that served cocktails. It was ideally located for visiting his ex-wife, Joan and for seeing Steven's grave.

On settling into his room, he unpacked before making a cup of tea, he rang Joan who sounded upbeat. She kept saying she was looking forward to seeing him. She insisted he let her collect him the following afternoon at six o'clock from the hotel. Her suggestion that he should go into town to see the revamped Whitgift shopping centre was dismissed. He had no intention of going shopping as he had other plans.

After saying goodbye, he looked out of the window of the second-floor bedroom and could just make out the Crystal Palace mast. Closer by was the large and mostly grassed area known as Woodside Green that was surrounded by Victorian houses. Large sycamore trees that were beginning to get their golden, rustic, autumn colours, towered into the South London sky as planes thundered up high above. Before meeting Joan the following day for dinner, he planned to walk the streets and take in a beer at one of the pubs that had once been his preferred watering hole.

He watched the news on the enormous TV and was impressed by the professional standard of presenting programmes. In Spain it was all a bit hit and miss with never-ending game shows or soaps that switched abruptly to advertisements.

Before running a bath, he rang the reception to reserve a table for his evening meal. He neatly folded the clothes he had travelled in and placed them in a large plastic bag. Standing naked in the bathroom he heard the jazzy call sound of his mobile and went to retrieve it. Swiping the caller screen, he smiled to see it was Martin calling.

'Hiya, you got there safely. Good flight was it?'

William was suddenly aware of his nakedness and had to check the screen to see if Martin had called him on Facetime. Relieved it was just a phone call and he was not visible to the caller, he still sat with his free arm dragged across his thigh. He drew breath and lied, 'Yes, bit bumpy but on time.'

'I'm bored and miss you.'

He ignored the remark, casting his eyes to the ceiling before enquiring what his friend had been up to.

'Oh, not that much, but I did see your girlfriend, Sarah. She was down on the beach with her friends. She was wearing a yellow one-piece bathing suit. She's quite a looker that one.'

'I'm really not interested and don't refer to her as my girlfriend.'

'Okay amigo, keep your hair on!'

Then a thought came to William, 'Where was it you lived in Penge? I may walk the streets and get a measure of the area.'

'You are a boring old fart, William. You are twenty

minutes on the train from central London and you want to visit Penge. If you really want to know, it is Frys Road. You can't miss our old family pad; Trevor House is next to a launderette. I was there four years ago and the town has gone upmarket with wine bars. Anyway, I must go now as this call must be costing me a fortune.'

* * * *

Having enjoyed his roast beef dinner, William retired to bed. The next morning, he awoke to the sound of a noisy helicopter flying directly above the hotel and cursed the busy area that he'd once called home. He pictured the scene in Spain with the early morning sun already lighting up his living room and the smell of freshly baked bread from the bakery two doors down. There was never any rush to have breakfast and he would sit on the balcony to glance down to the shimmering sea.

He took a shower and dressed in the new jumper and black jeans he'd brought especially for the trip. The temperature was definitely cooler, and his choice of clothes couldn't have been more different to his normal thin shorts and tee shirt. Down at breakfast he took pleasure in observing the other guests who included two businessmen in suits minus their ties. A small laptop precariously balanced on a chair was being regularly checked. Snatches of their conversation revealed they worked for the same company and both were struggling to meet targets. He heard them discussing the idea of persuading customers to overstock on their products.

On a table to the left of him, a mother and two daughters, who spoke in a broad Irish accent, delayed ordering their breakfast. Shortly a man who could have been the father appeared. He had a distinctive birthmark on the right side of his face and a mop of ginger frizzy hair that badly needed cutting. Lowering his enormous body onto the leather-backed dining chair, it was obvious he was short of breath. Addressing the woman, he made no effort to lower his voice informing that his credit card hadn't worked when paying the bill. All of this was music to William's ears as his brain recorded character and story lines for his future writing.

It was probably the best eggs and bacon he'd tasted in a long while. Spanish bacon always somehow tasted inferior and generally undercooked. He was pleased to be served with a teapot and topped up his china cup a number of times. In between mouthfuls of toast he tapped away on his mobile a text to Martin that read: *Have you registered online for your state pension, put the house up for sale and got info on getting teeth done?*

He was amused with the reply that shot back: *Get off my back, Mr Perfect.*

With breakfast now over, he made his way back to the bedroom. He became aware of the frenetic ringing tone that Martin had downloaded for him onto his phone. It was an awful sound and his preference would have been one that resembled a normal house phone. Swiping the screen, he stared at the number. It was a mobile and he nearly deleted the call, but something stopped him as he deliberated if it was Beth. He was right.

Clutching the phone to his ear he continued with his walking back to his room. 'Hello, Beth. Yes, I slept well thank you. Look can I be totally honest; meeting you again was a shock that brought back all the nightmares of losing my son. And, when you mentioned Steven's name I sort of freaked out.'

The voice on the other end of the phone was calm and she said how sorry she was for upsetting him. She made the point that she needed to return the watch and would understand if he didn't want to meet up. An arrangement was made to leave it with the reception desk.

Grasping the phone while he attempted to swipe the room card against the lock, he entered and sat heavily on the edge of the unmade bed.

'That's really kind of you. Are you sure you don't mind coming over here? That would be great as I have a busy schedule.'

On giving her the hotel address he ended the call feeling relieved he wouldn't have to see her again.

* * * *

Prior to meeting Joan for dinner, William walked the entire length of Portland Road before turning right by the railway bridge. It was familiar territory, but he still used the data on his mobile to locate Frys Road. He soon found the large Victorian bay-fronted house that was still known as Trevor House. There was no sign of the launderette as the building next door had now been converted into a smart looking town house. Two bay trees stood to attention outside the super shiny red front door. He studied the exterior of Martin's old house and was impressed with the expensive double-glazed sash windows and newly painted white brickwork. He understood his friend had been born in this house. Nearly twenty years ago, following a messy divorce, he moved out of the family home to a small rented apartment in Beckenham.

Martin worked as a creative director for an advertising agency in the West End and with his share of the money from Trevor House bought his property in Spain. It was in Penge that William first met Martin and the men built up a friendship.

* * * *

As William weighed up the street that certainly had gone considerably upmarket with a wine bar and smart delicatessen, he kept thinking about Martin's missing son. A plan was forming in his head – somehow, he was going to reunite father and son. It wouldn't be easy, but he was determined to repay Martin for all his kindness. The difficulty wouldn't be tracking down a man with a surname like Fudge, more in understanding the reasons behind the rift and whether a reunion was indeed possible.

* * * *

Back at the hotel when he collected his room key from reception he was handed a small padded envelope and he instinctively knew what was inside. Walking to his room he peeled off the sticky tape and gently encouraged Steven's watch to fall onto his hand. He held it to his cheek and felt elated to have it back.

* * * *

Joan arrived at the hotel at exactly six thirty and William, who was waiting in the car park, was genuinely pleased to see her. She brought her new red Mini to an abrupt halt over two disabled spaces and turned off the engine. Climbing out of the car she went over to hug her ex-husband and planted a kiss on both his cheeks. He was concerned that she looked tired and wondered if she might be ill.

Her first words to him were whether he liked the new car.

'It's great, but very red.'

Dismissing the remark, she stood back from him; he felt her eyes scanning his body.

'God, you are better looking every time you come over.'

'It's living in the sun, Joan.'

'You are so slim. Why didn't you look like this when we were together?'

Anxious to change the subject he nervously asked what time she had booked their meal at the Italian restaurant in Bromley.

'Change of plan dear, I've been out and got all the ingredients for a perfect meal. We are dining at my place. I even got a couple of bottles of that Rioja wine you like.'

He simply muttered a quiet thank you. Observing Joan in her white blouse and long blue velvet skirt that was practically sweeping the gravel driveway he inwardly smiled. He acknowledged that her safe choice of clothing hadn't changed since he first met her. The steely grey hairstyle was old fashioned as were the choice of large silver earrings. The round silver-framed glasses that perched on her tiny nose must surely have been an exact copy of the ones she wore all those years ago. But he still found her attractive despite her out dated dress sense. Her ventures into the modern world were reserved with her Mini car and smart phone. Where she lived in a flat at South Norwood, her living room was devoid of a television as her preference was to listen to classical music. Yes, Joan was still exactly as he remembered her when they were together. She had a heart of gold and he was sorry for the anguish he'd brought her.

Tucking his long legs into the cramped floor space of the Mini, he spied library books and a giant sixteen pack of toilet rolls on the back seat. As soon as he had fixed his seatbelt the car shot backwards as she engaged reverse gear. He was suddenly nervous of being in a car with her again as he recalled past times when she drove too fast. Passing the driving test after five attempts had really tested his patience. Her refusal to seek professional help and demanding he teach her had been challenging. Then there was the expense of buying her a car and a parking permit. He remembered the fights with the insurance company to settle minor accident claims that resulted in increased premiums every time it was up for renewal.

The early evening rush-hour traffic was manic with stop-start all the way. As they passed the swimming pool on the left, Joan suddenly became excited, 'You should have brought your trunks.'

He laughed and switched the subject to the shops that never seemed to change. These included launderettes, betting offices, cafés, newsagents and convenience stores. He shuddered as they passed a funeral business that had been one of his competitors. The memories of dealing with dead bodies unsettled him. He looked away changing his thoughts to the beautiful Spanish town he so looked forward to returning to. He just had to get through the evening with Joan and tomorrow to pay his respects to Steven. Then, after lunch, it would be back to the station to return to Gatwick for the flight home.

On arriving at the flat he was given a glass of red wine and inwardly sighed on discovering Joan hadn't even started to prepare the meal. It was going to be a long evening before the lasagne would be ready. He fretted at the prospect of not eating for another few hours and having to talk to her. Worryingly, she kept topping up their drinks and quickly became tipsy from the effects of the alcohol and no food. Perched on an uncomfortable, tall, wooden stool in her kitchen, he watched her peel onions and chop courgettes. Busy with her cooking and constant chatting, William struggled to get a word in edgeways. Eventually, the ingredients came together and she turned her attention to making the sauce before layering the pasta.

With her hands covered in flour she stirred the milk in the saucepan like a demented soul. He could tell she had the gas on too high and feared the mixture would congeal into a rubbery topping. When he cooked back home he took pleasure in creating a meal and left nothing to chance.

With a droll look on her face she said, 'I haven't prepared this dish before. The recipe said it was easy, but I'm not sure how many pasta sheets to use. I hope it tastes okay.'

At least five layers of pasta were sandwiched into the glass cooking vessel with the sauce leaking over the edges of the dish. He didn't have the heart to tell her that this was excessive. She had never been a natural when it came to cooking.

'I'm sure it will be fine; just go easy on the heat. You may want to put some cheese on top of the sauce. Possibly a few more herbs as well.'

He took a generous sip of the Rioja and nearly choked with what she said next.

'Do you ever miss sex with me, William?'

'Bloody hell, what sort of a question is that? It was all a long time ago and now we are divorced. Level with me please, hasn't there been anyone in your life since we split up?'

She shook her head. 'No, I never met anyone, or for that matter, felt the urge to get close. But when I saw you in the hotel car park, it got me thinking. Do you think it would be an idea if we had a special evening together like in the old days?'

William felt the sweat running down the back of his neck. God, what was she playing at? There was no way he would entertain such an idea and shook his head vigorously.

I could even come out to see you in Spain, if you like?'

'Oh… no… no… I think we are just fine as we are. There has been too much water under the bridge to make changes. We've managed to stay good friends all these years and that suits me.'

His body shook when she touched his arm and somehow, he just knew what was coming next.

'I think I still love you. I just want you to hold me. I meant what I said about visiting you abroad but only mean for a short time. I really do need company.'

She looked down to her blouse and back to his eyes. 'Don't you find me attractive?'

Of course he found her desirable despite the extra weight she was carrying and the baggy clothes. If things were different he would have whisked her off to bed, but he didn't love her any longer.

Trying not to hurt her feelings, he placed both hands on her shoulders. 'My love for you is different now. You will always be special, but I don't want to try again. It would ruin what we have. You do understand, don't you?'

She pulled away looking annoyed and muttered, 'I do, and I don't.'

Then, without any sign of emotion in her voice she mentioned their old business. 'That's another thing I also miss. We had a good steady company with such lovely customers and you wiped it all out.'

He nervously joked, 'But they were dead customers. I don't miss the work one bit. The thought of that grim business horrifies me.'

Maddened with him Joan snapped, 'It suited you just fine, that was until you had those affairs that destroyed what we had.'

'Oh, Joan let's not argue. I'm here to see you and tomorrow is a big day in the calendar for us both. How many times have I said sorry – you were right I cocked up big time.'

Joan dismissively waved a hand in his direction. 'Okay, it's clear you are not interested so I won't mention it again. Just don't expect me to come running if you change your mind.'

With at least an hour left for the meal to cook they retired to the lounge and much to William's relief she kept her word and there was no more talk of getting back together. He was confused by her sudden climb down from claiming never-dying love for him. They chatted about their past holidays recalling happier times when they were so much in love.

As he deliberated on Joan's proposal his foolishness with the prostitute in Girona also came to mind. The next woman he'd happily take to bed had to be someone he was deeply in love with. Sarah's name came to mind. There was something about her that felt right for him. He'd love to get to know her better, warts and all.

Joan's meal was surprisingly tasty and between them they washed down most of a second bottle of Rioja. She ordered a taxi for him and they made their arrangements for visiting the cemetery the next morning.

* * * *

After a poor night's sleep worrying about Joan's revelation, William was determined not to let it cloud over the reason for him being there. Following a breakfast of scrambled eggs, toast and coffee, he loaded his case into Joan's tiny car boot that was already quite full. There was no rush to reach the cemetery and they made a stop to purchase flowers from a local florist. Back in the car he spotted the new town houses where his business once stood. This time he was determined not to fret about the past. Life had moved on and they had realised a tidy sum from the sale of the large property and grounds.

On reaching the graveyard there was a delay before driving up to the parking bays as a funeral that was about to take place. The hearse had just arrived, and a young woman dressed in her smart black suit was heading up the proceedings. She was walking ahead of the car for the last fifty yards. How many times had William done this?

When it was convenient to park up, his eyes remained focused on the proceedings. He couldn't but help noticing the style of the dark veneered coffin and handles that had been chosen. In his mind he had a measure of the description and even the old prices. The size of the casket indicated this was a small person they were carrying into the church. Morbid thoughts of lined coffins, the smell of the body and all the tricks of the trade momentarily came flooding back.

Standing by Steven's grave, Joan clung heavily to his arm as they gazed at the wording on the stone. It saddened him to read the inscription of the plot to the side of where they were standing. The lady had reached almost one hundred years of age, unlike their poor lad who had died so young.

Over the last five years of making these visits he always said the Lord's Prayer before laying a bouquet of flowers on the base. Kissing their fingertips, they took turns to touch the gold wording on the gravestone to say goodbye to Steven. Living abroad limited William's opportunities to pay his respects. He knew Joan came every month, as he would have done if he still lived there.

Back in the car neither spoke. The moment was one of peace. Then there was an almighty clattering on the roof. The heavens opened and with the engine running they waited for a few moments before setting off for East Croydon station. There was a change of plan when she insisted on taking him to the airport. She was much calmer with her driving which pleased him. The journey gave them a chance to chat with him promising to ring her the following day on his arrival back in Spain.

As they joined the traffic on the M25, she suddenly took her left hand off the steering wheel and patted his knee. He felt every muscle in his leg tense as he wondered what she was up to.

'Look I'm sorry if I embarrassed you last night mentioning wanting you in that way. My head is such a mess at the moment with so much going on.'

'That's okay, but put your hand back on the wheel please. I thought you said we wouldn't be discussing that again.'

'I know I did. I just want to say that it took me years to forgive you, William, but recently I've been thinking a lot about you. Deep down I still love you and yes, I do miss you in that way. We used to be so good together.'

Annoyed and uncomfortable with what she was saying he snapped, 'It's never going to happen. We've moved on and I have a new life that doesn't include you.'

'Why don't you try and hurt me a bit more.'

'Look, I'm fond of you as friend but really don't want any of this. Now pay attention to your driving. You should be in the middle lane for Gatwick and watch that car on the right!'

Her mind was clearly not on her driving and entering the lane was tricky as she squeezed the car into the narrow gap between two other vehicles. Still not giving up Joan raised her voice. 'Is there somebody else in your life? When we talk on the phone you mention Martin's name a lot. You aren't gay, are you?'

Disgusted with the suggestion, William pushed his back hard into the seat.

'No, I'm bloody not! He's a great mate and that's as far as it goes.'

He lied with what he said next in an attempt to dissuade her from thinking he preferred the company of men. 'Actually, if you must know I've met a lady who teaches creative writing and we get on very well. We are taking one day at a time.'

Joan went quiet on him for the rest of the journey and on joining the airport dual carriageway that led to the terminals she muttered, 'I miss you.'

William said he was sorry if he'd hurt her feelings. She started to cry and he hurriedly extracted a tissue from his travel bag and passed it to her.

His mind was buzzing – this was the second person in the last few days who said they missed him. Martin was obviously hoping for more. How many times had he told him he wasn't interested? Fortunately, his friend had never stepped over the line or made any advances. He shuddered at the thought of another man fancying him. And now, Joan wanted him back. Why did life have to be so complicated?

* * * *

On the return flight William read the opening chapter of Sarah's latest novel. He quickly warmed to her style of writing, acknowledging her research on Finland.

The story was intriguing leaving the reader keen to follow the menacing tale that was unfolding. The Finnish girl from Tampere certainly had a secret and it kept him turning the pages.

Chapter 8

Relieved to be back to a place he now called home, William threw open the balcony doors allowing the gentle evening breeze to waft into his face. Down in the town the buildings were lit up like a fairy town with spotlights showing off the castle's sandstone walls. The tall fir trees up on the Vila Vella were covered in electric lights that twinkled in the night sky. The delicious smell of cooking coming from the restaurants that lined the beach road made him hungry. Judging from the loud music and raised voices, there was a party going on down below in one of the villas. He glanced up to the gloriously bright full moon, surrounded by an incredible array of stars and told himself it was good to be back in Spain.

This evening he took that bit longer cleaning his teeth as he stared at his reflection in the mirror. For a brief moment he hardly recognised the image that confronted him. He was surely a shadow of his old self, the man from South London who still courted a secret. With his mind still playing on his meeting with Beth on the flight out, it brought back the memories he'd managed to mostly shut out. The other disturbing thing was Joan's shock news that she still wanted and needed him. There was a time when she left him breathless with his passion for her, but not now. He decided against ringing her in the morning and reached for his mobile to send a brief text. There was no point in prolonging the agony, as she needed time to settle back into her life, as did he.

Just before retiring to bed he texted Martin with the message that he'd see him soon.

＊ ＊ ＊ ＊

The next morning, he wandered down to have breakfast in one of the newer beach cafés to read more of Sarah's novel. It certainly was a gripping story that had opened with the police questioning Pinja, a young office worker from Helsinki on the whereabouts of her boyfriend. This Finnish woman's bending of the truth opened up a web of lies. Sarah's skill of sowing into the mind the seedier aspects of living in Finland and dangers that lurked there was outstanding.

A few hours later he made his way to Sarah's villa to attend the weekly meeting, but soon encountered a somber mood existed with the other members. One of their writers, a woman called Sue, had just died of cancer back home in the UK. Her fellow writers were devastated, and a card was doing the rounds along with a collection to send flowers.

William stood around waiting for the class to start and waved at Sarah who smiled back. It was definitely cooler and most of the ladies wore jumpers and jeans. With the end of the season, the tourists had mostly gone home, returning the beautiful town to the locals. When the sun went in it was definitely cooler with a slight breeze bringing a few leaves pirouetting down onto the lawn. One of the ladies mentioned the next class in two weeks' time would be held inside the house in the lounge.

When Sarah banged her large plastic ruler on the chair, everyone stopped talking and sat down. A moving tribute was made for their friend and it became clear their leader was concerned for the woman's husband.

'I feel so sorry for him losing her like that. I know what it's like as it still feels like just yesterday that I lost my man. I turned to food and ballooned out to a crazy dress size.'

She looked down and patted the elasticated waistband of her trim red jeans and smiled. 'And now look at me – now I just can't seem to put on weight.'

William felt sorry for her. It was devastating to lose someone special. As for her once being a large woman he had trouble imagining such a thing. Despite her funny ways, she was a wonderful person, someone he wanted to know better.

Sarah's eyes scanned the writers individually. 'Now before we make a start, I need to know how many of you did the homework?'

A few limp hands were raised and she frowned.

William had worked on her prompt for a story about the man behind a modern-day Noah's ark. He proudly announced he'd completed his task and looked forward to reading it out.

Sarah appeared to ignore him and said, 'Ok, here's a short writing exercise on making every adjective count. And ladies, please limit the number of adverbs. Every word counts. Make your work shine and the subject is to feature the sea. You have ten minutes and then...'

The woman with the crazy haircut interrupted. 'Can anyone lend me a pen? I keep forgetting to bring one.'

There was a roar of laughter, prompting Sarah to reach down to retrieve her ruler. Three frantic cracks later, the peace was restored. She directed her words at the woman who was now frantically searching her bag for a pen. 'Just remember that the sign of a good writer is being prepared.' She then quickly added, 'And of course a lot of imagination and skill.'

She then passed over a pencil from her case which was passed around the group until it reached the woman whose face had turned a bright red.

With writing pads at the ready the class silently

worked on their task and on completion each read out their work. Sarah was pleased and praised absolutely everyone which came as a surprise to William.

At half time William stood at the end of the garden looking out to sea. He was joined by Sarah who asked if he was enjoying coming to the class. He nodded his head before confirming, yes. Triumphantly he told her he was reading her book.'

'Which one is that?'

'The Finnish one – *Wrong Side of Sanity.* It's brilliant.'

She looked pleased and momentarily touched his arm.

'Thanks for that. My agent has just confirmed my new novel has also been taken up by the publisher.'

'Wow, well done. You make me feel I should be writing a novel.'

'And, so you should. Now off you go and leave me in peace.'

****

On his way back to the apartment William spotted Martin entering a small supermarket on the corner of the square. Clutching his bag, he waited patiently for his friend to appear. They shook hands and Martin, in an excited voice, informed him that he'd put his property up for sale. The agent had apparently told him the market was slow. He'd also made an appointment with the dentist for the implants he so badly needed.

'You have been busy. What about applying for the state pension, have you done that yet?'

'I could do with you helping me do that online. You know what I'm like with computers.'

'Come tomorrow morning and we'll get it sorted. I'll

need your national insurance number and bank details.'

As an afterthought William dropped into the conversation, 'Hey, last week, I saw your old house in Penge. When did you last go back there?'

'Oh, four or five years ago. I do know the area has improved greatly with house prices rocketing. Is that old launderette still there?'

William ignored his question. 'Do you think your son Billy still lives in the area?'

The expression on Martin's face changed to one of sadness. 'Not sure I'll ever know what became of him.'

* * * *

Despite drifting off to sleep that night thinking about Sarah, William kept courting a nightmare so disturbing that featured his ex-wife Joan. This time he was once again living with her and her stunning admission was that she was carrying his child. Disturbingly, she appeared as a young woman but William was still his actual age. She kept patting her enormous stomach saying that when their son was born they should call him Steven. Adding to the chaos of this bizarre dream, it swiftly moved to visiting his old company. Oddly the staff acted as if he'd never been away and Steven was still alive. Then the setting switched to him collecting corpses from the morgue. His customers sat with him in the front of the grey company van and discussed their demise. Later they climbed into coffins never to say a word again.

William awoke from his terrifying dream dripping with sweat. He jumped out of bed and opened the blinds. It was light outside and he gazed at the dark grey clouds that were scudding across the sky. Winter was on its way although there was still some warmth in the air that felt like you were on holiday. Living here all this time had always seemed like an extended vacation that he never wanted to end.

He took longer than usual to shower. The bathroom was all steamed up and with a towel wrapped around his waist he left wet footprints all the way through the lounge on the colourful floor tiles. He checked his phone for messages and felt uneasy to discover Joan had texted him. It read: *Yesterday I brought myself an iPad like yours. Can I Facetime you this morning? It's urgent that we talk.*

Now he was worried. What was so important that she needed to tell him? He was also amazed she'd bought the device and wondered how she would master swiping the screen, yet alone use Facetime. Perhaps a friend was helping her with the technology for her new purchase. He hoped her broadband signal was powerful enough as on his visit she admitted to rarely using the laptop he'd given her before they split up.

He was on tenterhooks waiting for the ring tone. When it came through he readily accepted the call but there was no sign of her, just her voice and an image of the kitchen.

'Joan, I can hear you, but you are not standing in front of the camera.'

Then she came into view and he was shocked to see her worried face. She looked a mess with unwashed hair and was still in her blue dressing gown. She kept pushing her hair away from her eyes and was frowning.

'I'm still trying to get the hang of this thing. The girl next door set it up for me and she made the connection to your end.'

In an anxious voice William said, 'Is your neighbour still there?'

No, she's just gone. She's been showing me how to do e-mails and I think I'll get the hang of it if I read her

80

instructions. Look, I didn't want to do this on the phone but I've got something to tell you.'

'Okay, but what's so important that you couldn't let me know last week when I was over there?'

He could sense the tension in her voice as she struggled to form the words and momentarily moved away from the camera. He had to remind her to position the screen closer to her face and it was then he noticed tears running down her cheeks.

His heart went out to her. 'You take your time and remember there's nothing we can't sort.'

Observing her face, he just knew something awful was going to be revealed.

'Oh William, I didn't want to say anything but last year I was diagnosed with breast cancer. I've been in remission and now it's back again.'

Shaken with this news he lowered his voice to almost whispering, 'Joan, I'm so sorry – you should have told me. We may not be married any longer, but I always want to be there for you. How bad is it?'

William looked away from the screen as he heard her say she'd had a lump removed but the cancer had spread to the lymph glands. She'd undergone chemotherapy and had got the all clear; that was until the week before they met up in Croydon.

He was amazed she'd chosen not to tell him. At the time of his visit there were no signs of sadness in her face, completely the opposite, just the flirting that unsettled him. Creasing up his eyebrows he offered, 'I'm really upset you had to go through all this on your own. You say it is back again. Is there anything I can do?'

Staring hard at the screen, he watched her wipe her eyes with a tissue. She looked wretched and he wondered just what if anything he could do to help her. Life had served her a terrible blow with the uncertainty of whether further treatment would help. He had lived with Joan for many years and regardless of whether they were still married or not, he didn't want to see her suffering like this.

'Nope, everyone at this end has been great. I've seen the specialist and he's told me to stay positive as this could just be another hitch. But to be honest with you, I saw the look on his face and I'm worried this time it's really bad. I'm back for more chemo on Tuesday and suspect they will alter my medication.'

Trying to say something that would give her hope he stressed that the treatment was so good nowadays but deep down he knew things were going to be hard for her.

'I'm sorry for saying all those things about wanting you back. I just felt if you took me into your life again you'd look after me and I'd get through all this. I feel like I'm looking through clouded eyes and the dream is fading. I was wrong expecting you to drop everything and come running.'

He was making all the right sounds telling her things would get better, but why did it feel like emotional blackmail. He knew this wasn't her intention to unsettle him but there was no turning his back on her.

'Look I want to help. I could get a flight tomorrow and stay for a few nights. What you need at this moment is moral support with…'

Joan interrupted him, 'No, the purpose of the call was to keep you in the loop and for me to promise not to put you under all that pressure again. I'm pleased you have found someone to love. She must be a lovely woman and I've no intention of spoiling your relationship.'

William turned swiftly away from the iPad. He felt

bad about misleading Joan on his love life. Yet another lie.

'I'll be fine and keep you informed on how the treatment is going. It's not like I'm going to die or anything like that.'

Again, William turned away from the screen so she wouldn't see him welling up. He wished she hadn't mentioned anything about dying as it really upset him. As for lying to her about having a relationship with Sarah back in Spain, that was unforgivable.

Joan disturbed his train of thought saying she ought to go as the call would be costing a fortune. He explained the usage of this app was completely free and she should contact him whenever she felt the need.

As they said their goodbyes he observed her contorted face. She was obviously puzzled with something. 'How do I end the call?'

'Press the red button on the screen. Take care Joan.' That was the first and last time she used her device to communicate with him. Possibly seeing him so upset was too distressing for her. She returned to using the landline and true to her word she never mentioned her feelings for him again.

****

A few days later Martin visited the apartment for help on his state pension that should have been applied for some months ago. It was obvious he was extra hyper today. Sitting awkwardly on one of the balcony chairs he kept mumbling about someone he'd seen in town and then switched his attention fully to William.

'Great to see you. So, you enjoyed Benidorm?'

'Oh, Croydon you mean. Yes, it went okay, but there has been an upsetting development since I got back. Joan told me something that really upset….'

Martin looked away and it was like he hadn't heard a word his friend had said and excitedly poured out his own story.

'I saw her again down by the castle.'

'Who did you see; it wasn't Sarah was it?'

'No, not your writing lady. It was Kylie Minogue and her fiancé. Rumour is they are searching for a holiday home. That should raise the house prices with a star living here, especially with me selling. Perhaps they would like to buy my place.'

William laughed as he pictured the small untidy property.

'She was in front of me in the queue buying churros and asked for extra chocolate sauce. She turned to me and smiled. I wish I'd had my phone as I could have got a selfie. Her young man has an incredible beard, quite a looker that one. I adore my men with bushy beards.'

William ran his fingers over his smoothly shaved chin and nervously blurted out his own news about Joan's cancer. There was a change in Martin's expression as he attempted to console his friend.

'When did this all happen?'

'Unbeknown to me, she's been in remission for quite some while, that was until a few weeks ago and now it's back to the hospital for more chemo. She doesn't want me to help and I'm worried she might die.'

'Oh, God, that's awful news.'

'Yeah, what am I going to do? I don't love her but she's still dear to me. It's comforting to know she's surrounded by friends who are looking out for her.'

'Now I feel bad expecting you to sort out my pension. Let's leave it for a while. Poor Joan. Treatment for cancer is so good and I'm sure she'll come through all of this. You have to remain positive and respect her wishes.'

'Thanks, Martin. I intend to be there for her. It's just so frustrating with me living here and not being able to pop around to see her.'

'I'm not trying to sound cruel, but you have to get on with your own life. You enjoy your writing and going to see Sarah, don't you?'

Hearing her name sent a shiver down his spine. What was wrong with him? He'd seen her a few times and his initial impression hadn't been good. She was noisy, a bit of a bully and he had wondered if she had a drink problem, but recently, he couldn't stop thinking about her. Then a thought ripped through his head – what if he made a fool of himself trying to get close to her and she rebuked him. Would it then spell out the end of attending her class and any further contact? His inner voice kicked in asking what the rush was all about. Surely, it was wiser to gradually get to know her and see how things developed.

****

'Am I too early?' enquired William. Sarah stood in the open doorway of her villa and momentarily looked puzzled. Dressed in jeans and a thin red, woollen jumper she looked gorgeous. She stepped forward with a dazzling smile and an outstretched hand. Aware of the wonderful smell of perfume he kissed both her cheeks. Staring at her perfect skin and tiny nose, he knew this was the first time since leaving Joan that he truly fancied another woman. Although, she was much younger than him, he wondered whether she just saw him as an older man with no chance of becoming her partner.

In an excited voice she greeted him with, 'Oh, hello,

William, it's good to see you. Have you forgotten there is no class today? Come inside and have some coffee.'

Feeling embarrassed for forgetting that Sarah had told everyone the meeting had been cancelled as her new kitchen was being fitted, he limply apologised. On entering the warm hallway, he heard the sound of banging. The whine of an electric drill droning away in the kitchen made it hard to make conversation. Stacked against the passageway were kitchen doors, work surfaces and a radio that was blasting out pop music.

Once in the lounge with the door closed to lessen the noise, he was invited to sit down, but chose to stand. Sarah attended to the coffee maker she'd earlier carried through from the utility room.

'I'm sorry, I got the days mixed up.'

Her cynical reply annoyed him. 'You obviously weren't listening when I made my announcement. You really do need to pay attention.'

William's back tensed making him wonder if he should cut short his visit. He was relieved to see a smile developing on her face.

'Just kidding, it's great to see you. In fact, I'm glad you called as I was thinking of coming over to your place.'

'Oh, why would that be?'

'Well, to encourage you to start writing a novel. I believe with that first short story you read us, it could be a brilliant start for something much larger.'

Leaning forward he quietly mouthed, 'Do you really think so?'

Handing him his drink she nodded her head and then patted the fabric of the cushions on the sofa for him to join her.

Before sitting down he placed his drink, that was too

cold for his liking, on a table. He observed her taking a sip of the coffee and the frown that followed

'This time it's me not concentrating – I'll put some more on. I think I must have switched off the machine earlier – sorry about that.'

She scooped up his cup from the table. Raising her voice, she continued, 'Going back to my suggestion for your novel writing, I want to offer my services to mentor you. It will be hard work, but I know you can do it.'

'Really!'

'Yes. Keep in mind though, I can't guarantee you'll get published as it's really hard getting a break. If I think it's good enough we can send it to my agent to test the water. What do you think?'

He coughed nervously. Sarah was right about the story he'd read out as it had a hook that teased the reader. Yes, he was thrilled with the prospect of getting started, but just how much would she charge for all this mentoring? He certainly didn't want to run up a huge bill with her.

She smoothed the fabric of her jeans and not waiting for him to reply spoke first. 'Don't look so worried; I can read you like a book. My interest in you is not financial as I just want to help you. You are a kind man and I've taken a shine to you. If I can be of assistance in any way, then it will be a pleasure.'

William moved closer to Sarah and smiled. 'I don't know what to say. Yes, I'd be thrilled to have your input. In fact, I'm so excited about it that I'm going to start writing as soon as I get home. One thing I will do is plan the plot out fully to craft the novel correctly.'

'So, you have been listening at my classes. Now, how about that coffee?'

Feeling confident he joked about the second cup

being warmer than the first.

His eyes strayed around the beautifully furnished villa with the mixture of both antique and modern furniture. A bookcase was crammed with paperbacks and it was apparent she was an avid reader. He spied her laptop on a desk that was cluttered with many documents and an old large black printer sat on the tiled floor. The oil paintings were mostly modern-day images of the Costa Brava and not to his liking. He wondered to what extent the furnishings were her brother's choice. The villa certainly appeared to have her womanly touch and not that of the older sibling he'd met just the once after the fire.

His reveries were interrupted as Sarah enquired, 'I don't even know your surname.'

Fearing his name sounded terribly boring he quietly mouthed, 'Jones, plain old Jones.'

'And do tell me what you did back in London. You weren't a tax inspector, were you?'

Panic set in as William desperately tried to think what to tell her. He hated lying, but this is what he'd done in the past when he was put on the spot. It was his way of cushioning his dreadful secret.

So, like so many times before he bent the truth. 'Nothing spectacular like that I'm afraid. I worked for a small company in their office. To be honest I was never happy with my lot and following the divorce I sort of escaped over here.'

'Sorry, I touched a nerve there. My story is probably similar, but I won't bore you with the details. Living here for me is all about making a new start.'

Both looked up as a workman appeared in the doorway. The young man with a screwdriver in his hand looked worried. His broken English was difficult to comprehend and William was impressed with Sarah's ability to converse in Spanish.

With no sign of emotion in her voice she turned to William as she translated. 'He's just said whilst fitting the oven he's broken the glass door. I'll have to cut things short here and see what has got to be done.' She shook her head. 'I thought it had gone quiet out there.'

William immediately got up from the sofa. 'Look, I'm sorry there is a problem. Of course, I'll let myself out. I'll say goodbye.'

There was no response.

Sarah had already switched to her old bossy self and waved a dismissive hand at the workman for him to show her the extent of the damage.

Leaving the villa William zipped up his fleece. A slight breeze chilled his cheeks, but nothing could possibly spoil the wonderful time he had just spent with Sarah.

****

Two days passed, and William was back on Sarah's doorstep ringing the bell. It took a while for the door to be opened. She was wearing a white bath robe with red fluffy slippers. Grasping the beautiful bouquet of flowers, he'd purchased in town, he averted his eyes from her body to mutter, 'Oh, I'm sorry. I've picked the wrong time to call – these are for you.' Placing the gift on the floor by his feet, he was about to say goodbye then hesitated. 'I hope you like the roses. I wanted to thank you for helping me with my writing.'

'That's really kind of you, but there was no need. I haven't done anything yet, have I? Come in and wait while I get dressed. The kitchen man has finally finished leaving me to tidy up, so I'm a bit behind with everything this morning.'

Following her through the hallway he tried to make polite conversation. 'And the oven door, was it repairable?' She laughed. 'You could say that, but my translation wasn't quite as good as I thought it was. It turned out that the hinges weren't lining up, but it's all fixed now. You go through to the kitchen and have a look at the superb job they have done. It's the last door on the left.'

Off she went leaving him to see the newly refurbished room. The generously proportioned kitchen afforded ample cupboard space with new white goods and a cooker. He crossed over to the window to gaze at the garden with the headland just visible behind some trees. A table positioned at the far corner of the room was packed high with storage boxes containing chopping boards, pans and various utensils all ready to be unpacked for use. On the work surfaces tinned food and spice jars were waiting to be stored.

When Sarah returned she was dressed in jeans and a shirt that complimented her figure. Today her hair was tied back and she wore no lipstick. For the first time he noticed a tiny birthmark on her cheek and just how small her ears were. She was, unquestionably, the most beautiful women he'd ever met. The thought of getting to know her thrilled him, as did the desire to hold her in his arms. A nagging voice inside his head shot out the cruelest of insults. *What makes you think she could even begin to like a liar like you and what about your overlapping teeth? It's hardly a turn on is it? She's far too good for you William.*

She topped up the coffee machine before searching frantically in one of the boxes for cups.

With her back to him he plucked up courage and said,

'I was wondering if you would like to join me tomorrow for lunch. There's a new German restaurant I've been to at the top of town that is really good. I can vouch for their grilled chicken and their apple and cinnamon pancakes are to die for.'

Sarah swung around to face him. 'I don't normally eat at lunchtime, but those pancakes sound great. Thanks, I'd love to come, but I insist on paying my way.'

William deliberately applied a harsh voice. 'This time I'm the one in charge and I say no. This is my treat. It's a long time since I've entertained a beautiful lady for lunch, or any woman for that matter.'

With a giggle in her voice she said. 'It's been a while since I've been on a date with a good-looking man like you.'

Excited by what she had just said, he kept staring at her taking in the wonderful body and the lips that he so longed to kiss.

'Shall we meet by the bakery off the main square at one o'clock and walk up from there?'

'Are you sure Martin won't mind you taking me out?'

William bit his lip and possibly a little too rudely snapped, 'I beg your pardon. What's it got to do with him?' He could sense she was embarrassed but still replied, 'You know, with you two being an item.'

Reining in his anger William whispered, 'I wish people wouldn't go making assumptions like that. Just because I have a friend who is gay, it doesn't mean I am that way inclined.'

'I'm really sorry. It was just seeing the two of you together so much that I got the maths wrong. Look, can we change the subject back to those lovely pancakes you are going to give me for lunch?'

Feeling relieved that this misunderstanding was out

of the way, he smiled at her then nodded his head. 'You won't be disappointed, I promise.'

'Great. Now I've got my blogging to do this afternoon then onto putting the laptop through its paces on my new sequel.'

William wasn't sure what the term blogging meant and decided against asking for an explanation. He left her standing in the kitchen and let himself out of the front door. Feeling like a young man in love, he couldn't wait for tomorrow to arrive.

****

Making his way down the steep path that led to the seafront, the view would normally have made William really happy, but his mind dwelled on the possibility that some people thought Martin and he were more than just friends. Even Joan back in Croydon had aired her suspicions. And whilst on the subject of Joan, wasn't today the first of her chemotherapy sessions; he would have to ring tomorrow to check it all went okay.

First though, he needed to get back to the apartment, as he'd promised to help Martin with his state pension. Later he would type up a detailed plan for the plot of the novel he was determined to write. The genre would be romantic fiction with the title: *Someone and No-one.* He estimated it would take around eight months to complete.

****

It was gone midday before Martin arrived carrying a plastic folder with his pension details. In a cheerful mood he demanded a cold beer and settled down on one of the sun loungers on the balcony.

Martin eyed his friend with suspicion. 'Are you okay – you look worried?'

'Me, oh no, I'm fine. I've a busy afternoon ahead of me as I'm writing a novel and it's really hard work.'

Martin's vacant eyes travelled up to the ceiling. 'I'm not into reading.'

'Yes, I'm aware of that. Can we get started? Remind me to talk to you about the money for your dental work. I plan to transfer it to your bank account, I just need your details.'

As the pension website loaded Martin tapped the edge of the table. 'About that money, I'm really grateful for your help but it has to be a loan or I'm not taking it.'

'Give me strength, I know it's a loan.'

'Some other news is that the agent selling my house says it could take ages due to the economic climate. When it eventually goes through, I'll be in pocket and can then move to a smaller place.'

'There, I told you things would work out, didn't I? Let's now concentrate on the job in question.'

Checking the connection signal, he frowned at the laptop. 'This wretched broadband signal is so annoying. How is anybody expected to use the internet when it keeps going this slow?'

'Can I give you some advice on what I'd do?' offered Martin.

'No, you can't.'

'I'd press enter twice.'

William ignored him and proceeded to reload the site. What did Martin know about computers? He struggled to use his phone let alone sort out an internet issue.

Frustratingly, the computer crashed many times involving the tedious task of re-entering the entire data again. Eventually, the bank details were accepted and confirmed as being set up for regular monthly deposits to his account. The remaining task was to transfer funds to Martin's bank for the work on his teeth.

William put a thumb in the air, 'Well that's us done.'

'Thanks a million, I would have struggled without your help. It's much easier for younger guys like you to get your head around using all those programs. I'll leave the technology to you.'

****

The afternoon panned out differently to what William had expected as he struggled to work on his plan for the novel. He had dreamt up too many sub-plots as well as walk on characters that may confuse the reader. He'd need to jot down a table of sequences that took the story along a logical path and satisfying ending. Sarah was correct in saying he had the perfect beginning, the problem remained in where it was it going. He recalled her words on the difficulty of getting published with the market so heavy with writers seeking deals for their debut novels. He was determined not to be deterred. With Sarah's encouragement, he instinctively knew he'd find a home for his book.

A while later he put through a call to Joan. He was pleasantly surprised to hear her upbeat voice and that the ordeal had not been too bad. He read somewhere that for many people the early sessions of chemo don't affect the patient greatly. As time goes on, sickness with lack of energy can kick in. He prayed she would remain positive about beating the aggressive cancer and settle back once again into the safety net of remission.

****

Lunch at the German restaurant proved to be an eye

opener for William. Sitting next to Sarah he felt the chemistry growing between them. Their conversation hovered between living in Spain and the effects of Brexit on the UK economy. On finishing the main course, he became concerned about the amount of wine she was consuming. She kept topping up her glass and he had foolishly ordered a further bottle. She'd become loud and kept hanging onto his arm and, while it felt good, he was having difficulty in finishing his meal. Talkative as well as flirty, it was obvious she'd had too much to drink. Fortunately, they were the last people in the restaurant, but William was aware of the German proprietor who kept glancing over in their direction.

Slurring her words Sarah waved frantically at the owner with the handlebar moustache and shouted, 'Two… two pancakes with app… apple please.'

In perfect English the reply came back that they were out of apples and would crème caramel do. Sarah laughed loudly saying what kind of a restaurant ran out of apples. William was uncomfortable with her conduct, which left him wondering if further outings with her would be this challenging. He pondered on the reality of her actually being an alcoholic as Martin had suggested? He cast his mind back to the occasion in the bar with her friends when she had clearly been loud and off her head. Could he really cope with someone with an illness like this? He hung onto the hope that most of the time she acted fairly normal and that possibly the drink went to her head too easily.

Sarah suddenly sat bolt upright and amazingly her speech became calm again making it easier to understand what she was saying.

'I've spent most of my life living in the Basingstoke area. Have you ever been to Basingstoke William?'

'Just the services on the M3 – have I missed much?'

There was no reply and he detected she was processing her thoughts. A look of sadness enveloped her face. 'I moved to London to be with my partner who sadly died. We settled in Lewisham and were so much in love, then my life fell apart.'

William hung his head low. He felt sorry for her loss and momentarily placed an arm around her shoulder. She shuddered as if an electric shock had flown through her body but then relaxed by cuddling up to him. She stroked the side of his neck and went to kiss him. Feeling this close felt wonderful, but it wasn't his intention to take advantage of her following her divulgence about her sad past. Turning his face away she sank back in her chair.

'God, you have had it rough. It's the hardest thing getting over losing someone.' Not wishing to linger on that topic, he switched the subject back to where she used to live. 'Lewisham, well that's a place I once knew terribly well. I used to visit a supplier to pick up things.'

'What sort of things?'

He had to think quickly and answered without pausing too long. 'Metal work and furniture accessories – nothing exciting.'

For a moment his mind was back in his old trade collecting some urgent handles and pins for securing the lining for the coffins. He knew the owner well and always got a good deal as well as a cup of tea. The two men had remained friends and he had even buried Sam's wife who had died of cancer. He had been tempted to call in to see him when he visited Joan but feared it might be too upsetting revisiting anything to do with the funeral world.

Sarah broke his chain of thought as she insisted he bought her another drink. He made her promise this was to be her last before taking her home. That one glass of wine set her back again leaving William with little doubt she had a problem. Just how long had she been like this and was she drinking every day? He was saddened as this addiction may well prevent him getting to know her better. What if he couldn't help her and the love that was blossoming in his heart wasn't enough?

When they left the restaurant, she was in high spirits and then there was the unmistakable and embarrassing sound of her breaking wind. Bursting into uncontrollable laughter she placed a finger to her lips and said quietly, 'Oh dear.'

William glanced briefly at her and then in the direction of the castle that was peeping through a gap between two hotel buildings. Uncomfortable with her conduct, which he still put down to the drink, he was beginning to wish he'd never suggested they go out for lunch.

She suddenly stopped in her tracks and yanking on his arm said, 'I'm sorry, it must have been the apples in the pancakes. They sometimes have that affect on me.'

'But they weren't serving pancakes today!'

With a vacant look on her face she giggled, 'Oh, yes, that's right.'

In essence, the lunch had been a disaster due to her being noisy and lounging around in a drunken state. When they eventually reached her villa, she thanked him for the meal and reminded him to come to the class the following week. Dropping her keys, she bent down to retrieve them and fell over. William helped her onto her feet, then unlocked the door and said goodbye.

Chapter 9

Over the next week William shut himself away in the apartment to write his novel. He deliberately ignored Martin's calls and texts because he needed space from thinking about his friend and for that matter Sarah.

Engrossed in his work all thoughts of her were put to one side. He hadn't given up on her, but just for now he would take a break from making contact and took the decision not to attend the writing group. She'd no doubt wonder why he hadn't shown, but so be it. He wondered if she would recall her drunkenness the previous week at lunch. What was puzzling though was how one moment she appeared to be extremely inebriated and the next, without reason, she was back to normal. It didn't make any sense. Maybe not seeing her would put things into perspective, but there was no escaping the fact that he longed to be in her company.

The high pitched sound of the intercom made him jump and bought his thoughts back to the present. What if it was Martin; should he ignore whoever was calling? Whoever it was, was obviously not going to just go away because they made at least six attempts to get his attention.

'Yes, hello, who's there?' he asked, the frustration was obvious in his voice. He was shocked to hear Sarah's voice.

'It's me, can I come in please?'
Wondering how she knew where he lived and just what she wanted, he activated the door release. In she walked carrying her coat and what looked like a bag containing shopping. Today she looked different with a

new shorter hairstyle enhanced with blue streaks. He was also surprised to see her wearing glasses for the first time. They really suited her beautiful face and her small mouth looked so inviting. As she smiled at him he pondered over the purpose of her visit. Observing the smart navy-blue trousers and white-buttoned blouse that showed off her gorgeous figure, he made a conscious effort not to stare.   Settling down on the comfy sofa she looked around the lounge as if conducting an inventory. 'I love your apartment, especially that view of the sea. I can't get over how quiet it is here. Where I live I hear the jet skis and that wretched banana speedboat.'

'I'm sure it's not that bad. How did you know where I lived?'

Sarah drew breath. 'Hardly a secret, I asked Martin this morning.'

Momentarily William cursed his friend who had no right to pass on his address without asking him first. He vowed to back-pedal on his contact with him. Over the years they had slipped into spending too much time together, no wonder people presumed they were an item.

'What's with the visit, Sarah?' he said a little to abruptly.

Her lips tightened as she looked up at him quizzically, 'I don't need an appointment to see you, do I?'

'No, not at all.'

She reached down to the bag by her feet and produced two bottles of red wine.

When William saw this he groaned inwardly as recollections of their lunch came thundering back. Was she expecting to stay and finish off all that drink?

'These are for you as a thank you for that lovely meal. I think the wine must have gone to my head and I hope I wasn't too much of a nuisance. I promise you there will be no repeat of me getting tipsy again. I was just enjoying myself.'

She lay the present on the sofa and smiled at him before placing a hand on his arm. Nervously he gazed down at the expensive Rioja then back to her face. Plucking up the courage to tackle the delicate subject of her drinking he said, 'That's very kind of you. How did you know what my favourite wine was?'

Looking pleased with herself the reply shot back, 'Martin was most helpful.'

He felt his body tense at the mention of the name. 'Sarah, please excuse me for asking, but how much do you drink?'

She snapped, 'Please stop this questioning as I'm feeling uncomfortable with where this is all going.'

William nervously straightened the cushion between them. 'A few times I've seen you in a bad way and I'm a little concerned. It frightened me seeing you at lunch like that. It was embarrassing witnessing you in that state. That is one of my favourite restaurants and I could sense the owner was unhappy. Be honest with me please, how often do you drink?'

She stroked her lips and whispered, 'I just have the odd glass. It's not like I have a drink problem, is it?'

William looked down at the bottles. 'Please believe me when I say that I'm looking out for you. It's so easy to slip into a regular drinking habit. Years ago, we had a friend back home who drank too much. She was hit by a car as she staggered across the road and died later in hospital. She left a husband and a two-year-old daughter.'

'Oh, that's really sad. You are right, I do hit the booze a bit too often, but I'm not an alcoholic. I get the urge to have a drink and then I'll have nothing for three or four days. It's mainly when I get a bit down that I turn to the bottle.'

'Well done for telling me that and I suggest that you just need to slow it down a bit. There are some excellent non-alcoholic wines and beers that you could try between having the real stuff. I don't want to see you falling down in the street hurting yourself, or your reputation for that matter. I care too much about you to let things get any worse.'

'That's really kind of you to say that.'

Then she did something that made his body tingle. She kissed the index finger of her left hand and stroked it against his lips. She kept it there for some time. The feeling was sensational leaving him with little doubt she had feelings for him. Her power over him was unreal. He told himself this must surely be a signal to take their friendship to another level.

'You are a really lovely man, William. I want you to know I carry a lot of baggage from my past and I get moments of sadness and sheer desperation, but I can handle it. You are not to worry about me. Is that understood?'

With this she high-fived him and yet William was concerned she was saying what she thought he wanted to hear.

Her reference to excessive baggage resonated with him. He longed to tell her about his own slipups, but it wasn't the right moment. He'd have to see how things turned out before revealing his darkest secrets.

Then she shocked him with, 'I might not see much of you for the next month and I'll be cancelling the writing classes for a while. I've messaged everyone but didn't have your e-mail to tell you. That's why I called in to see you.'

Downhearted at the thought of not seeing her he drew a deep breath. 'Oh, that's a blow as I was hoping we could spend some time together. What have you got organised, is it your writing?'

She nodded. 'I'm always writing and I have a deadline for the new novel – this one could be my best. I'll catch up with you sometime. There's no urgency for us to meet up, is there?'

Her vagueness and sudden lack of interest irked him. Prior to her arriving this morning he wanted to back-pedal on seeing her but now, well, he felt like a teenage boy fancying the new girl in class. The thought of her avoiding him for a while was breaking his heart. Why was she sending out these signals of wanting more? It was a classic case of Jekyll and Hyde with her obvious split personality. He became aware that Sarah's attention was now solely on checking her mobile.

'Are you waiting for a call?'

With a look of helplessness on her face, he wondered what was coming next.

'No, a text. It's my brother. I don't know if I have mentioned that he owns the villa, not me. Well, he needs to raise some money by selling it. It could take ages to get a buyer though.'

'Oh, surely not, it's your home. Is that what's been bothering you? I could help.'

He certainly wasn't prepared for the sharp reply that spilled from her lips. 'No, I said I was busy, didn't I? Back off please. What's with all the questions?'

Raising a hand in the air he said, 'None of my business… sorry.'

She shuffled around on the sofa and spoke quietly, 'I may have to rent a small place in Tossa, but after living in that beautiful cliff top house, I couldn't bear to end up in some titchy bedsit with no view. The other option is for me to move back to the UK.'

The possibility of her moving away was a frightening thought. Momentarily, he began to wish he'd never answered the door to her. Had he not, he would still be doing his writing and oblivious to the woman who was causing havoc with his emotions. Trying to focus on preventing her leaving Spain he asked, 'Haven't you some savings? I thought with you being a famous author you would be living on your royalties.'

She coughed and shrugged a shoulder. 'My savings have dwindled, but I still have the income from the travel articles. As for earnings on the books, I'm doing reasonably well but…' She paused, and the hint of a smile appeared on her face. She laughed loudly, 'I'm hardly the next J. K. Rowling, am I?'

'No, I suppose not. I'm going to make some coffee.'

As he filled the kettle he panicked thinking that he couldn't actually help her, and certainly not financially. It felt like she'd been teasing him before backing off. Sarah was the first woman in years who had unleashed these feelings in him; feelings he hoped would never fade.

Chapter 10

As sad as William felt with the uncertainty about whether Sarah would continue to live in Spain, he still felt inspired to concentrate on his story. Part of his day was spent researching on the internet to firm up setting the scene for the novel. He was tempted to edit the text but remembered the advice to do this on completion of the first draft. Disappointed not to be receiving the mentoring Sarah had enthused about he was resolute in becoming an author so decided he would press on with or without her.

Just before the weekend he chose to ring Martin. The break from not seeing him had put things into perspective and now it was time to meet up again. The venue was a local bar on the promenade.

When William greeted Martin, he was moody and sarcastic with his comments about why his best friend had been avoiding him. Seated in the packed bar the music drowned out their conversation. A decision was made to finish their drinks and walk up to the Vila Vella to take in the view from the Pandora statue.

Up high on the castle battlements the wind was blowing hard and the seagulls were squawking overhead. A hint of dark, low clouds in the distance suggested rain was on its way. Winter would sooner see the town experience mixed weather. As they walked past the huge iron cannon that faced out to sea, Martin dropped a bombshell. 'I don't want to upset you, but your Sarah has a new man. I've seen them a few times this week and they looked really happy.'

'What did you say? That can't be right. I know she is not attached.'

Martin flapped his hands up and down like a heavy bird trying to take off. 'Keep your hair on old boy – what did you expect? She's a good-looking woman and should have a partner. I've tried enough times to get you two guys together, haven't I?'

'It's complicated. I feel something for her, but she's not keen. Who's this man you mentioned?'

'I've seen him going in and out of her villa. It looks like he's made himself at home.'

'How can you be sure they are an item?'

'Because they had arms linked. I also saw them in a bar together having a good time. He's a bit younger than her and what a dresser. He's really attractive, tall as they come, with long hair tied back in a ponytail and wears an earring. What I wouldn't do to meet a man like that.'

'You are observant. You say the pair were in a bar? Was she drinking?'

Martin looked tired with his questioning. 'Suppose so.'

He then suggested they continue walking the coastal path, but William disappointed him by saying he had to get back to his writing.

'Well, when will I see you? Be honest with me – have I upset you?'

'No, I just need space from everyone.'

Judging by the look on Martin's face the penny finally dropped. 'All this is about her, isn't it?'

William remained silent as he gazed across the water to a small red and white fishing boat that was riding the waves. The sky suddenly darkened overhead threatening heavy rain. The two men increased their pace down the castle slope as the drizzle quickly turned to heavy rain. As they passed the statue Martin patted the wet bronze lady saying he bet she'd been a real heartbreaker in her day.

William's thoughts returned to Sarah. Heartbreaker didn't come anywhere close to how she'd treated him.

* * * *

Living in a small town, sightings of Sarah and her new fancy man were hard to ignore. Each time William saw them together they were either dining in a restaurant or strolling along the promenade. This younger man was elegantly dressed and with his hair tied back he looked really cool. In total contrast to him, William was verging on being elderly and far from being cool – what could she possibly see in him?

Whilst he still had feelings for her, it was crystal clear she wasn't interested. The confusing thing was one moment she could be so close to him and the next as cold as steel. Hadn't she said she was busy with her work and yet she found time to court this man and not him? When would he see her again?

He wasn't even sure if the writing group would reconvene, or whether he would even feel like attending?

* * * *

The weeks flew by and on a cold and windy morning, William visited the Thursday market to buy some vegetables. The plastic covers on the stalls were billowing around in the wind and an earlier downpour had created puddles along the road. The stalls were full of leather goods, clothes, household items, fresh bread and local cheeses. There were some good deals to be had and he bought a new wallet from a hippy couple that lived in a commune close by.

Entering a supermarket, he headed for the back of

the store to buy groceries and toilet rolls. If he wasn't mistaken he could hear Sarah's voice. She was asking if her partner wanted steak for their evening meal. Not wishing to see her he quickly reached into the cold cabinet for some yogurt and was about to make tracks for the checkout.

'Hello, William, how are you?'

Feeling uncomfortable about her seeing him looking so scruffily dressed and unshaven, he nodded before muttering, 'Fine thanks.'

His eyes then travelled down to their shopping basket. He was dismayed to see four bottles of wine. Was this new man in her life also a heavy drinker?

Gazing back to the man beside her, Sarah smiled. 'This is Scooter and he's staying with me for a while.'

Scooter, an exceptionally tall man held out a hand to greet him. In an American accent he spoke kindly, 'Pleased to meet you, sir. If my memory serves me well, you're the guy, or should I say author, who's writing a book. Sarah says your work is awesome.'

William blushed. He was flattered to be referred to as an author but unsettled to be addressed as sir. It brought home how old he must appear to these younger people. He sighed as his eyes focused on the immaculately turned out man in the three-quarter-length blue winter coat. His tailored, black jeans that covered his wafer-thin legs accompanied polished, black, narrow shoes with white laces. How different to William's old soiled trainers that had been through the washing machine too many times. Scooter's face was perfectly shaved, unlike his own with prickly stubble. The last two weeks had seen a cursory scraping of his face with a razor. He looked and felt a mess.

He addressed Scooter. 'Well thank you for that but

I'm in the early process of writing my first novel, not like Sarah with all her books and brilliant reviews.'

Nodding his head spiritedly, Scooter placed an arm around Sarah. 'That goes without saying, she's ace.' He paused briefly then excitedly said, 'Do you think we should tell him our news.'

'No, not yet,' replied Sarah awkwardly.

William's thoughts were working overtime with his inner voice squealing inside his head. *How many times have I told you that she doesn't want an old fart like you?*

As he made his exit he heard Sarah say, 'His friend is Martin, the neighbour I've spoken about. He's the older man living on his own a few doors down from me.'

Scooter's sarcastic reply really upset him. 'No, I haven't seen him. Tell me Sarah, are all the guys you know as old as him and William?'

* * * *

It was a further two weeks before William saw Sarah again. On this occasion he looked smarter than the last time they met up. She insisted he join her in a bar for a coffee. Her face was radiant with a smile that looked like it was never going to leave her. She wore a long grey woollen scarf that was wound around her beautiful swan-like neck. This time there was no sign of Scooter. Today she was friendly and keen to chat. Once out of the cold they ordered drinks. Sipping scorching hot lattes, they settled down at a table in the window looking out at the locals going about their business. To say he was apprehensive on being in her company would be an understatement. He was pondering on her obvious split personality traits wondering where all this was leading. Not knowing if she was going to be all over him or totally cold, he settled down into the comfy leather chair to listen to her news.

'I would have brought Scooter, but he's washing his hair. I've never come across a man who spends so much time in the bathroom as him.'

Her face now took on a serious look. 'I hope you don't think I've been avoiding you. I've had so much on my plate with my brother selling the villa and, of course, work. The last few weeks have been great having Scooter in my life again. He really is an adorable man.' She hesitated to say, 'You don't look very happy, what's up?'

William felt he'd had enough of having his face rubbed in the dirt. If he never heard Scooter's name again that would suit him just fine. Now aware of customers entering the bar, he leant forward and spoke in a low whisper, 'If you must know, I'm pissed off with our friendship. One minute you are giving out signs and the next you don't want to know me.'

Sarah's jaw dropped and her eyes looked like they were going to pop out of her head. 'I'm not with you.'

He focused on her eyes. 'I thought we were getting on so well and had a chance together. I know I'm much older, but you must know I have feelings for you - then you take up with Scooter leaving me high and dry.'

She laughed. 'I do believe you are jealous.'

'And what about when he mentioned you had some brilliant news? How do you think I felt imagining you were in love with him?'

Sarah fiddled with the buttons on her coat. 'Oh, my God, I've been a complete shit with my moods and now this with Scooter. He's my literary agent from London.'

'Literary agent – why didn't you tell me.'

She shrugged her shoulders. 'Believe me there is no

love affair. He's taken two weeks off work to do some writing and is staying at my place. Scooter is gay and is a wonderful man. The news he was referring to was that I've been nominated for the Morray Mayer Literary award.'

'Ruddy hell, that's brilliant news.'

'Yeah, my novel that was set in Finland is doing really well. I'm literally flying. As for treating you so badly, I want you to know I also have feelings for you. As for you being too old for me, the answer is no. In such a short time I've become attracted to you and can't sleep at night for thinking about you.'

Before William had a chance to reply, she stood up from her chair and leant over the table to kiss him. It was an age before she pulled away leaving him feeling dazed and wonderfully satisfied.

They were about to order more coffee when they spotted the woman with the crazy haircut from the writing group making a beeline for their table.

'Oh God, what does she want? Every time we meet she keeps hitting on me.'

When their unwelcome visitor stood by them she smiled at William and ignored Sarah. 'Can I sit with you?'

Sarah was annoyed and her face took on a stern look. 'Take a hint darling and leave us in peace. I'm trying to have a one-to-one conversation on William's writing.'

Still not taking the rebuff, she pulled a chair and placed her bag on the table. 'I won't stay long. I'm glad I spotted you as I wanted to give you my mobile number and an invitation. I'm having a small gathering at my place.' She paused and as an afterthought turned to Sarah, 'And you can come too, if you want.'

Shaking her head and frowning Sarah remained quiet.

William adopted a firmer tone saying he didn't want her number and would she stop pestering him. The awful woman rose from her chair and looked like she was about to explode with anger, 'Charming!'

As she was about to leave she pulled a face at Sarah. 'As for attending your class I won't be coming any longer.'

They watched her leave and Sarah punched the air with her fist and not caring if other customers in the bar overheard her, she triumphantly shouted out, 'Yes. That's what I call a result.'

* * * *

With his arm around her shoulder they walked back to his apartment. Entering the warm interior of his home, he gently pushed her against the wall to kiss her. He loved the feel of her soft skin and the fragrance of the expensive perfume she wore. She responded by wrapping both arms around him and pulling him tight against her body. She then pulled away to place one of his hands on her blouse.

Tugging on his belt, he could hear her heavy breathing.

William struggled to unbutton her shirt. 'Damn these buttons – I've never been able to undo buttons.'

Sarah excitedly said, 'I'm sure you've had no complaints from your past girlfriends.'

Brimming with excitement, he stepped out of his trousers leaving them on the tiled floor. He led the way to the bedroom where they both removed the remainder of their clothes before collapsing onto his large double bed.

Their lovemaking was fast and furious with much

frantic kissing. Sarah certainly knew how to make a man feel good. Their bodies glistened with sweat as they fulfilled their passion. Cuddling and feeling happy and contented they drifted off to sleep. It was one of the best sleeps William had experienced for a long time. He dreamt about Sarah, but this time he was the man beside her.

* * * *

The next few days William and Sarah spent as much time together as they could. She was more adventurous in bed than any other woman he'd ever known. Her undies were skimpy and exciting unlike his ex-wife's high-waisted ones. Making love with Sarah was incredible but exhausting. Her dynamism and appetite for sex astounded him and made him feel like he needed to sleep for a very long time to recover from all the activity. He wondered how many lovers she'd had? The main thing was this was the woman he wanted to be with and he thanked God for bringing her into his life.

* * * *

Over the next few weeks there were numerous dates as they got to know each other. Fortunately for William there were no more awkward questions on his past working life. Both of them were thinking about the present and taking one day at a time.

Whilst out shopping, Martin spotted the pair walking hand-in-hand along the seafront and quickly joined them.

'Hello, this all looks terribly cosy. Are you two an item?'

William broke into laughter. 'Tact was never one of

your strong points, Martin. Yes, if you must know we are dating and exceptionally happy.'

'That's great news. I just wish I could find someone to settle down with.'

Sarah let go of William's hand and put a motherly arm around Martin. 'I'm sure you'll find the right person.'

With a twinkle in his eye, William couldn't help saying, 'It's a pity you don't want the company of a woman. There is an ex-writer from Sarah's group with a crazy haircut that's doing the rounds.'

Sarah was in hysterics at the preposterous suggestion. 'That's cruel. I wouldn't wish her on anyone.'

It was obvious Martin sensed this was a private joke. 'Very funny, I don't think. Tell me you guys, when is the wedding?'

Pretending not to hear him, William changed the subject to the three of them having lunch the following day.

Continuing with their walk, Martin left them when they reached the main square. He was taking the bus to Girona for his first consultation to replace the worst of his buckled teeth. William felt guilty having forgotten about the dentistry requirements. Normally he would have been offering moral support and even accompanying him to the surgery. More recently he had just one thing on his mind and that was when he'd next see Sarah. Nothing else mattered.

Chapter 11

Sarah decided to have one final writer's meeting at the villa and she went to a lot of trouble and expense to lay on a buffet lunch for her students. The newly painted cream walls brightened up the large room with the furniture repositioned to make way for the extra seats required. A splendid selection of mouthwatering food was on display that included canopies and fancy sandwiches along with fruit drinks and sparkling wine. It was warm enough to open the bi-folding doors and a gentle breeze swept through the large lounge. Some of Sarah's typed sheets pirouetted down from a shelf and William along with others retrieved the documents from the floor.

The guest speaker was Sarah's agent Scooter, who had recently returned to Spain. Everyone was interested to learn more about the role of a literary representative.

There was only one other person in that living room who was not a writer but who was spellbound by being in the presence of this speaker. Martin's eyes never left the wonderful man who was entertaining them with his revelations. He listened passionately to Scooter's amazing life in the literary world and how he'd encouraged Sarah to become a best-selling author. He proudly informed the party that she had been nominated for the highly prestigious Morray Mayer Literary award. There was much clapping from everyone, although judging from some of the puzzled faces it was obvious they had never heard of this prize. Scooter raised a hand in the air and added that Sarah had a book deal for two further novels.

When it came to the break for coffee and biscuits, Martin sidled over to Scooter to introduce himself. Many of the other ladies were also keen to meet the agent, but he patiently waited until it was his turn. William had been observing his friend and noticed the obvious attraction between the two men. They were chatting away like old friends. If he wasn't mistaken Scooter handed him a card that unquestionably would have included his mobile number.

Scooter addressed everyone again and it became obvious that the agents held the key to achieving a publishing deal. He stressed that a writer's work had to be of exceptional quality as many thousands of manuscripts were sent through each year for consideration. William inwardly groaned as he acknowledged that getting published was going to be hard, if not nigh impossible. Was he, at his age, really up to plastering his walls with rejection letters and still remaining positive? The difficulty was in striking a balance between enjoying his hobby and dipping his toes in the waters of the publishing world.

When it was time for the guests to leave, Sarah shocked them by saying there would be no further classes for a while. There were gasps from everyone. William already knew these details having had the discussion with Sarah. With her busy schedule she assured him their love would survive the odd trip abroad. Her writing career had taken off big time leaving him wondering if there would be room for him in her life.

* * * *

Due to Sarah's workload it soon became clear in the next month she would be away for at least a couple of weeks. She was returning with Scooter to London to meet up with the publisher to sign the new contract. This time a generous advance was to be made, which would undoubtedly help Sarah with her finances.

Sales of the earlier novel had gone through the roof with international translation rights for four countries being granted. The Amazon ranking placed her book high up in the must-read charts and was bringing in the sales. Book distributors were looking forward to selling more from this author. Along with book signings in various cities and towns in the UK and Finland, Sarah was going to be kept very busy. But all this meant she'd be away from William for quite a while staying with a friend in London.

Downhearted with the prospect of not seeing her, he still kept congratulating her. With her improved income, he hoped she would be in a position to buy the villa from her brother. The nagging question that tortured his mind was whether, with all this fame, would she change and not want him? The thought of living without her was unbearable.

* * * *

With the buildup to Sarah's trip, William booked a surprise short break to Barcelona, a place he loved to visit. After a longer than scheduled journey, the bus drove along the dual carriageway past the high-rise flats into the city. They took a taxi to their hotel close to the Plaza Mayor. Entry to their accommodation was through an enormous brown wooden door that led to a steep staircase and the reception. The view of the ancient square from the bedroom window was breathtaking. Street vendors and flamenco dancers plied their trade each one intent on relieving visitors of their euros.

Gazing down to the alfresco restaurants with waiters dashing from table to table, the incredible aroma of food being served wafted upwards and the smell of grilled fish made them hungry. Spanish music and loud chatter from tourists added to the ambience. Despite the cooler weather in November, there was no shortage of holidaymakers taking in the wonder of this incredible city.

Rather than rush down for a late lunch, William drew Sarah to his side and told her he loved her before laying her on the bed with the hideous purple cushions. This time there was no frantic lovemaking, just the closeness of lying still and listening to the music that was drifting up from three floors below.

Later they walked the entire length of Las Ramblas to take lunch in a tapas bar off the Placa Catalunya. Surprisingly, they were the sole diners and chose a table looking out onto the busy streets. They stared out at a musician who was setting up his guitar. He waved at them through the window before unpacking an amplifier and fold-up seat.

Over a mouth-watering meal of tortillas, patatas bravas, ham, cheese and chorizo washed down with freshly squeezed orange juice, they watched the world go by.

'Are you going to miss me when I go to London?'

William frowned and went on to kiss her forehead. 'What sort of a question is that, of course I'm going to miss you, but I know it's really important for you to go. I know I'd jump at the chance to become an author if I had your skill.'

'I keep telling you it takes a lot of effort and even more luck, but I'm convinced you will get there. My one regret is I promised to mentor you and here I am gallivanting off around Europe. I promise on my return to keep my word and help you.'

In an anxious voice that must have sounded like he was desperate for her to stay, he muttered, 'You couldn't cut the trip down to get back to me sooner, could you?'

'Are you for real? It's just a few weeks and I'm looking forward to being in Finland again. It's been a long time since I was there.'

Her mention of Finland prompted him to tell her again what an incredible read her book had been.

'Thanks, that means a lot to me.'

William was now holding her hand. 'We may have been together for a short while, but I will be counting the days until your return.'

'Believe me, the time will fly. We'll talk on Facetime every day and I'll tell you about how the trip is going. You just have to remember I love you and I'm in for the long run, so stop worrying.'

William forced a smile. 'Got that. Just bring me back a signed copy of your novel.'

Sarah suddenly looked deep in thought as if she'd just remembered something. 'I keep meaning to ask how your ex-wife is getting on with her chemo.'

'She's well into the treatment and from what she's said it seems to be going well. I'm hoping she'll be back in remission any time soon. It must be awful having this hanging over her.'

Nodding her head Sarah whispered, 'It doesn't bear thinking. Let's hope she gets the all clear.'

* * * *

Later that afternoon, the light was fading, and a cool breeze whipped through the tall buildings and avenues that lined the approach to the Sagrada Familia. Glancing up at the towers of Gaudi's unfinished cathedral, an idea suddenly came to William.

'Hey, I just thought of something. As you are going to Finland, how about, once you've completed the British book signing, I fly out to Helsinki to join you for a few nights?'

He paused and lowered his voice. 'It's going to be really cold there. I read that the sea freezes over and it gets dark terribly early in the afternoon. I could keep you warm.'

Sarah's face lit up. 'I really believe you would go all that way to snatch a few hours with me. Yes, of course I want you there, then I will return to London for a meeting with my editor before coming home.'

'Then it's agreed. I'll get on line when I get back home and book a flight. You'll need to give me the hotel details.'

'No problem. I will change my booking for the two of us. I've got two book signings in the capital, so why don't I tell Scooter that you and I will add a further day or two to the trip. We can travel up to a super lakeside hotel in Imatra for the night.'

She smiled and wagged a finger in the air. 'Just one thing though – if you attend the book signing and I sign a copy for you, please don't kiss the author.'

Chapter 12

Having arrived in Finland, William booked into their hotel before meeting up with Sarah who was busy completing some research in the city. On donning his new anorak with the fleece lining and hood, he set off for the port to have a look around. Contrary to his understanding the temperature in December in Helsinki was just above freezing. As magical and picturesque as it would have been, the sea around the port had not frozen over. A dusting of snow on the magnificent high-domed churches and palaces added to the thrill of being there. It was still very cold with a northerly wind whipping the dark clouds over the city.

Wandering around on his own, William's first impressions were of a welcoming city with an attractive waterfront. Old warehousing had been converted into trendy clothes' shops and restaurants while the stunning white cathedral with green domes dominated the city skyline. He was thrilled to see the Uspenski Russian Orthodox cathedral that sat high on a hill to the east of the city. On arriving at the port there were no ferries or liners to be seen. Sarah told him that in the warmer months, the crossings to Tallinn, Stockholm and St Petersburg were numerous. This being William's first visit, he was enthralled by the graceful architecture, elegant gardens and the unique island fortress. Walking along the road away from quay, he gazed at the white and pastel green government buildings with soldiers in their smart grey uniforms and black peaked caps. He was shivering with the cold and wished he had listened to Sarah's advice about wearing gloves. The snow was now falling much harder and settling on everyone's hats. He increased his pace along narrow roads that eventually widened into the main shopping area. Cobbled streets with restaurants, covered food halls and shops made this an attractive place to visit. On reaching Senate Square, the market was atmospheric, and his eyes lit up on at seeing so many Finnish craft, food and Christmas gift stalls. The sound of live music heightened the experience as he braved the cold weather. Eyeing up the crispy sausages cooking on grills, the smell reminded him of the delicious steaks they served back in Spain.

It was then that he saw Sarah in her bright purple, long coat, red gloves and scarf. Crossing to where she was standing she became excited to see him. They hugged and on pulling away she patted the sleeve of his anorak.

'I like the coat, it should keep you warm. Now what did you think of our hotel?'

Stamping his feet to keep warm he was aware of people staring at him. 'You couldn't have described it better. I love the room and now I'm wishing I'd brought my swimming costume to wear in the sauna.'

He looked shocked when she corrected him.

'You can still take the sauna as they don't bother with any clothing. It never worried me, even in the mixed sessions.'

'I'm not sure about any of that unless it is just you and me there.'

* * * *

Ready for a warm up and something to eat, they entered the covered Food Yard and marvelled at the variety of pies and cold meats available. The sizzling strips of steak cooking on the wood-burning stoves smelt amazing and Sarah had to stop William from buying lunch out in the open. She told him she knew a small restaurant close to the railway station. In the pine-clad eating house, traditional Finish food was laid out in a buffet. Not to be missed was the lohiketto salmon soup prepared with milk, potatoes and dill. Their main course, kalakukko, consisting of rye pastry with herring, bacon and onions, was a treat. It was obvious from the menu that Finnish people liked their fish, but for William, the giant reindeer cheeseburgers appealed even more.

Sarah insisted on a visit to the infamous Moomin Café that was part of a chain found in various cities throughout the world. It took its name from work of the Finnish illustrator who created the popular children's picture books and comic strip; the loveable roundish fairytale characters with their large snouts resembled hippopotamuses. Watching the children play, William and Sarah enjoyed sipping their hot chocolate drinks and sampling the cinnamon buns. Sarah took a selfie and posted it on Facebook prompting many comments from her friends.

****

The ride in a taxi back to their hotel came as a little bit of a shock as the blond-haired Finn with the bushy beard had plenty to say in his perfect English. With their backs pressed hard into in the seats of the Volvo, they were surprised by his tirade.

'You do know what the problem is with British people?'

Possibly too feebly William replied, 'Mmm, no.'

The man's voice grew as he expanded on his theme, 'You all appear to have an opinion on most things and think you are the only people in Europe and this attitude is not good.'

Sarah put a hand out to stop William leaning forward

and replying. She whispered, saying that the man must have had a bad session in his sauna and burnt something. Fortunately, their driver with the extraordinary attitude remained silent for the remainder of the journey. Thankfully this man was not typical of the charming Finns they had already encountered in the shops and restaurants during their trip.

Arriving at the hotel, the greeting they received was much more pleasant than the one they got from the taxi driver.

Back in their warm room Sarah drew the curtains and to William's delight turned down the duvet on the bed and started to undress. With his excitement growing he watched her slip out of her long blue skirt, dropping it on the carpet along with her blouse and jumper. Naked, except for white knickers, she climbed into the massive bed and closed her eyes. Dropping his clothes around his feet he quickly joined Sarah. She smelt wonderful and running his hands over her smooth skin his desire to make love to her grew in intensity. He felt like he was in heaven. Making up for not seeing each other for two weeks was fun, just like the first time they discovered each other. Later, they lay back very much out of breath but feeling content and so much in love.

* * * *

Sarah had lived in Helsinki for a year when she was a young woman and consequently knew all the haunts. Later that night she led the way through the port to a steep hill where what looked like a prison came into sight. With high walls, the building was now a hotel that was popular with tourists. They made their way past the merchants' houses and large industrial warehouses that had been converted into flats. The snow had stopped falling, but the wind chill was getting too much for William who pulled on his scarf in an effort to keep warm. Just before the road came to an end, they came to a small restaurant and went inside. Relieved to be under cover and seated at a table next to a roaring log fire, the magic of this truly Finnish restaurant unfolded for the two tired travellers.

They dined on buckwheat pancakes, known as blinis, filled with sour cream and mushrooms and enjoyed just one glass of white wine each.

Although Sarah had already given him details of the UK trip he still wanted to know more. 'Everything you said about your time back home in the UK sounded great. Was it tricky getting around to the various locations?'

'No, not at all, Scooter guided me through everything. He even travelled with me up to Birmingham, Manchester and Edinburgh to the bookshops where I did the signings. The odd thing was the northern trip seemed more successful than London. They were large stores and loads of people came to see me. Whilst we were up there, I got a message from the publisher who confirmed my book deal for two further novels.'

'That's what I call a result. I'm proud of you.'

William reached down into his coat pocket and produced a small red box. 'I have a present for you.'

Sarah, all excited, opened the gift to discover a beautiful gold dress ring. He tried to place it on her finger but unfortunately it was too small.

'It's lovely, it must have cost a fortune.'

'I just wish I'd picked the correct size, let's hope it can be altered and...'

They were interrupted by William's mobile ringing. He glanced at the screen and muttered that it was Martin.

'Martin, old boy, how are you? Can I ring you tomorrow as we are eating at the moment?'

He ended the call and smiled. 'Sorry about that, he's always ringing me. You'll have to tell me about what I should do at the book signing tomorrow.'

Fingering the narrow gold band of the wonderful ring, Sarah raised her eyes to the ceiling and back to William. 'You can get the ball rolling by buying a book but promise you won't go telling everyone you know me personally.'

* * * *

Entering the Forum Centre in the heart of Helsinki's busiest shopping area, Sarah was thrilled to catch sight of a large colour poster with a photo of herself. The wording read: *Book signing on level three in the Gotti suite. Best-selling author Sarah Barney's acclaimed novel 'Wrong Side of Sanity.'*

Riding the escalator and clutching Sarah's workbag, William gazed at the incredible department store with the modern Finnish furniture and gifts. There was also a model reindeer mounted on a base with a background depicting the Northern Lights. Following the instructions in the document from Scooter, they presented themselves at the customer services desk and it wasn't long before the director of sales for the store appeared to greet them.

Immaculately dressed in a navy-blue pinstripe suit, the bearded man with a huge birthmark that covered the entirety of his left cheek welcomed them. He spoke impeccable English and ushered them into his office. With introductions over, he congratulated Sarah on her captivating drama that featured Helsinki. He claimed it had touched many people's hearts in their country and that it was a frightening insight into how easily things can go wrong. He was keen to know if a film would be made of the story.

The venue for promoting the book was in the Gotti Suite and a table had already been set up with a poster similar to the one they'd seen earlier. William could sense Sarah's nervousness as she straightened the piles of books ready to be signed.

'What happens if no one turns up?' Sarah said with a look of panic in her eyes.

William placed a reassuring arm around her. 'Don't be silly. The ones in England went well. Keep remembering what the director just said about how successful you are.'

'Yes, but all this fame has happened so quickly. I've always had a lot of my books selling, but this is surreal. A few weeks ago, I would never have dreamt I'd be in demand like this.'

It was time for the event to start and the tall white doors creaked as they were opened. There must have been over a hundred people waiting to come in.

Even William was shocked as he quietly mouthed, 'Bloody hell.'

Fortunately, there was a member of staff who took the money and restacked the books for signing. More and more customers joined the queue with a number asking the author if she'd mind posing for a selfie. Sarah was happy to oblige and answered questions as she endorsed the inside page of her book. She thanked everyone for making the purchase.

William hung back but couldn't help noticing a man of similar age to Sarah who was waiting in the wings. He looked Finnish with his long blond locks and blue eyes. He was staring at her and clutching a small bouquet of bright red roses that must have cost a fortune. With winter bedding in, flowers had to be imported and carried a hefty price tag. Who was this mystery man? Possibly a fan who enjoyed her book who was waiting for the crowd to disperse to speak directly to her.

When the last of the people left, the man in the designer black jeans and three-quarter-length coat with large shiny buttons moved in to speak to Sarah. As he reached the desk, Sarah gasped and put a hand to her mouth. 'Oh my God, is it really you Pavvii?

* * * *

The late afternoon journey in the rental car to reach the hotel in Imatra was over one hundred miles north of Helsinki. Driving past rich green forests and lakes there were plenty of *'beware of elks'* signs on the roads and unpronounceable town names that displayed massive use of the letters A, I, K, J, L and P. The location for their stay was in a forest by a lake. It was getting dark when they booked in and the welcome given by the receptionist was a little strange. Her multi-tasking included managing to avoid eye contact and checking her mobile phone for messages. Not once did her sullen face break into even a half-smile. To all intents and purposes, it was like the newly arrived guests weren't even standing on the other side of the counter.

To their amusement, for the duration of their two-night stay, they were issued with a book of tickets for the breakfast, dinner, gym, complimentary bar drink, parking permit and the sauna suite. However, during their stay not once were the tickets requested for the various services the couple enjoyed.

Ravenously hungry, they joined a handful of diners in the cavernous pine-clad restaurant. The room was chilly, and badly lit. Had they switched the heating off? It soon became apparent that the receptionist with the poor communication skills doubled up as a waitress and that she was multi-tasking taking orders and serving the food. It took nearly an hour to get their meals and they wondered if the same lady was doing the cooking. The reindeer stew with steaming hot potatoes was delicious. Neither of them drank any alcohol as they were exhausted from their travelling and eager to get a hot bath before going to bed.

Retiring to their Superior Room with a view of the lake they kissed and fell asleep immediately.

On opening the curtains the following morning, much to their annoyance, an enormous yellow skip lay in front of their window, totally blocking out the scenery. When they mentioned it to the girl on the desk she seemed totally unsympathetic saying they could still see the trees. Their efforts to change rooms fell on deaf ears as they were told all the accommodation was fully booked.

Sarah's voice rang out, 'Now hold on there, you told us there were four other couples staying. You also said it was the last week of the season before you closed, surely you can move us.'

The receptionist, who was wearing an anorak with a fur-lined hood, refused to be drawn into the conversation and returned to reading e-mails on her mobile.

* * * *

On closer observation, both the hotel's interior decoration and outside wooden cladding were in need of much attention. Hadn't Sarah said this was a super hotel? Walking down to the lake the real beauty was there to be seen with the picturesque log cabins with a dusting of snow on the roofs. Nestled in the woods that bordered the shoreline were trails that ran through the forest. Despite the cold weather, there was much evidence of wildlife with birds still in abundance and red squirrels busy hunting for acorns to store for the winter.

Walking hand-in-hand William wanted to broach the subject of the mystery man at the Helsinki store who had kissed Sarah's cheek. It was obvious the two knew each other and after a brief chat both exchanged cards and off he went.

'That man at the end of the afternoon who didn't buy a book, but seemed to know who you were – who was he and why was he giving you those roses?'

Sounding sheepish with her reply, Sarah broke away from his side. 'I didn't even think you'd noticed. I left the flowers on the desk. It was my ex-boyfriend Pavvii from the time I lived in Finland. We lived together for the last six months of my time here. He read in the paper I was promoting my book, so popped in to say hello.'

'Oh, I see.'

'Pavvii worked for one of the big newspaper companies as a literary critic. If he hadn't encouraged me to follow my dream, I don't think I'd be where I am today.'

William slowed his pace to a crawl. 'Did you break up with him and that's why you returned to England?'

'It's complicated. I met someone else, an English man who was visiting Helsinki. The rest you know. He became my partner and I told you that he died. I was in mourning for a number of years, that is until you came into my life.'

Reaching out for Sarah's hand he excitedly said, 'And that was the best thing that ever happened to me.'

He paused as his thoughts went over the possibility that her old friend Pavvii may try to keep in touch. He continued, 'Is this guy married?'

Sarah burst into laughter. 'I do believe you are jealous. For heaven's sake change the record and look around at all this beauty.'

* * * *

That evening the hotel was remarkably busy preparing for a local dance club to hold their meeting. Multitudes of people descended on the restaurant area in preparation for the ballroom dancing that was due to start at seven o'clock. Anxious they wouldn't get a table William tackled the receptionist who, unexpectedly, had already made a reservation for them. On this occasion she made a point of telling them to bring their tickets to gain entry to the dining room.

Hungry, and with tickets ready, they sailed through the restaurant entrance without being asked for the poorly photocopied vouchers. On this occasion they were pleased to see an abundance of staff serving the many diners. Close to the oblong wooden dance floor, two men were setting up speakers and other electronic apparatus. It appeared they were disagreeing on something as both were frowning. Eventually, the younger Finn snatched a cable from his colleague provoking an angry shaking of his head.

The heating was definitely turned up high, probably not for the benefit of the guests, but for the dancers. The beautifully laid out soups, grilled meats, fish and roasted potatoes on large tables were kept warm in heated trays. Rather strangely, prior to eating, their young waitress brought over the desert and two enormous spoons.

Worryingly, this evening Sarah was knocking back the drink and at times was rather loud, which William was starting to find embarrassing. Trying to tell her to quieten down failed to have the response he had hoped for as she became even more excited. Talkative and fidgeting with the tablecloth, it was obvious she was becoming extremely hyperactive.

Trying not to talk too loud in fear of being overhead, he pleaded, 'Why don't you slow down on the wine, darling? I don't want you getting too drunk.'

Slurring her words and reaching out for the wine bottle she was giggling. 'I... I... don't know what you mean.' She paused and then stood up to smooth down the front of her dress and rather too loudly announced she was going to find the toilet.

William watched her wobbly walk along the edge of the dance floor stopping occasionally to chat to other diners. Suddenly the dancers took to the wooden floor in force and at least twenty couples wowed the onlookers with their quickstep routine. There was much clapping and tapping of feet which went on for some time. He watched Sarah in the reception area as she came close to entering the men's room before locating the right door.

Above the noise of the music, William was suddenly aware of her mobile on the table that was glowing and vibrating. He leant forward to grasp it and was shocked to read a text: 'Urgent. Ring Pavvii as soon as possible.'

His heart skipped a beat as he cursed the man who just the day before had leant over the desk to kiss his woman on both cheeks. He had witnessed the swapping of cards and now he was contacting her. The burning question was why she was encouraging him to keep in touch? He was also annoyed she hadn't introduced him to this man, instead they'd chatted and ignored him as if he wasn't present. Even if the guy had noticed him, he may have just thought he was her agent or just some old man waiting to chat.

Waiting for Sarah to return, he turned his attention to the elderly group of dancers who were enjoying their tango. Sarah came back and, like many times before, as if by magic she had sobered up. Acting as if nothing had occurred she returned looking fresh and in complete composure of her senses. What was protecting her from slipping into the realms of becoming an alcoholic was indeed a puzzle. William stood up for her to sit and calmly said she'd missed a call. In a disinterested manner she swiped the screen on her phone. On discovering Pavvii had sent a text this made her smile.

'Can't think what he wants. I suppose I ought to ring him.'

'Who dear, ring who?'

'Oh, just Pavvii, the guy at yesterday's book signing. You wait here and I'll make the call from the lounge area where the signal should be better. Won't be long. Have another drink and I'll be back shortly.' She paused. 'Hey, the dancing is really good, isn't it?'

William looked on helplessly as he watched the woman he loved grasping her phone and leaving him sitting there while she went off to speak to her ex.

Ten agonising minutes later she was back at the table looking pleased with herself.

'You will never guess the outcome of that call. It turns out that he wants to write an article on me. As my book has resonated with many people here he's keen for me to tell my story as an author. The interview tomorrow will be in a private press lounge in the airport. He's also bringing along a photographer. The coverage will help my writing career no end.'

Trying to disguise his worried voice he nervously coughed. 'I'm sure it will. That's incredible news and well done. Will there be time before your flight for the interview though?'

'Not a problem because I'm scheduled to fly out about two hours after you take off. It will be a good way to pass the hours before boarding. I'm so excited getting this break. What a stroke of luck meeting up with Pavvii again.'

* * * *

The following morning, they took a short walk by the lake before setting off for Vantaa airport. Back in the car William concentrated on his driving whilst Sarah slept for the entire journey. Soon they were on the shuttle bus having returned the hire car. In a short space of time he would be leaving Sarah alone and possibly at the mercy of her ex-boyfriend. He wished they were on the same flight allowing him to remain in the airport whilst she was being interviewed, but that wasn't the case and there was nothing he could do about it.

When it was time to make his way to the boarding gate, he became emotional and clung to Sarah saying he didn't want to leave her. She kissed him hard on the lips telling him there was just another three days before she'd be home. She also told him she loved him more than anything else in the world.

Waving goodbye as he walked towards the gates he suddenly stopped in his tracks to look back, but there was no sign of her.

* * * *

It was gone midnight before William let himself into his apartment and sent a text to Sarah to say he arrived back safely. Exhausted from his two flights, he collapsed into bed and slept until after nine the next morning. He awoke to the sound of the road cleaner truck directly outside in the street. Dragging himself into the bathroom he glanced at his reflection in the mirror. He'd definitely put on weight and vowed to eat less in an attempt to look slimmer. Literary man Pavvii was super-slim with boyish looks, unlike himself who was carrying a heavier load. It was imperative for him to remain trim and attractive if he wanted to keep Sarah interested.

Checking his phone over breakfast he was relieved to discover a text from her but was shocked as the message lit up the screen: *Still in Helsinki. Flight at 11.00 this morning. Facetime you later.*

William slung the mobile onto the table before swearing loudly, 'Bloody Pavvii, he's obviously persuaded her to miss the flight last night.'

Out on the balcony he stared at the view overlooking the bay. Unfortunately, he couldn't see the beauty in what he was seeing. All he could think about was Sarah and Pavvii.

Feeling sick with worry, a cruel scenario flashed incessantly through his mind. Was she was slipping away from him already and had that creep encouraged her to drink further glasses of wine? Possibly in an intoxicated state, she may have followed him along the hotel corridor. He pictured their fast and furious lovemaking with just the necessary items of clothing removed. William was torturing his mind as he imagined her yelping with pleasure as the strong young man satisfied her. Pavvii, with all the energy that youth offers, was once again to take advantage before collapsing next to her to sleep.

William raised a hand to his face and pinched the unshaven cheek hard in an effort to empty his head of the horrendous thoughts that he knew must be just his imagination running wild. What was wrong with him distrusting her like this? Surely with their love for each other she wouldn't have been disloyal? He muttered, 'Get a grip man.'

* * * *

It was mid-afternoon before William ventured out into the streets to visit the local supermarket to buy bread and top up on groceries. Inadvertently, he had gone out without a coat and cared little about being soaked by the persistent drizzle that was turning heavier by the minute. He walked slowly towards the mini-market, but his thoughts were interrupted as Martin caught up with him.

'It's going to pour and you've got no coat. Get that arse of yours into gear and let's get under cover.'

William obediently followed, increasing his pace to reach the store. Once under cover they robustly shook hands. It felt good to meet up again. The two men stood in the doorway watching the heavy rain thundering onto the awnings and making rivulets on the road. They kept moving to one side to allow shoppers to come and go.

'Go on, tell me how was Sweden?'

William laughed loudly, 'Actually it was Finland old chap. You were never any good on detail, were you? It was an amazing place to visit. Sarah is really motoring with her writing; she's actually quite famous. Hopefully she'll make a lot of money with the royalties from her books. Anyway, more importantly, how did your visit with the dentist lady in Gerona go?'

As they entered the store Martin pointed to the badly buckled and yellowed teeth. 'Oh, next week these will come out so the implant preparation can begin. She reckons it won't be too painful, but I'm not that sure. It will be worth all the aggravation to look good.'

William was about to respond with some reassuring words when his friend touched his arm and said, 'Going back to what you were saying about Sarah's climb to fame, she probably needs the press to interview her. There might be a newspaper or magazine that can put together a good article on her. If those guys show interest they won't let go without delving deep to get the story. What do you think?'

There was no answer, just the feeling of nausea creeping up into the back of William's throat. He turned away and stared at the shelves of cleaning materials in the entrance of the shop. The suggestion of anyone like Pavvii paying any attention to his woman was too much to bear.

Chapter 13

Coping with the poor broadband signal in Spain was never easy when using the Facetime app, due to the screen continuously freezing. The initial connection was frustrating with the uncertainty of whether the person at the other end could see or hear the caller. On this occasion it took three attempts to make contact with vertical lines appearing on the screen followed by the message *'poor connection.'*

When the picture finally settled, Sarah was frowning. 'It doesn't get much better does it? It's great to see you. Are you missing me?'

'Miss you; of course I'm missing you. You didn't get your flight then?'

He watched as she shrugged her shoulders, 'Just one of those things that happens – some technical problem with the aircraft. The flight was cancelled but they did put me up in a reasonable hotel.'

Trying not to show how stressed he felt about her staying over another night with that man hanging about, he turned his face away from the screen. 'I wondered if your interview was delayed and you had to stay over. Did Pavvii know your flight was postponed and did he wait in the airport with you?' he asked tentatively.

Watching Sarah's face for her reaction, she raised her eyes quizzically. 'And your point is William? Look it was a great interview with him highlighting how I first got published and the success that has been building. Of course, yes, he kept me company, but stop reading things into it. We had dinner in the airport. He even got me a taxi to go to the hotel. I'll say this once – nothing happened.'

Feeling cross with himself for imagining the worst, he made a concentrated effort to banish any further ridiculous ideas from his mind. He forced a smile and lied, 'Ignore me; I'm okay with everything. This editor guy could be useful for promoting your book, so bring it on.'

'For just one moment I was worried because you sounded jealous. It was a lucky break meeting up with him again. He's a really great person and put me at ease. He forked out for a really decent bottle of wine at dinner that must have cost a fortune. I think I had a bit too much to drink as I can't even remember going to sleep that night.'

William shuddered on hearing her say this. He interjected with, 'I hope you were careful. I should have been there.'

'It was just business. I now have to get to London. Some good news though, I'll be home on Thursday as I'm cutting the trip short. The editor has agreed to see me earlier than scheduled. Are you still on to meet me at the airport?'

* * * *

On the day of her flight back, William stood around in the airport terminal scanning the arrivals screen. Fidgeting with the rental car keys, his heart was quite literally aching with longing to see her. He kept telling himself how silly he'd been worrying about her being unfaithful. Of course, she'd stayed true to him and was now coming home. Hopefully this Finn's assistance would add to Sarah's reputation as a writer, but he also hoped there would be no further contact from the man.

When Sarah finally came out wheeling her red case he was in for quite a shock. Her hair was cut really short which made her look even younger. Despite the cooler weather she was wearing a short-pleated skirt, the hemline definitely exposing more of her legs than ever before. Perched on new red high-heeled shoes she looked taller and it suited her. When he reached her, they hugged briefly.

'Your hair, what have you done to your hair? And is that a new skirt, or should I say belt?'

'Very funny; this is my new image. I'm still young and half decent looking and I thought you'd like the skirt.'

The little voice in William's head secretly whispered, *You can't keep your eyes off her, can you? Lucky man.*

Now in control of her luggage he listened as Sarah chatted incessantly about her trip and the new book deal. The publisher was pushing her to complete the new novel, so the pressure was on.

Determined to get a word in edgeways, William raised his voice to compete with the noisy airport. 'I'm so glad you are home. I've been lost without you.'

'Oh, you poor thing. We saw each other just a few days ago in Helsinki. The time has flown for me what with the interview and then London. By the way, my agent Scooter sends his regards and get ready for a shock; he mentioned he has been in touch with your friend Martin quite a bit and they hope to meet up soon.'

'Good for him, he never mentioned anything when I saw him the other day. That really pleases me, especially if they get together. Martin needs someone in his life and Scooter could be the guy to make him happy. I saw how well they got on at your place, but he never said a word to me about this.'

Out in the airport car park, William had a senior moment and forgot the make and colour of the rental car. He was unsure where he'd parked it. The paperwork with the details of the number plate had been left in the vehicle along with his wallet. Sarah's cool-headed intervention kicked in as she demanded the key fob. Soon the small white Ford lit up with orange flashing lights.

The road back to Lloret de Mar was along the new carriageway and driving in the pitch dark was tricky. William missed the turn off for the town, which involved having to find a side road to turn around in. He took the steep road that led through the hills to Tossa and kept saying they would soon be home.

On reaching Sarah's villa he could see how tired she was and suggested she get straight to bed and they'd talk in the morning.

Before entering the villa, she pulled him close and his feelings were soon aroused. With his hands firmly around the waistband of her skirt he longed for more but knew he'd have to be patient. Determined she should catch up on her sleep, he kissed her forehead before gently pulling away.

* * * *

The rest of the week was magical for William and Sarah with long walks along the cliff and taking meals in neighbouring towns and seaside restaurants. Importantly, their relationship appeared to be enough for Sarah, as mercifully she moderated her drinking. There was always the worry that on her own she secretly turned to the bottle.

Over dinner one evening in his apartment, William was thrilled to hear her say she wanted to spend the rest of her life with him and they should tie the knot. She also spelled out the necessity for balancing a life with him and meeting deadlines for her new books. Once again, she mentioned not helping him with his writing. Her plan was look over his recent text and offer constructive help. He didn't have the heart to tell her for the last two weeks he hadn't even opened the lid of the laptop.

* * * *

Sarah's brother travelled over from the UK with a potential buyer for the property. Scooter, Sarah's friend and agent, had fallen in love with the quaint Spanish home and was over to sign the papers. His intention was to holiday and occasionally work from this location.

Scooter kindly invited Sarah and William for dinner at a local restaurant. The calamari starters although frozen, were delicious as were the steaks with patatas fritas. This particular evening the couple chose not to drink but kept holding hands and whispering words of love. Scooter made a further announcement that a new friend of his would be joining them for a drink.

In marched Martin in a pastel blue jacket with open shirt. Smoothly shaved and smelling of expensive aftershave, that he later revealed had been a gift from Scooter, he pulled up a chair to join the group. With a cheeky grin on his face, he thanked the host and proceeded to eye up what everyone was drinking.

Smiling at his guest Scooter said, 'I suppose I should tell everyone that you and I are really good friends.'

William patted Martin's arm. 'Does this mean you will stop hitting on me now you have a new man in your life!'

There were roars of laughter from everyone as William glanced around the busy restaurant at the other diners who found their conversation amusing. On ordering further drinks Scooter momentarily closed his eyes before saying, 'Last guest to arrive pays for these.'

Martin looked embarrassed as he checked his wallet. Staring at the small number of notes, he joked, 'In that case darling we may have to change that Rioja to lemonades.'

* * * *

On the day William proposed to Sarah, he placed a beautiful diamond ring on her slender finger. She leant forward to kiss him then whispered in his ear that she loved him. Celebrating with a glass of champagne they donned jumpers to stand outside to take in the view. The Villa Vella looked spectacular in the late morning sun with a cool breeze that was gently swaying the geranium baskets on the sandstone castle walls. They could see and hear the elderly Spanish residents dressed head to toe in obligatory Mediterranean black who were out enjoying their stroll. Colourful flashing lights attached to many of the buildings had transformed the fairytale town of Tossa into a wonderful place to spend Christmas. There was even a shop in town that was selling artificial trees and decorations. The single thing missing was Father Christmas, but William was convinced Martin would know someone who owned a red outfit for the occasion.

With the vegetables peeled and the joint of beef cooking slowly in the oven, William left Sarah in the lounge to ring his ex-wife to check on her health. He'd heard that the chemotherapy had been successful and she was back in remission. As he dialed her number, he prayed that she would remain in good health allowing her to enjoy the rest of her life.

When Joan picked up, she sounded flustered. Having just commenced with cooking her Christmas lunch the power had gone off. The electricity company was estimating a three-hour window for restoring the service. William sympathised with her but was still interested to know if she'd bought a whole turkey for just her and the reply pleased him. A new man called Ray had entered her life and at that precise moment he was on his way over to join her. Her opportunity to find happiness with someone was great news allowing him to stop worrying about her. He held back on disclosing details of his engagement and ended the call feeling relieved that all was well.

* * * *

The next few days were busy attending drinks parties at friends' houses. William certainly knew many people, mostly British couples who'd settled in Spain. Whilst Sarah had integrated well into the local community, she had remained a bit of a loner concentrating on her work. She recently admitted missing running the writing group and vowed to e-mail the members with a new timetable for classes when things became less busy. William carefully reminded her that some of the writers must be concerned over the uncertainty of the lessons continuing. One matter still needed to be addressed though – where was she going to live? For the meantime Scooter had kindly agreed she could stay for a short while in his newly acquired villa paying a minimum rent.

Chapter 14

William stared in disbelief as Sarah pointed to the images on her laptop.

'A tattoo!' he shrieked. 'What do you want to have one of those for?'

'Calm down, won't you. Everyone's having them done. It's quite safe. It really won't hurt and we'll get them done together.'

Unsettled with the suggestion of having anyone pricking his skin with a needle, he shook his head. 'Look, I'm much older than you and the last thing I want is one of those things.'

'Many of the ladies in my writing group are your age and they have butterflies on their arms, necks and legs and a few other unmentionable places. It's fashionable and nobody bats an eyelid anymore.'

'Everyone except me.'

'I'm asking that you to have a small one with a picture of a sunflower and the first initial of my name. I'm going to have you on my arm, so stop making such a big deal about it. You do love me enough to do this for me, don't you?'

'Well if that's not emotional blackmail, I don't know what is.'

Sarah, obviously seeing the funny side of what she was about to say, laboured her words. 'And don't go worrying about having the first letter of my name on your arm. If you left me you could always look for a girl with a name like: Sheila, Sally or even a Sabrina.'

'Stop mucking about. You know I don't want anyone else. Okay, where do we go to do the terrible deed?'

'I've booked us into a place in Lloret de Mar. It is

also a vape bar that serves cocktails.'

William laughed loudly, 'Great, so if the dreaded needle doesn't finish us off, the vapour from those ruddy electric cigarettes will.'

* * * *

Ron's Vaper Lounge & Tattoo Studio was situated in a row of shops close to the petrol station in town. It was housed in a poor looking building that had seen better days. The windows were plastered with examples of their work and vapour accessories for sale. Hanging from two chains, a flashing sign with the wording *Vape Shop* swung in the mid-morning breeze. Entering the tatty premises, they were greeted by a young man with short jet-black hair and tattoos that ran up both sides of his neck. As Sarah had booked the appointments, there were various forms to be filled in before entering the main lounge.

To the left of the tiny reception, the poorly lit vaping bar was devoid of any customers, but there was loud music playing. A young girl was stacking shelves with all the various products associated with electronic smoking.

William settled into the comfy chair that was showing signs of wear with slits on the leather armrests and the smell of the tanned skin. It reminded him of Martin's sofa. All that was missing were the cigarette burns and grubby cushions that his friend insisted added character to the room.

He was startled by a loud voice as a man entered the shop. The South London tone sounded familiar. On turning to get a better look, to his alarm there stood James Moorfield, someone he used to know back in Croydon. The man who was that bit younger than him was the publican who used to run the Goose and Bear

145

pub. The old Victorian drinking house had been directly opposite William's undertaking firm and was well attended by many of the local office workers. James hadn't changed one iota with his belly that still overhung the waistline of his faded jeans. Totally bald with a shiny forehead, his narrow lips twitched as his voice boomed out.

'Bloody hell, fancy bumping into you. You've lost so much weight and a new shorter haircut, just like mine. But, I knew it was you. How the hell are you old man?'

William cringed wondering what he should say to the man who was holding out a hairy hand to shake.

'Who's your friend?' Sarah asked quietly.

William reluctantly grasped James' greasy palm. He promptly drew it back to the side of his trousers to wipe his damp fingers.

Turning to Sarah, he made the introductions saying he knew James back in London.

'That's right. I still run the pub near to where he worked, or should I say used to! I never thought I'd see him again. I know he's divorced, but had no idea where he had moved to. Are you on holiday like my wife and I?'

Sarah smiled and stood close to her man. 'No, we live out here.'

In a triumphant voice James told them that he and his wife owned an apartment in Lloret which they rented out.

'And where do you two live?'

Sarah was first to answer. 'Tossa de Mar.'

'Much quieter than here then. We should keep in touch and next time we are out here let's meet up for a meal.'

William panicked. There was far too many questions for his liking. He just wished the tattoo man would call them in for their appointment to escape the interrogation. This was going to be tricky with this old acquaintance knowing so much about his past. What if Sarah was to discover what the nature of his old profession was? He should have told her about his work but with the rawness still biting deep he had been ashamed.

William steadied himself on the side of the chair and looked anxiously in the direction of the receptionist willing him to announce they were ready to see them.

He was relieved to hear the young man say that Sarah should go through first and he stood up to let her go in.

She bid farewell to James and was shown into the treatment room.

Then the cross-examination began again. 'You managed to sell your business very quickly which surprised us all. That was a grim old trade if you don't mind me saying.'

'Tell me about it. I needed a change.'

'I was sorry to hear about the trouble you had and all that bad publicity. It was in the papers and local TV. How did you manage to bury the wrong man? You also lost your son as well. I'm sorry for your loss.'

The nightmare was starting all over again and the perspiration started to run down William's forehead. Launching himself out of the chair his intention was to leave the shop to escape any further agony. Sarah would be furious, but he was at breaking point.

James was concerned he'd upset William by mentioning the loss of his son and apologised profusely and persuaded his old customer to sit down. He quickly changed the subject to his sister. 'She bought one of the town houses they built on your old site. Paid over six hundred thousand. The three-bedroom ones sell for just over seven. What a rip off as none have garages and are on that busy road.'

William stuttered, 'Seven hundred thousand!' He was shocked at learning the true value of the land he'd sold wishing he'd hung out for a better return. The contractors had managed to squeeze these homes onto his old site and made a fortune.

'Have you not thought of retiring James?'

'Me, God no, I can't afford to retire. I'm much younger than you. I also enjoy living in Croydon.'

William suddenly felt terribly old and ran fingers over the stubble on his chin. He'd got up too late to shave and now felt uncomfortable.

He said the first thing that came into his mind. 'I imagine you are waiting for a tattoo like me.'

'Yep, that's the plan. It's my last day before we fly home and I'm going to surprise the wife by having one done. She's got them all over her body, and I literally mean all over.'

James was next to go through to one of the booths and they said their goodbyes. Just before he left, he thrust a card into William's hand. 'E-mail me some time. When Marleen and I are out here again, we'll sink a few beers with you and catch up on old times.'

* * * *

When Sarah came out he asked her if it had been painful and she shrugged her shoulders. He left her reading a magazine while he went in for his turn. She certainly didn't look in pain, but she still wished him good luck.

In the cramped area with pictures of dragons, birds, faces and flowers, William became nervous. After a brief discussion with the man with the long hair tied back and denim blue shirt with various metal badges, the leftover hippy told him to relax. He mentioned the legislation and all the safety rules required for running the business. Pointing to the certificate on the wall with the registration for their practice, William noticed the date on the document was over ten years old.

'Sit on the couch please and take it easy. This will take just under an hour and it shouldn't hurt. So, it's the same sunflower as your wife had with the first letter of her name, Sarah. Is that right?'

William liked the reference to wife and nodded his head in agreement. He did, however, request that the image didn't need to be too big.

The man inspected his arm in great detail before reaching for his electric shaver to remove the hair for a smooth surface to inject the ink. The area was disinfected and William's body tensed up as he felt the first prick of the needle on his skin. It was a process that left him feeling sore. There was much dabbing and to add to his distress there was evidence of blood that kept forming on the partly completed tattoo.

'Relax, sir, we are nearly done.'

A short while later the image was finished and despite William's earlier worries, the bright sunflower and letter didn't look too bad. The affected area was wrapped in cling film with the instruction to leave the dressing on until he showered the following morning.

Back in the waiting room Sarah was looking at the pictures on the wall. She joked that the serpent with the long winding body would look great on her leg.

Back in town they bumped into James again. The swirl of his vapoured breath wafted in their faces which really annoyed William.

'Small world. Looks like we are destined to meet up

regularly. As I said, message me.'

'Sure thing,' came back the disinterested reply.

Walking swiftly up the street, the card he'd given to William was popped in a waste bin. He had no intention of meeting up again.

* * * *

The bus ride home through the hills was as spectacular as ever. The steep road climbed allowing views of the sea and the magnificent countryside. Driving past farms and white painted villas it wasn't long before their seaside town came into sight. Unlike Lloret de Mar, there were no high-rise buildings or large shopping centres to spoil the view.

After a late lunch in the apartment they both concentrated on their writing. It was not long before William gave up due to the soreness on his arm. In the other room, Sarah just kept tapping away at the laptop and even through the closed door he could hear her singing.

An early evening meal in a typically Spanish bar in the Villa Vella started off well but despite William's insistence that wine wasn't necessary every time they dined out, Sarah overruled him. Over some superb tapas that included tuna filled empanadillas and chorizo mini pies they discussed their visit to the tattooist.

'Tomorrow, I'll show you mine,' said Sarah in a sexy voice.

'Not so loud, someone will hear you.'

Sarah took another sip of her wine. She then placed both hands in the air in an act of defiance, speaking even louder than before. 'But the restaurant is empty, there's nobody here. Even the waiter is still out the back watching the TV.'

Having consumed just one glass of wine, Sarah was getting hyper and this unsettled William. After downing her drink in one go, her hand disappeared under the table to squeeze his knee. It felt good but he was still embarrassed in case the waiter spotted them. She leant over the table and the straining of her white blouse ballooned the material and showed off the whispery white bra she'd bought the previous week. With a cheeky grin on her face she whispered, 'And this is for being a good boy this morning. It didn't hurt that much, did it?'

'Sit up properly as I don't want you looking like that' William said rather abruptly.

It was at this point he noticed her face had turned red. She jumped up and holding a hand to her mouth rushed to the ladies' toilet. It was some time before she returned. 'I've just been sick. It must have been the tapas. Are you okay?'

He nodded and wondered just how one glass of wine could possibly have affected her in this way. She had shown signs of drunkenness followed by sickness but surely, with so little alcohol in her system, this shouldn't have happened.

* * * *

Twenty-four hours later, William removed the cling film bandage from his arm and stared at the dry blood and scabbing to the tattoo area. The small bright sunflower accompanied by the first letter of Sarah's name wasn't too bad to look at. He was pleased it was positioned high up on his arm so as not to be seen when he wore short sleeved shirts.

Sarah inspected the picture. 'See, it looks great. You also met up with your old friend. That was a bonus, wasn't it? He mentioned his pub was near your work – what exactly did you do? I've hung back all this time on pushing you further as I know you had a bad time. Do you think you can tell me now?'

William took a deep breath. It was time to be upfront and disclose more about his life. He'd hold back on revealing details on the mix up of the bodies, as this would undoubtedly freak her out.

'I worked in the company my grandfather started. For a number of years my father taught me the trade. I never enjoyed the nature of the work and longed to take up a different profession.'

He took a deep breath and continued. 'It was an undertaking business in South London.'

Sarah definitely looked surprised and sat down heavily on the sofa. 'Oh, I see. I wondered when you said it was a family business, but not this.'

'I ended up having a breakdown, my marriage broke up and I lost my son. I've told you about Steven, haven't I?'

Nodding her head, she whispered her acknowledgement.

'I didn't want to tell you because the work was really quite grim and people tend to be shocked on discovering what I did. In truth, I hated my career and resented my father for stopping me from working in a bank. Figures have always been my forte as you already know.'

'Yes, you don't even own a calculator. But hey, you should have told me about your job. The bit I did know was that you had a breakdown and lost Steven. In future, you really must talk to me.'

'I even considered suicide but didn't have the guts to go through with it. If it hadn't been for Martin, well I don't know what would have become of me. The change in my life coming out here to live has given me a whole fresh start. Back in London I was overweight and now I feel so much better with the way I look, so this is the new William.'

Sarah ignored the reference to his transformation to becoming a healthier person. 'I can't pretend I'm not stunned to hear you worked in that trade, but I suppose someone has to do it.'

'My sentiments too, I just followed my father's instructions and within a number of years it was my turn to take over the reins. I can't explain, you just sort of slip into the work. I never revealed any of this to Martin but will do soon.'

'Well, I'm glad you've told me.'

'God, I don't know what I'd do without you. I love you so much and I'm over the moon knowing you have agreed to be my wife. Are you sure you still want to marry me?'

Sarah rose from the chair and hugged him. 'Behave; of course I want to marry you. No more surprises like that or I'll insist you have another tattoo.'

Plucking up courage William muttered, 'There is something else I want to discuss with you.'

'Oh no, there's not more about your work, is there?'

'Definitely not. It's because I love you that I just wanted to say there are times I get worried about you drinking too much.'

Sarah pulled a face. 'What exactly do you mean?'

'When you have too much wine you get really drunk and then the amazing thing is you recover so quickly. I just don't want you getting ill and needing help. Please don't think I'm suggesting you are an alcoholic.'

'Well, I'm pleased to hear that. If you must know, I've been like this for some time. I enjoy drinking and experiencing the high of feeling good. It's a bit like a drug, but I'm not hooked or anything like that. As a younger woman in Finland, I used to smoke cannabis and now I suppose I've swapped the weed for booze. As you said after a short while the effects of the alcohol soon disappear.'

'Now don't get upset with what I'm going to say next, but have you ever considered counselling?'

'No, I haven't! Please don't mention that again.'

Acknowledging that enough had been discussed on this sensitive subject, William leant over to kiss Sarah on the lips. 'Just as long as you are okay, I'm happy with that.'

He was relieved to have told her his news, but he had still disguised the truth. The day would come when he would have to tell her the whole sad story.

* * * *

That night William had trouble sleeping and listened to Sarah's gentle breathing. Lying there, his mind was doing somersaults recalling his past. Memories of working with Steven appeared so real, with his son popping out to the local café to buy a snack for their mid-morning break.

The smell of the salty bacon in the enormous bap was overpowering. Beth his secretary was a vegetarian and had a canister of air freshener on her desk. Her frantic spraying of bouquet of summer flowers in the hallway always amused them.

A typical week saw the embalming process of at least one new client, something William never got used to witnessing. Every effort was made to improve the appearance of a corpse. The face and hue of skin were restored to a natural state suggesting the deceased was simply asleep. He would never forget the ghastly smell of formaldehyde and disinfectant spray that lingered in the back of the building. The mortician's draining of blood and fluids from organs and chest was necessary, but unpleasant and just thinking about it now was enough to make him throw up. It was no wonder he had chosen not to disclose details of his profession to Sarah for fear of losing her.

In the past, much of William's working day had been spent helping relatives come to terms with their loss. It was quite common for requests to dress the dead person in their own clothes along with special keepsakes being laid in the coffin. Planning the service and hymns always took time, as everything had to be just right. Their chapel of rest had seen thousands of visits over the years, but on one occasion the world had come tumbling down and changed his life forever.

William frequently reminisced about the past. The memories were possibly a fraction cloudier but they still refused to go away. When he arrived in Spain, in an effort to free himself of these terrifying thoughts, he'd sought help from a psychiatrist. The woman's questioning about his childhood and relationship with his parents irked him and three sessions later he vowed to face his demons on his own.

☐

Chapter 15

The February issue of the Finnish magazine, Film & Book Arena, included a double-page spread on Sarah's path to becoming a best-selling author. It was well written with an insight into her time spent working in Helsinki. The same article was published in Sweden and the UK. Book sales were rocketing with a major television channel requesting an interview at their Manchester studios. There were also the radio slots in London and Birmingham to cover. Scooter had messaged Sarah to confirm travel details. Worryingly, he was also applying pressure on her to mail over the middle section of the sequel that Sarah was struggling to complete.

Over the past few days she was suffering from writer's block, saying she needed a break to charge her batteries. She was annoyed there hadn't been time to work on the finer details for their wedding. Over a leisurely breakfast, William took a sip of his coffee and smiled at Sarah. 'I've read all the reviews and you are flying high. That man from the press in Finland has really sparked off even more interest in you.'

'Yes, he was certainly instrumental in raising my profile. The exciting news is people are buying my earlier books, too. I must find a way to thank Pavvii.'

William tried to hide his disappointment by calmly saying, 'Oh, I'm sure there's no need for that, he was doing his job.'

'I'll rattle off an e-mail or Facetime him later,' she said ignoring his last comment.

Sarah's expression then changed to one of annoyance as she retrieved a message off the inbox on her phone. 'I could do without this e-mail.'

With a confused look on his face William said, 'Sorry, you've lost me. I thought you were thrilled with all the publicity.'

'No, it's nothing to do with work. I just heard from my brother – Scooter has pulled out of buying the villa.'

'I thought your agent was intent on having a bolt hole in Spain, what changed?'

With a droll smile on her face the reply came as a shock. 'So did I, but he's now buying your friend's house instead. It seems they have been seeing a lot of each other and are prepared to share the property.'

'Just the sort of news you don't want to hear. I'm sorry it has put a spanner in the works for your brother. Martin and Scooter must be serious about their relationship.'

'You could say that.'

'I haven't seen much of Martin, so I'm not privy to his comings and goings. I suppose this is the way he can still remain in his house. My concern is if they argue or split up, where's he going to live then?'

In a disinterested voice Sarah said, 'Whatever. That's his problem, not ours. We have enough on our plate without worrying about him.'

Of course, she was right. Her brother would still have to dispose of his holiday home but it may buy Sarah more time to live there. When push came to shove she could always move into his apartment. However, with her need for an office to write in, the place could soon become cramped and untidy. Another thing to think about was the necessity for her to fine-tune her work commitments. Recently the pressure to complete the novel had impacted on their marriage plans. On a positive note, by delaying the wedding, it would give them more time to find a larger apartment where they could begin married life.

His thoughts were interrupted when Sarah said she needed to make some calls. As he loaded the dishwasher with the breakfast things he was aware of her talking on the phone.

'It's great to speak to you. I can't thank you enough for that article as it's really helped increase sales of my books. Yes, it would be great to meet up again when I come to Finland. That's right I will be on my own so we can catch up big time. We'll have to get a date in the diary. I'm in London shortly so I'll be in touch.'

* * * *

Over the next few days William's self-esteem plummeted to an all-time low. Nagging away in his head was the hold Pavvii appeared to have on Sarah and the consequences that could evolve. Why couldn't she see all of this was hurting him? Yes, he knew he was bitter and may well lose her if he didn't rein in his emotions, but what if this man plied her with drink and the worst happened?

The difficulty for him was accepting that Sarah had to network to seek out opportunities for her writing career. There was also the matter of whether marrying a man like him, with so many hang-ups, was such a good idea. With him creeping into his late fifties, possibly he was too old for her. She was still a relatively young woman and probably needed more space. Their lovemaking was always exciting, but was it enough for her? These negative thoughts constantly nagged away at him.

Whether he liked it or not, she needed other friends and more importantly his trust. Frightened of being alone again and losing the love of his life, somehow a balance would have to be struck. And whilst on the subject of friends, recently he'd distanced himself from Martin. Now he appreciated the importance of their friendship and with Sarah's business trips leaving William on his own again it made sense to team up.

* * * *

Eight days after the deadline, Sarah forwarded the last editing section of her novel to the publisher who told her in no uncertain terms that he was annoyed by the delay. The sign off for the cover had already taken place and the printer's proof was impressive. The eye-catching image of a young woman beating her fists against the closed front door of a modern-looking house also revealed an older man staring from a window. His expression was one of terror as he grasped a young child to his side.

* * * *

The morning that Sarah rang saying she needed to come over to see him concerned William. He suspected she was worn out with the constant strain of completing her work. Then again, a few days ago, to his amazement, she was talking about her idea for another novel.

When Sarah let herself into the apartment, she sat down in the lounge and called out to the kitchen. 'What are you cooking? I love the smell of burnt toast.'

'No need for sarcasm. I like mine done well and I'm warming up some tomato soup for our lunch. Good morning was it?'

'Yep, nearly got this one nailed. Just a few more

corrections and then I can think about the next one.'

He popped his head around the door. 'Oh yeah, what's that one going to be about?'

She joined him in the kitchen and lent against the fridge door. 'I have an idea for a story about a doctor that will involve doing some research and I thought…'

With his eyes raised to the ceiling, William interrupted her, 'Ah, research you say. That will mean more time away from me, won't it? Would it just happen to be in Finland again where that ruddy man lives?'

Rising from her chair she looked annoyed and snapped, 'Bloody hell! What's wrong with you? We are talking about my writing and you are reducing it to a sordid romantic episode with Pavvii.'

'I just don't like the guy.'

'Oh, behave, won't you? You've not even met him. Everything I do is professional and bloody hard work, as you well know. You have some crazy notion that if I see him I will end up in bed with him. He has a wife and two children. I'm certainly not interested. Aren't we supposed to be engaged? Get a grip or we're done as a couple and I mean what I say.'

She grabbed her coat and headed towards the door. 'You enjoy your rotten old lunch. I've told you before I don't like tomato soup. I'll catch up with you tomorrow when you have had a chance to think about whether we take this relationship any further.'

Desperate not to make matters worse, William muttered a gentle sorry which she never heard. The door slammed and he returned to the kitchen with a heavy heart and a voice screaming incessantly in his head. *You've really done it this time. Of course she doesn't want you. She's leaving you for a younger man.*

He poured the contents of the soup down the sink

and stared at the ghastly orange mess that had splashed onto the draining board. It smelt foul. How was he to know she didn't like tomato soup, or perhaps he hadn't been listening? Glancing over to the roses he'd bought her that lay on the worktop, he burst into tears.

* * * *

Two days can be a very long time being apart from the one you love. There was no word from Sarah and any plans to contact her were dismissed. He prayed that the break from him would heal the rift between them. He'd leave it until mid-week then go around and say sorry. In the meantime, he'd keep busy with housework and do some reading.

When the intercom buzzed his heart raced and as he thumped the call button he prayed it would be Sarah.

'Hello, mate. Any room for another geriatric up there?'

Trying not to sound too disappointed, he greeted his friend and activated the door release. Today Martin's hair hung loose around his shoulders and with a smile on his face he kept pointing to his mouth. 'What do you think of these little beauties?'

It took a moment to comprehend what all the excitement was about. 'Oh, your teeth, I had no idea you'd completed the treatment; they look great.'

'Thanks. I couldn't have done it without your help. Oh, and I haven't told you, Scooter is buying a share of my property. We are going to live together when he comes over.'

'Yes, I heard all about it through the jungle drums, it sounds a great idea. I really hope he is the guy for you.'

'Goes without saying, he's ace. Now, how have you

guys been? Since you took up with that beautiful woman I've hardly seen anything of you. I hope you weren't avoiding me.'

'Me ignore you, no chance. We'll have to make up for lost time as Sarah is having to work hard on her books and wants me out of the way.'

'Oh, poor old you, on your own.'

'Not so much of the reference to old. How about we have dinner tonight and a few beers; how does that sound to you?'

'Sounds like a plan. The reason for coming is to tell you that soon I'm going back home to spend time with Scooter in London. It's hard with him being over there and me here. Long term, I may even move back to the UK. I just have to be really absolutely sure about us as I've been hurt before.'

'Yes, best to be sure.'

Here was another person who may be leaving, yet he couldn't stand in the way of his happiness. If he made the move and Sarah also left, how would he cope living alone in Spain?

Martin picked up a photo of Sarah from the sideboard and smiled. 'Now you two were made for each other.' He paused and then added, 'Solid as a rock.'

William suddenly felt terribly sad and muttered, 'Would you like some tea?'

'No thanks, but I could murder one of those beers you keep in the fridge.'

Out in the kitchen the two men stood around drinking from their cans. Martin's eyes strayed to the wilting roses that were still in the wrapper.

'Just a tip old mate, those flowers would last longer in water. Are they a present for her?'

'I didn't get around to giving them to her. We had a

row and now she's not talking to me. I thought I'd ring her tomorrow.'

'Oh, that's awful. Scooter gets moody with me and I give him space; it works every time. The making up is always worth the falling out. How about tonight I cheer you up? We'll eat at Bar de Mar at seven. The owner Jeremy will be there and he's celebrating five years with his partner so we may get a free drink.'

'Sounds okay to me.'

Off went Martin clutching the straps of his bright blue shoulder bag. He hesitated before opening the door to leave and smiled, 'When I'm in London, I plan to take your advice to find my son. All these years without any contact I now have to give it my best shot.'

* * * *

Just before William left to meet Martin for dinner there was a text from Sarah asking him to ring her. Thrilled at the prospect of speaking to her, he made the call.

She sounded upbeat as she greeted him. 'I didn't disturb you, did I?'

'No, I'm just so happy to hear your voice.'

'I was hurt you thought there was anything going on between Pavvii and me. You do know that's nonsense, don't you?'

Again William lied, 'What was I thinking? It's just me getting all mixed up and emotional and I'm sorry. Can we meet up tomorrow?'

'I was thinking of tonight. You haven't got anything planned, have you?'

'Nothing I can't cancel. Why don't you come over here.'

* * * *

Sarah placed her glass of Rioja down on the kitchen table. The soft dim light cast a golden glow around the room as William took her hands into his own. He unbuttoned her shirt and eased it off her shoulders. Struggling with the clasp on her bra she leant forward and the flimsy garment slipped onto the cold tiled floor. She was like an animal as she wrenched his belt open and encouraged him to strip off his clothes. It was a hurried affair but left them both feeling satisfied, if rather cold.

Moving back to the lounge William put on his dressing gown and fetched a blanket, which he wrapped around Sarah's shoulders. Concerned her feet would be chilly he brought out his large red tartan slippers encouraging her to wear them.

'Oh, you are funny. They are enormous, you really have large feet.'

'They are size eleven. More to the point, I don't want you catching a cold. I'll make some coffee. Are you hungry? I've got one of those lasagna meals with garlic bread. It's in the oven warming up.'

Giggling she replied, 'As long as it's not any more of that stinky tomato soup. Have you washed the saucepan out.'

'Not sure, I've my mind on other things right now.'

'Yes, I noticed. Just promise you won't burn the lasagna. I could murder a drink. These last few days I've been very good and not touched a drop. I've been depressed as I really thought we were over.'

William was concerned to hear about her feeling so low.

'We can't have that, can we? I will have to give you lots of attention.'

164

'You just need to keep me happy like earlier. The lounge worked well tonight. How about the hallway or out on your balcony?'

William had a big smile on his face. 'You say the balcony. Now, that's an awesome idea, just a bit on the cool side at this time of year though.'

Sarah retreated to the bathroom to get dressed and soon returned with his gigantic slippers, which she dropped on the floor with a clatter. 'Possibly your past love life may have been different if you hadn't wooed your young ladies with these monsters.'

'Very funny, I got those in London. I thought they looked fashionable.'

Sarah kicked one of the slippers and sent it skidding along the tiled floor. 'Now you are showing you age. The description 'old boy' comes to mind but undeniably you have the passion of an Italian man. You are so hot.'

Sniffing the air, he triumphantly said, 'Now talking about heat, I need to check that meal as it smells nearly ready.'

Sarah's face then switched to one of concern. 'When we were apart I got to thinking that I hadn't been exactly fair with you. Breaking my promise to mentor you on your writing was cruel. Let's diary Friday afternoons to get things moving.'

Possibly a little too firmly the tone in William's voice rose, 'No, I'm okay. You are far too busy and I've also been doing some thinking. Seeing the stress you put yourself through I'm not keen to tread that path. Even if I got a lucky break and did manage to get my book published, the thought of meeting deadlines scares me. One serious writer in the family is enough and I'll just enjoy my hobby.'

'But you are really talented. I'm sure Scooter would

be interested to read the first few chapters.'

'My mind is made up. I would, however, love to attend your classes. Your students must be straining at the bit for news on when you are starting up again.'

Sarah muttered, 'Oh yes, the classes. I'd forgotten all about them. I have too much on my plate with the trip to Manchester and London next week without worrying about all that.'

'Yes, your radio and TV interviews, I bet you are really excited.'

* * * *

With the sound turned up on his iPad, William stared at Sarah as she appeared on the breakfast TV show and he felt so proud of her. He was a regular watcher of the programme and was used to seeing the news presenters. Today, it was his lady who was sitting on the red couch being interviewed. Dressed in a smart navy-blue skirt that showed off her shapely legs, she looked so attractive and young. Her hair had blonde highlights and she was wearing the new glasses she had recently bought in Helsinki.

Responding well to the questions, she revealed her passion for writing had started as a young schoolgirl. Over many years the hobby had evolved into a full-time job. She talked briefly about the Finland experience saying this had been the turning point of her career.

This prompted one of the presenters, a tall woman with short blonde hair, to wave Sarah's best-selling novel in the air and say, 'Having read your fascinating book it is not hard to understand why so many people have been captivated by the story. The two main characters could easily be people any of us could have known. Just where did you get your idea for writing the Wrong Side of Sanity?'

Sarah nodded briefly. William could tell she was thinking before answering. 'I've always been a people observer. For this particular story I had the good fortune to be living in Finland. It was late afternoon and during an appointment in a bank, unbeknown to two employees, I witnessed their heated conversation. The young woman was definitely in trouble and trying to cover her tracks. The story came to me in a flash and the rest is history.'

The male presenter summed up the interview by saying, 'And what a reaction to your novel there has been. Printed in four languages and selling well in America, we look forward to see what you do next. Sarah Barney, thank you for coming in and now over to Sashi with the latest weather.'

Swiping the screen, the live TV show faded. His fiancée was already an author but now she was famous. He wondered with her new busy life if this would affect their relationship and tear her away from him.

Later that afternoon she phoned and it was evident she was on a high with her news. Pleased that William had managed to catch the show she said, 'Was it okay?'

'Of course, it went really well, I'm that proud of you. I would kiss you if you were here.'

'I've just got a meeting with the publisher in London tomorrow and that radio interview in Birmingham and then I fly home in the evening. I had a chat with Scooter this morning and there's a bank transfer going ahead for my advance on the book deal. It's not mega bucks but enough for some of it to be put towards a short break. How would four days in New York suit you? I think we ought to arrange it as soon as I get home.'

'You are kidding. That's been my dream destination

after listening to Scooter reminiscing about his life over there. Did you know he lived in Brooklyn?'

'Sorry, I'll have to cut you short. The car is waiting to take me get the train. Love you lots.'

Chapter 16

Sarah's offer to visit New York thrilled William. He'd never ventured further than Spain and a trip to Paris with Joan on their honeymoon. Recently, he had listened intently to Scooter's recollections of living in the Big Apple. He was wowed by the descriptions of the architecture and lifestyle. According to Scooter, he had lived close to the Brooklyn Bridge, which sounded an incredible place to grow up. His claim to fame was meeting Billy Joel a number of times in a diner and the gift of a pen from him. Scooter's party line was boasting that the sleek silver pen may well have been used to write some of those incredible songs.

Born of Italian parents, Scooter's real name was Luigi, which had changed when he joined a band and the name stuck. He was no musician, more of a writer who penned a number of travel articles that were snapped up by the press. With a degree in English literature he accepted a job with a Manhattan literary agency working as an agent. Over a period of ten years he represented a number of successful authors. Then the call to move to London to join an enterprising firm in Mayfair and that was when he first encountered Sarah. Ploughing through the enormous number of manuscripts that landed daily in his inbox, he found her letter of introduction intriguing. The passion demonstrated for creating a story by this relatively unknown writer was outstanding. Reading the initial three chapters, he was enthralled by the brilliant opening description of the main character. His intervention became the catalyst for her novel developing into an international best seller.

* * * *

Terminal four of JFK was heaving with passengers and when William and Sarah eventually retrieved their cases, the queues for taxis were horrendous. Making their way to the subway, fortunately the crowds thinned out and it wasn't long before they were taking the ride to New York City centre.

The journey took fifty minutes to reach Grand Central station. William marvelled at the magnificent marble floored concourse with the famous Oyster Bar close to the ticket offices. Painted platform signs harked back to a bygone age with wonderful destination names highlighted in gold lettering. Taking the Lexington exit out of the station, their first view of the city was the Chrysler Building on the opposite side of the street. Gazing upwards, the glass in the upper section of the iconic skyscraper sparkled in the late afternoon sun.

It was pleasantly warm with just a hint of white cloud forming over the tops of the high buildings. Not surprisingly, everything was on the large size with enormous advertising hoardings and skyscrapers. The streets of Manhattan were chaotic with cars, yellow taxis and trucks with many of the drivers beeping their horns. It seemed that everyone had an agenda, unlike Sarah and William, who patiently waited to cross the busy roads to walk the four blocks to their hotel on East 39th Street.

Heavy trucks sporting Chevrolet and Ford badges roared along Lexington as the streets of Manhattan took their daily pounding. There were no end of police sirens that shattered any chance of a peaceful walk through town. Extraordinarily, with space at a premium, there were still a number of building sites with swinging cranes. Gigantic billboards announced further developments of apartments being built.

Walking past delicatessens, liquor stores and diners, they wheeled their small cases along the crowded sidewalks. It was not hard to believe the old saying that New York never slept, as the city was vibrant and noisy but undoubtedly one of the most incredible places to visit.

They reached their block, but the hotel was a fair walk down and the pair were exhausted from their travels. The silver-fronted exterior had seen better days, but once inside the plush reception with comfortable seating was inviting. Taking the elevator to level twenty-six, a hall window afforded a wonderful view of the city with both the Empire State and Chrysler buildings stealing the show.

Inside their spacious bedroom it was evident that no expense had been spared by Sarah in reserving a deluxe room. He felt bad about her financing the trip, but she insisted it was her way of thanking him for all his patience with her. In truth wasn't it the other way around? Hadn't she been the one who put up with his moods and bouts of jealousy?

Seated in the bar on level twenty-eight with a glass of champagne they discussed plans for their wedding back in Spain. It was to be a small affair in a local hotel.

Early evening found them wearing their warm coats and hats as they walked to Times Square and Broadway. The sidewalks were full of people staring up at the illuminated billboards or viewing the fronts of theatres. All the restaurants and bars appeared busy with the incredible aromas of every style of food wafting into the air. The temptation to enter was hard to resist. Interestingly, many of the signs on the shops and diners were lettered in both English and Spanish. It was clear the Hispanic community featured high in this city.

Eventually, the restaurant Scooter had recommended, came into sight.

The bold frontage boasted the claim of serving the best burgers in the whole of NYC. Once seated, a waiter quickly appeared to take their order on his tablet, but there was a long wait before they got their meals. Sipping monster glasses of cola, they had time to take in the ambience of their surroundings.

When the prize burgers arrived, the mountain on the plate was clearly too much to eat, even for William who had a healthy appetite.

Happy, but feeling very tired, the conversation switched to which guests to invite to their wedding with Sarah reeling off her list. 'My father has said he will definitely come. You'll get on well with him.'

William's face grimaced as he had already seen a photo of the friendly-looking man who looked younger than he did. How was this guy going to feel about someone around his age marrying his daughter?

'And have you given any thought to who you want to invite?'

Aware that he had to raise his voice significantly to be heard, he leant forward. 'Oh, you know just Martin and Derek and his wife from the apartment below me.'

'Surely you should invite someone from back home. A friend or relative or even an old work colleague.'

'You don't really want me bringing someone from my old line of work, do you?'

Sarah shuddered and shook a finger in his direction. 'I think you are probably right. But, what about that man we met at the tattoo parlour who runs the pub back home? Do you think he and his wife would like to come?'

Ignoring what she had just said, William got the attention of one of the servers to make up their bill. The large young man, with the open white shirt and a hint of a vest underneath, insisted they grade how good their meal had been. Giving him a score of ten the waiter smiled and asked if they would like to try the apple pie and cream.

Declining the offer, they left the restaurant to head back to the hotel. Walking arm in arm and bracing the cold wind that was whipping up, they stared up at the Empire State Building that was lit up with lasers. Waiting to cross the block for their hotel, a police car with sirens and lights flashing swept past them. The vehicle came to a sudden halt with a screech of tyres before accelerating off again at high speed. Sarah yawned. 'Busy place, don't you think? I'm shattered. Let's go and get our heads down.

* * * *

Waking up in the enormous comfy bed with the red padded headboard, there was no rush to get up. Although back home Sarah still had deadlines to meet, the prospect of a further two full days in New York was exciting. Even their mobile phones had been switched off for the duration of the trip. Sitting up with the duvet pulled up over their shoulders, the breakfast news featured an interview from the White House. Footage of the President commenting on the Middle East was the top story. William switched off the TV and activated the electric curtains to reveal a gloomy day outside. He snuggled up to Sarah and gently kissed her. It was the most wonderful feeling just being there with her. There was no necessity for lovemaking, just a closeness that made him very happy. He could feel her heart beating and reminded himself on just how lucky he was having her in his life.

* * * *

Sheltering under Sarah's umbrella, avoiding the puddles was tricky, especially when waiting to cross the roads as the heavy traffic thundered by. It was possibly not the best of weather to take the ferry to the Statue of Liberty. Taking the subway to Bowling Green and then the short walk through Battery Park, the persistent drizzle continued to soak their coats. In need of a hot drink, they entered a small bar and settled down with a coffee. With dampness creeping up William's trouser legs he started to shiver, prompting Sarah to comment on the awful weather.

'Hey, it's not your fault. I'm sure the rain must be lessening.'

'That's what I like about you, forever optimistic.'

Eyeing up the food that was being served, William sipped his hot drink. 'Do you fancy one of those pizza slices, they smell incredible?'

'Surely you aren't hungry after all that breakfast you put away. We'll get lunch back in town after the ride. Come on let's do Liberty.'

The visibility outside had now improved as they made their payment at one of the booths. It came as some surprise to discover the excessive attention to security that was in place. The men and women carrying out these tasks had expressionless faces and reacted in an abrupt way to any conversation.

As the boat rode the choppy waves, the view back over Manhattan was outstanding with many of the tops of the skyscrapers engulfed in cloud. In the distance, two orange painted ferryboats heading for Staten Island encountered the rough waters of the East River. On reaching Liberty in her copper green coat, it became apparent just how large the monument was. The outstretched arm with the torch appeared to be welcoming them. Up on deck Sarah was taking photos on her mobile. On disembarking she took a selfie of the two of them promising to send him a copy to his phone.

The view from the crown was spectacular, but it was particularly cold, so it wasn't long before they were back on the ferry for the ride back to the city. It was extremely windy up on deck but exhilarating as the boat was hammered by the wind. With the rise and fall of the ferry as it coped with the massive waves, William was suddenly overcome by a feeling of nausea. He remembered his father's advice to keep the eyes focused on the horizon, unfortunately today it wasn't helping. Concerned he was going to be ill he made his way to a toilet and was violently sick.

* * * *

Later that afternoon the view from the observation deck of Rockefeller Centre of the Hudson and East rivers was breathtaking. The sun was dropping into the horizon as the light started to dim. The outline of a crescent moon waiting for its turn to light up the sky became an incredible backdrop. The ferryboats were still busy and in the distance a liner was preparing to enter the port.

Just before queuing for the elevator down they visited the gift shop. William bought a wallet with a picture of the Empire State Building for Martin and a key ring for Sarah. Grasping his street map and coat he commented on how expensive things were in America and then handed Sarah her gift.

With a droll smile on her face she said, 'Wow, a key ring, just what I didn't want.' With this she kissed him on the cheek. 'What am I going to do with you?'

* * * *

The following morning the contrast in the weather brought sunshine with a slight breeze that rattled the bushes in Central Park. The welcoming sound of the clip clop of horses pulling beautifully painted spoked carts added to the enjoyment of this wonderful open space.

New Yorkers and visitors all year round enjoyed the 843 acres of the beautifully laid out gardens and lakes. William had read up on the stunning eighteen-acre lake that was used for ice-skating during the winter and boating in the warmer months. He encouraged Sarah to climb the ancient boulders in the park, but the height frightened her and she had to be guided back down. Walking along the paths they marvelled at the ornamental trees, plants and shrubs. Here was this enormous garden encased by all the chaos of the city and it still felt like the countryside. Within the massive acreage tranquility and peace ruled. It was true what they said about Central Park that, along with all the other wonderful green areas in New York, it served as a back garden for residents who mostly lived high above the ground.

Lunch was a simple meal of thinly sliced pastrami on rye bread followed by a generous slice of cheesecake. They sat for almost two hours gazing out at the grass verges and tall trees lining the park. For the first time, William disclosed details on his childhood. He chose to make reference to the family business and the school holidays when his father took him into work. He always thought it strange that he hadn't been allowed to wander around the offices and adjacent rooms. There was always a peculiar smell about the place especially the back of the building that was out of bounds. It soon became obvious that his friends' parents' occupations bore no resemblance to his father's work. On leaving school, the process of being inducted into the business became a reality. He was expected to join the firm, learn from the bottom and eventually take over from his father when he retired.

William's intention to give Sarah an insight into his working life certainly filled in a few of the gaps.

'Thanks for that, but as I've said before, it's all a bit grim for my liking. I accept someone has to do the job, but with you being so secretive about your past, I swear I never guessed this was what you did.'

'Yes, and I'm sorry for not being upfront with you right from day one. When I was growing up I was proud of my parents. They expected me to follow in their footsteps and it all kind of fell into place.'

Sarah placed a reassuring hand on William's cheek. 'I think I'm beginning to understand and now you've told me I'm fine. Let's just not talk about it too often. The important thing is we no longer have any secrets. We love each other and that's all that matters.'

'Yep, all that history of mine has finally gone in the trashcan. It's the future that now counts.'

His fingers played with the edge of the white plastic tablecloth. In his head he silently repeated the word trash. There was no need for her to learn about the events that led to his illness. Acknowledging that this was the moment to move on from those awful memories, he muttered quietly, 'Got that.'

* * * *

Shopping at Macy's, eating pizza in Little Italy and walking the streets of Chinatown were some of the highlights of their trip that thrilled William. Time was running out, leaving the last afternoon free to call in on

177

Scooter's parents in their apartment in Brooklyn. They both felt a little apprehensive about turning up at someone's home that they didn't actually know. Sarah's agent had insisted they visit. Scooter had mentioned he'd spoken many times to his parents about the talented author he was representing and they wanted to meet her.

Close to the bridge they stopped outside a church to consult the map and stared up at two horribly grotesque gargoyles carved directly into the stonework. After walking two blocks they took a right and the apartment block came into sight. Rusty railings on the steep pitted concrete steps led to a badly painted black front door. At least ten letterboxes, some with doors hanging precariously from hinges, did little to enhance the entrance. The brick-fronted building had seen better days with deteriorating wooden window frames. Sarah pointed out the graffiti under one of the bay windows that read: *Taxation sucks.*

She drew breath as she acknowledged that this was where her agent's parents lived. Somehow, the picture Scooter had painted was of a tree-lined street with terraced houses and children playing on the sidewalk. On the contrary, this run-down area of Brooklyn was in need of redevelopment. From where they were standing they could see a glimpse of the bridge that was a good two blocks down.

Standing close to the rusty grill of the intercom with a number of bell pushers, they waited as the speaker went through a series of bleeps and hissing of air.

'Hello, is that Mr Martinella? It's Sarah Barney and my fiancé from England. Your son Scooter told us to call in this afternoon.'

With no trace of an Italian accent, the deep voice sounded excited. 'You guys come up to level four and we are apartment ten.'

There was no lift, only an antiquated dark wooden staircase with handrails that must have been varnished so many times over the life of the old building. Sarah pointed out that the walls had been recently painted and the telltale splashes of white on the much worn purple carpet. It was quite a climb mounting those stairs leaving William out of breath. On some of the landings there were bicycles, raising the question how anyone could possibly manage the arduous trek up and down?

Sarah gazed up the staircase. 'Scooter is really quite wealthy; I've seen his mews house in Pimlico. Surely, he wouldn't have left his parents to live in this place. I'm really shocked.'

'Yeah, I know what you mean. Perhaps they didn't want to be helped. God, just look at the plaster on this wall, it's coming away in chunks. That's got to be damp. It makes me feel really grateful to be living in our lovely homes in Spain.'

They were suddenly aware of a man on the next landing who was leaning over the banister. On reaching him they stared in disbelief at his tracksuit bottoms and jumper with holes in the sleeves. In his mouth an unlit cigarette hung crookedly from thin lips. William gauged his age to be older than himself. The deep voice was undeniably the result of heavy smoking and his unruly head of dark brown hair was accompanied by bushy eyebrows and an unshaven face. William immediately warmed to the man who spoke with the New York accent. Judging from the appearance of Scooter's father, it was obvious he had fallen on hard times. He wondered just how their son could bear to see them residing in this awful place.

In the doorway stood Scooter's mother who looked

older than her husband. Dressed in a long skirt, chunky sweater, her long steely silver hair hung loosely over her shoulders. She spoke with an Italian accent. They observed her smile that lit up the wrinkled and liver-spotted face and immediately took a shine to her. Slightly overweight and walking with the aid of a stick, the woman ushered them into their home. Attempting to close the heavy front door she sighed. The frame obviously needed attention as something was sticking.

Turning to her husband who was in the process of relighting his cigarette, she pleaded, 'Salvatore, give me a handa to closa the door.'

There was no response as he puffed out a cloud of smoke that wafted in their faces. William noticed he was wearing a hearing aid.

Feigning a cough from the dreaded nicotine, William went over to help.

'Here let me see what I can do, sometimes the wood swells and it needs a good push.'

Leaning against the wooden door he was unable to close it. His next attempt he slammed it so hard, it shut with an almighty bang. The loud meshing sound of wood against the frame was worrying.

Mr Martinella looked embarrassed. He explained his landlord needed to fix the door as well as the hot water tank.

Inside the narrow hallway, the smell of nicotine was overpowering and they momentarily glanced up at the yellowing ceiling before following the couple to the lounge.

'You don't mind me smoking, do you?'

William inwardly groaned. Uncomfortable with breathing in the contaminated air, he muttered. 'No, not at all.'

Not wanting to stare, he took short glances at the poorly decorated room and shabby furniture. It was obvious this couple were struggling with their finances. There were no luxuries to be seen. Even the TV was one of the old ones with the back of the set being so deep it reached far into an alcove. Despite the starkness of the apartment, the place was immaculately clean.

They were invited to sit and offered coffee and the pair went off to the kitchen.

When Scooter's parents returned, they carried two gold-painted trays loaded with expensive pastries. William caught the look on Sarah's face and knew exactly what she was thinking. What wonderful hosts these people were spending their money on cakes for them.

Passing out the plates, the kind lady proudly said, 'I tolda my son we'da looka after you. Taka one of the cinnamon rolls they are delicious.'

The refreshments must have cost them a fortune and between taking mouthfuls of the luscious, buttery mixture topped with a drizzle of cinnamon, Sarah replied, 'These are really incredible, but you shouldn't have gone to all this trouble.'

Coughing, Mr Martinella raised a dismissive hand in the air. 'Nonsense. Any friend of our son is welcome in our home. Scooter has told us you are a famous author. He said your writing is awesome.'

Blushing, Sarah stared at his nicotine-stained fingers. 'Oh, I don't know about famous. I've just had a lucky break and I wouldn't have got this far without your son's assistance.'

She paused and turned to William and added, 'And, of course, my fiancé's encouragement and patience. Tell me, sir, do you work?'

'Me, I got laid off five years ago and am still trying to

find a decent job. Nobody wants an old guy like me, especially with my chest problem. I keep getting ill. Currently, I'm busting my ass off working as a casual worker with a cleaning firm, but they just reduced my hours.'

'I'm sorry to hear that.'

William took a chance and asked the question he felt needed an answer. 'How often does Scooter visit you?

Mr Martinella reached for his wife's hand. 'He doesn't! We haven't seen him since he left to live in the UK and that was twelve years ago. Our finances don't stretch to flying over to your side of the pond.'

He suddenly looked worried. 'Look here mister, please don't tell Scooter I told you anything about all of this. The last thing we want to do is upset him.'

The quietness that filled the miserable and cold living room was unbearable. Eventually Sarah went for it. 'But he's always talking about you. I can't understand why he hasn't been over. Any son would want to see his parents.'

The strained expression was an indication of how difficult all of this was for this couple. 'He can't return to New York,' sighed Mr Martinella.

'Can't, I'm sorry I'm not with you. He painted an incredible life growing up in Brooklyn.'

'The bottom line is our son can't bear the thought of returning home. You probably don't know that his partner died close to the bridge when a driver shot a red light. He was devastated losing the guy he loved. But look, we speak every few weeks on the phone and he always ships a hamper at Christmas. It's hard not seeing him but we are convinced that coming back could push him over the edge.'

* * * *

As they waited out in the street trying to catch the attention of a Yellow Cab driver, William put an arm around Sarah. Still feeling moved by their visit and the desperation Scooter's parents must feel every day of their lives, he felt his eyes welling up with tears. He kept thinking about the costly cakes and the wonderful reception these people had given them.

Sarah looked up to his face. 'He doesn't know how his folks are living, does he? I think we should tell him. I find it incredible he has no idea of their plight.'

'Now hold on there. It's not our business to interfere with families. Losing his partner still remains a big problem for him. He's a good son keeping in contact, but I agree it is strange he doesn't see them. My guess is with him regularly keeping in touch on the phone, they have never told him about their struggle surviving on so little money.'

Relieved to have found a taxi, William held the door open for Sarah. He became annoyed with the driver who abruptly said, 'Where to Mister? It's gotta to be local as I'm off home in twenty.'

'Drop us at the block where Lexington 39th meets 3rd Avenue, if that's not too much of an inconvenience to you.'

The car shot off at speed unsettling them both.

William nervously turned to Sarah. 'Soon be there dear, don't worry I am sure he's really a safe driver. Look, if it's alright with you when the time is right I'll speak to Scooter. I'll carefully drop in what we learnt today. I know he'll be devastated to hear our news. More than likely he will be pissed off with me for meddling in his affairs.'

'You will have to tread carefully and not tell him

what to do, like you do with me. Remember I have to work with this guy.'

'Now, hang on there. I don't tell you what to do, do I?'

'You know what I mean, you are forever offering me advice.'

'Do I?'

'Just a bit.'

'Mmm...I wasn't aware I do that. Anyway, going back to Scooter, I can understand his aversion to coming back here, but not helping them out with the fares to London is unforgiveable. When I tackle him I will mention our visit. I'll be careful not to comprise your relationship with your agent. I'm just trying to help the guy.'

Sarah was always proud of William's care for others and told him that Scooter was due over next month in Spain for the signing of his property agreement with Martin.

During the taxi ride, William's mind was working overtime. His friend Martin hadn't seen his son in years and now there was this business with Scooter's parents. Thoughts of bringing about a satisfactory outcome for both parties featured high on his wish list.

Chapter 17

Back in Spain, although it was a particularly busy week for Sarah, she still found time to arrange a meeting for her group. There was much interest from both old and new members as news had got around about the TV interview that had been posted online. Keen to bring in copies of her book for sale, she positioned them on her desk. William observed the sixteen-strong party. There were a few new faces including a youngish man with an unfortunate stutter who was writing a radio play. Sarah remained patient as she listened to Robert struggling to form his words.

The oblong dining room in the villa was too small to accommodate everyone and some of the writers had to stand in the hallway. Despite bringing in the green plastic chairs from the garden, there were still not enough seats and a few disgruntled ladies moaned about having to stand.

William handed around the coffee and ignored the query on the absence of the cakes that their tutor normally provided.

Sarah banged her plastic ruler on the tiled floor and all went quiet. 'Thanks for coming. Just to let you know that I intend to alter the frequency of the meetings from weekly to monthly. Current demands on my time are to blame. It is imperative that I have your e-mail addresses as there will be occasions when I have to cancel.'

There were a few sighs from some of the group who were probably hoping that after a break of two months since the last session, this meeting signified a return to the normal weekly get-together. There was a fair amount of chattering going on between various people.

Once again, the sound of the ruler brought about a hush in the room. 'Can we have one conversation at a time please. As you will appreciate this room is too small should everyone wish to attend. I'm not using the lounge at the moment as my brother has stored loads of his gear. Therefore, it is with regret that just my current most regular students will be able to come along in future. It has been great seeing some of my past writers again, but I can't accommodate everyone.'

There were gasps, as people must have been weighing up if they were to be included in future classes.

'Another piece of news is this villa is being sold. Possibly the English library will let us use their room; I'll let you know shortly. My charges for course fees have not increased in the last two years. If I have to rent somewhere there will have to be an adjustment.'

William who was standing at the back of the room overheard an older man comment to a group of women. 'No problem if I don't get a place as there's nothing she can teach me. I read her book and didn't think that much of it. Can't see what all the fuss was about. I still got her to sign my copy though.'

William sarcastically addressed him. 'I don't believe Sarah is going to miss you coming along. Perhaps you should leave now.'

'I beg your pardon, who do you think you are talking to?'

Sarah was obviously aware of the slight altercation and observed the man hurriedly collecting up his bag to leave. She called William over.

She whispered not wanting others to hear her. 'What was all that about?'

'Ignorant pig; we won't be having any more trouble from him.'

'He's always had a chip on his shoulder that one. Anyway, no more heated discussions with my students please.'

Sarah took control of the class informing everyone a writing exercise had been planned and that they had twenty minutes to complete it.

At the end of the session she chatted with the students saying she would mail over dates for further classes. When everyone had left she winked at William as he tidied up the chairs and collected the cups. With a smile on his face that felt good, he joked, 'At least that awful woman with the mad haircut didn't come today.'

* * * *

Without question, the highlight of the year in Tossa de Mar was always the Fiesta de San Vicente that took place in spring. Although it had been banned by the Spanish dictator, Franco, due to the boisterousness of the celebrations, following his death the locals soon reinstated the popular festival. The celebrations included colourfully dressed riders on horseback parading through the town, followed by street parties, traditional music and the seductive dancing of the sardana. The fiesta attracted the locals and brought in visitors from the whole region, as well as holidaymakers. Something that William always loved seeing as they partied on into the night were the fireworks that lit up the castle walls casting a myriad of sparkling colours over the old town.

Experiencing the festivities was all about being in the streets and mixing with the crowds. The festival was renowned for its mouth-watering food and wines. It never disappointed and for many it was a time to rejuvenate the spirit signifying the coming of spring and a return to hot weather.

Standing in a doorway of the main square, William, Sarah and Martin were impressed with the horsemanship as the magnificent animals were put through their paces. It was Saturday morning and coachloads of tourists had flocked into the town. Street vendors were plying their trade with delicious smelling snacks, which included barbequed pork strips wrapped in bacon and cooked in honey. The churros pastries coated in sugar with the obligatory thick chocolate drink were always hard to resist. William purchased three portions and they moved away from the crush of visitors to wander the backstreets to eat the messy treats.

Sarah's attention moved away from her sugary fingers. 'Hey, isn't that your friend we met in the tattoo shop?'

Focusing on the publican from Croydon, with the bald head and nervous twitch of lips, there was no mistaking it was James. William turned his head in a dismissive way and lied, 'No, I don't think so.'

'Oh, come on, it looks just like him. Go over and say hello. It would be rude to ignore him.'

Reluctantly William handed his churros to Martin telling him not to eat any of them. With a strained smile on his face he dodged the onlookers to tap James on the shoulder. Startled, the man took a moment to realise who was engaging him in conversation.

James' first words to his wife were, 'Look dear, you remember William who used to run the house of death opposite our pub.'

'William sheepishly stared at the couple and replied, 'I think what he meant to say was that I was the funeral director from across the road.'

She nodded and accepted the outstretched hand,

which she briefly shook. 'As if I would forget you, James said you were living out here now. Fancy seeing you after all this time. It's a great carnival isn't it? Are you here on your own today?'

'No, I'm with Sarah over there in the yellow top.'

Sarah waved and waited for a convenient moment to make her way through the crowds. Martin followed clutching the two portions of churros in both hands. The grin on his face was accompanied by a smudge of chocolate sauce on his chin.

When Sarah joined them, William grasped her hand. 'You remember James who we met in Lloret de Mar. This is his wife Marleen.'

Sarah observed the woman with the black curly hair and hideously large sunglasses and smiled. Seeing her highly tattooed arms and legs made her wonder where else on the fake-tanned body the designs appeared.

Marleen was determined to be heard above the noise of the festival and her screechy voice was painfully annoying. 'I remember William coming to our pub – gin and tonic with no ice, wasn't it? I also recall he had a liking for pie and chips. I must say he's lost a lot of weight, he was huge when we knew him.'

William was inwardly cursing this woman who had a habit of saying it just how it was. He remembered how she used to ask him about the details of his business. Her weird fascination for all things morbid had always troubled him.

Martin stood in the background attempting to extract the last of the sugary churros to stuff into his mouth, while still holding onto his friend's portion.

Sarah suddenly came out with, 'How's the tattoo you had done James, can we see it?'

Above the sudden increase in noise from the crowd

who were cheering some dancers, the man shouted back, 'Afraid not. This one is out of bounds, like most of Marleen's.'

'Oh, let's not go there then. When we last met you said you had an apartment in Lloret. Are you over for a few days?'

'Yes, but it's literally a flying visit as we have a pub to run. We are hosting a beer festival next week back home, so have loads to prepare. I still have your old man's e-mail address and when we come over again, which won't be long, I'll message him to meet up.'

William groaned inwardly and mumbled to himself, 'Oh, great.'

* * * *

Pleased to be on their own again, having also said goodbye to Martin, Sarah spoke about the earlier meeting with the publican and his wife. 'They were crazy people but fun. It would be a hoot to see them again. What do you think?'

'If that's what you want to do that's fine with me, but be warned they can be a bit full on. As for his Marleen, I just know she'll press me to talk about the horrible side of my old business.'

'Well, we will just have to steer the conversation around to what part of their anatomy the rest of their tattoos ended up on.'

William pulled a face. 'I think I'd rather not know. Now, it must be time for a siesta before the evening celebrations. I can't wait to see the fireworks – it will be so romantic with you by my side.'

* * * *

Sarah managed to avoid going to London to see her publisher which pleased William. Handling all the meetings with the help of conference calling was proving to be beneficial. On the whole, her time management was working well. She was back on track and drinking less.

Her new project lay in returning to Finland to carry out research for the sequel novel. She planned to stay with her ex-flat mate Alana on the outskirts of Helsinki for two weeks. All of this would take place well before the wedding that had been rescheduled for the second time.

Discovering more about each other was essential to their happiness and William urged Sarah to divulge more about her life before she met him. Reluctant to discuss such matters, the information she offered was patchy; then surprisingly she opened up. Her story was one of a happy childhood with loving parents who encouraged her with her studies. Achieving a BA with honours for English Literature had been an excellent grounding for becoming an author. For a period of five years she worked on the news desk for a medium-size newspaper group, but always aspired to greater things.

A rash decision to quit her job cost her dearly in finding work with a publisher. There was so much talent out there and, with so few positions available, she struggled to secure employment. Not to be deterred from her goal, for the period of one year, she worked for a major high street clothing store in the women's wear department. It paid the rent but the weekend shifts were difficult leaving little time to catch up on her writing. One benefit of working in the retail trade was the opportunity for her to observe her fellow staff and customers. Sketching them into her mind gave birth to many a character for her storytelling. Witnessing the flaws and acts of kindness in people was valuable information she could put to good use.

Sarah alarmingly revealed a story about her own eccentric ways. Working on the returns counter she became frustrated with a customer. The man had insisted she gave him six complimentary clip hangers as he was a regular shopper in the store and wouldn't take no for an answer. Having read the recent bulletin from the manger on the expense of these products, she ignored the instruction to limit the number given away. Instead she smiled at the fifty-something-year-old man in his hideous orange tee shirt with the picture of a lion emblazoned on the front. She made an excuse to go out to the back room where she placed the six hangers in a carrier bag having first snapped each one in half. The man went off happily and miraculously never returned to complain.

William listened intently and was stunned by her revelation. 'You could have been sacked for gross misconduct if you were caught on the security cameras damaging company property.'

'If you think that was bad, what about the time…'

'Bloody hell, it gets worse'

'No hear me out; this one was a hoot. I was between jobs and decided to impersonate a shoe shop assistant. The store was hellishly busy and I homed in on a woman who was after a pair of trainers. She'd already kicked off her shoes and I suggested she walked over to the racks to make her choice. I quickly removed the laces from her muddy, tattered footwear and left the shop carrying the shoes.'

'You did what!'

'Yeah, and then I stopped a lady in the street and asked a favour. Could she go into the store and give the shoes to the customer with the red hair? I asked her to say we no longer had her size and would these do?

William was taken aback. 'I really don't know what to say. I'm hoping you've made all of this up.'

'Definitely not; I've always had a wild side to me. Do you want to hear what else I got up to?'

He wondered if she was indeed one of her supposedly fictitious characters that featured in her books. Could she possibly even be the main character in the Finnish novel with the split personality that delivered the terrifying outcome?

Sarah giggled. 'Oh relax, haven't you ever done anything crazy? It was nothing really.'

'Well, of course, I've mucked around as a teenager, but nothing like you described. It's like you got a kick out of it.'

Looking puzzled by his response, Sarah raised her shoulders and in a disinterested voice retorted, 'You asked me to fill you in with my life story, so I did.'

'Yes, but I still feel I don't know much about you. Those episodes you just related was a bit odd, don't you think?'

Beginning to look bored she snapped, 'No, not really. Anyway, that makes us even. Look at your past. There's loads I still don't know about you.'

She was right, of course, namely the full truth regarding his earlier days. The mundane things like his interest in stamp collecting or the film club, he was sure would hold no interest and make him sound even more boring.

* * * *

The day the solicitor completed the joint ownership on Martin's house, Scooter came over for a long weekend and arranged a small gathering to celebrate.

Holding a glass of champagne in the air he toasted his friends saying how excited he was to have a share of the villa. He looked over to Martin and directed his words at the man he loved. 'Are you going to tell them our news?'

All eyes were on Martin who looked incredibly smart in his blue corduroy shirt buttoned to the neck.

'Well, Scooter not only has a half share in the house, but also my heart. I'm going to spend a few months of the year living with him in London and the rest of my time here.'

He proudly held up his left hand to display a narrow silver ring with a tiny diamond set into the band that glistened in the bright sunshine. 'He got me this little beauty when I was over in London.'

Moving closer to inspect the ring Sarah whispered, 'Wow, just look at that stone, it's really beautiful. That's the best news we have had in a long time.'

She held a hand in front of his face. 'Come on big boy, let's have a high five.'

William was trying to take in the news and quickly added, 'Here's to your new home and of course to you both.'

Pleased for his friend he was still concerned about the merits of relinquishing an equal share of the house to his new partner. What if the relationship fizzled out without an amicable agreement being reached? He recalled just how upset Martin had become in the past when his partner at the time disappeared off the scene. The last thing he wanted was for him to be hurt again. Scooter certainly seemed a decent person and the empathy between them was obvious, but would it be enough after such a short time of knowing each other.

Having not seen Scooter for some months, William had hoped to speak to him about his parent's difficulties living in New York. It was hard to believe he had no knowledge of their predicament, but wondered how his interference in the matter would go down. Today was obviously the wrong time to have such a conversation. Instead he turned his attention to Martin saying he was over the moon that he'd found someone special.

The reply, which everyone heard, was moving. 'At my age finding love was something I had dreamed about. He is the right guy for me. I've never been more convinced about anything in my life.'

Opening his mouth, he tapped on one of the gleaming white new teeth. 'It must have been these little beauties that did the trick.'

* * * *

An amber moon was fading over the hills signifying the start of a brand new day. The online weather forecast confirmed it was going to be hot in the Costa Brava. Intending to make the most of his day, William planned to sunbathe and take a swim. Before setting off, he texted Sarah to say he would come over to the villa after lunch. The return message that flipped straight back excited him – *why not pop over now.*

He changed into something smarter and applied the expensive aftershave she'd bought for him in New York. This was the second time this week she'd surprised him with an invitation like this with exactly the same words. As he walked along the castle path, his mind was full of just how exhilarating their lovemaking had recently become. It was like she was on fire experimenting with different ways to make him feel good. She was much more experienced than he was. Yes, he'd had his moments with women but nothing on the scale of his time with Sarah. For him, in the past there had been many disappointments with the fairer sex. His mind went back to the call girl in Girona who measured enjoyment by the number of Euros spent. Sarah was the one who pressed all the right buttons. She was the person he treasured more than anything in the world. Today he was going to take the lead and show her a thing or two.

He let himself into the villa and heard her say she was in the bedroom.

As he pictured her in a state of undress, he eagerly shouted back, 'Do you want me to come in?'

'No, I'm nearly dressed I'll be out in a moment. I'm having a problem with these tight jeans. It's all your fault fattening me up with all those incredible meals. I've put on four pounds in the last two weeks.'

Trying not to sound too disappointed with not having another treat he limply offered, 'I thought you said I should pop over, you know like the other day. I must have got the wrong idea, silly me.'

She appeared in the doorway struggling with the zip of her jeans. 'Don't you think of anything else but sex? You'll wear me out. I sent the text because I wanted to tell you I love you. Now tell me what else were you going to do with your day? I'm afraid I have to work.'

'Well, I was going to sit on the beach for a while, have a swim, then do that lovely walk that leads to that gorgeous village in the hills where we had those ice creams. Are you sure you can't join me?'

'Wish I could.'

William shrugged his shoulders. 'I suppose someone

has to earn the dough to pay for the wedding. I'll just go out and enjoy myself. Seriously, I don't want you worrying about paying for our big day as I've got my savings.'

'Yeah, I know that, but I just wish the publisher would get his arse into gear and chase up my royalties. People wouldn't believe me if I said it was a hard way to make a living joining the right words together.'

William laughed. 'Now you see why I changed my mind about becoming an author. It's all pain and more pain.'

Sarah frowned at him and simply said, 'I didn't have you down as being so defeatist.'

'Give me a break. I just love to get up in the morning with my head full of bright colours and no agenda whatsoever. The icing on the cake is receiving a text from the girl I love telling me to get over as quickly as possible to her place…' He paused. 'There's no chance of a cuddle before you hit the laptop, is there?'

Sarah eyes brightened and he knew he was on to a winner. With a wink of her eye he watched her fingers undo the buttons on her blouse. 'I think I need to do a security scan on the computer and it could take up to thirty minutes.'

As he leant down to kiss her, to his dismay there was the smell of alcohol on her breath. He pulled sharply away leaving her looking confused.

'Have you had a drink this morning? I thought you promised me you had it sorted.'

She looked like she was going to cry and William's heart went out to her. It couldn't be easy slipping every so often.

'Just the one at breakfast to steady my nerves. Getting my head around the writing has been terrible.

Sometimes I sit in front of the laptop and my mind freezes. I've lost my inspiration for doing the planning for this story. And the other thing I could do without is the publisher mailing me all the time with the same message – *how is it going?*'

'Oh God, you should have told me. Perhaps I can help?'

Sarah wiped her eyes with a tissue as she sarcastically snapped at him. 'And you darling with all your experience in writing are going to give me advice. I don't think so.'

With a hurt look on his face he placed both hands on her shoulders. 'I wasn't talking about your writing as well you know.'

'Sorry.'

'All I was trying to say was I'm here for you. It's not easy seeing you this upset. Let's hope you get your creativity back soon.'

He let go of her and she wandered over to the window. 'I think I'll bring the research forward and get over to Helsinki. I got a call from Pavvii yesterday who reckons he can pull a few strings for more publicity. That was really kind of him thinking of me.'

With anger building up in his head, William still managed to control his feelings. 'I just don't want you adding any more stress to your busy workload, but I'll understand if you think it is necessary to go.'

It was like she hadn't heard him and was staring intently at the garden. 'I swear to God that bloke next door has lowered the bushes on my side. His house is more visible and that affects my privacy. What if I want to do some sunbathing?'

He moved over to join her and focused on the garden and muttered, 'Oh yes, but soon you'll have to move out so it won't be an issue. I promise when we look for a new apartment it will have a private balcony.'

There was no reply from Sarah who seemed to be in her own little world. He kept wondering just how much drink she had in the villa? It was a miracle she wasn't already an alcoholic with all she put away. She claimed she solely had a drink just when she felt down, but this wasn't entirely true as even in the good times there had been incidents. The menacing thoughts in his head were now laying out settings that included her horrible friend in Helsinki.

Leaving Sarah, he went out to the kitchen. Opening the fridge, it came as no surprise as three bottles of white wine came into view. Next to the swing bin was an empty bottle. He wondered if this was the start of the end. No amount of nagging would change her habits, yet he couldn't give up on her. He pondered about the chances of getting her to attend a local alcoholics meeting. Perhaps they could help to stop her slipping any further. He'd researched such groups on the internet, but the last time he'd made the suggestion she threatened to stop seeing him if he mentioned it again.

Living with the consequences of Sarah's obvious addiction would never be straightforward as one way or another it always managed to impact on their lives. The necessity to seek help was paramount and he was determined to tackle her again about the subject. He deliberated on the fact that there were times when she didn't appear to drink at all, or had she been she lying to him. And to add to their problems, she was now planning to go overseas supposedly to carry out some research. The stark truth was he was going to lose her if he didn't trust her. She said she loved him and that would have to suffice.

He went back to Sarah to give her a big hug and said he would be back the next day after she had rested up.

Chapter 18

As is usual with life, there is always another issue waiting around the corner. William's ex-wife Joan was poorly again prompting him to fly to London. It came as quite a shock receiving the call from her, as he thought the treatment had been successful. Fearing the worst, he just knew his duty was to support her. Sarah had been fantastic about him going and was genuinely concerned.

* * * *

Having taken the first flight back to England, he wondered if when he saw Joan she would look terribly thin and exhausted from her ordeal. He suspected that sadly she had run out of time and this was to be their final farewell.

After a restless sleep in a hotel bed that was not that comfortable, he chose to have a simple breakfast and spent the morning in the lounge area reading. Just before lunch he set off for the walk to Joan's flat.

He homed in on an undertakers' business on the opposite side of the street. It was a company that he'd never heard of before and watched an empty hearse being driven under an arch into the premises. Hectically his mind started to process the world behind those walls where the business of preparing for funerals was undoubtedly going on. Crazy thoughts saw him inside the building directing the staff and enjoying every moment. In truth he was experiencing his usual nightmare and hurried away along the pavement. Living in Spain had greatly helped to remove some of the anguish of his past; it was coming back to the UK that brought it all thundering back.

He turned his attention to the dilapidated wooden window frame of the Chinese restaurant he and his son used to visit. Still after all these years the hideous potted plants with enormous rubbery leaves and fish tank were on display. Joan disliked oriental food and preferred to stay at home for her meals and watch television.

Reaching the flat William rang the bell and he didn't have to wait long before the door was opened by a familiar face, Carol, one of Joan's friends who he hadn't seen for many years.

The tiny woman with short, red, hair and a small birthmark on her chin greeted him as if it had been yesterday since they last met. She looked surprised to see him and said, 'I hardly recognised you looking so slim and no hair.'

'Carol, how super to see you again. I didn't expect you to be here, I thought you lived in Brighton.'

'I still do. I come up to help Joan now she's this poorly. You have just missed her sister who stayed here last night.'

'Oh, that's a shame.'

'Come on through and see Joan.'

Hesitating in the doorway William nervously said, 'Joan and I speak on the phone every so often. I honestly thought the chemo had done the trick. She never mentioned she'd come out of remission. When I got her call, I instinctively knew I had to come.'

'Don't beat yourself up. It's difficult when you are divorced and you know how independent she can be. I should tell you she's hardly eating anything and wasting away. She's not got much time left so it's good you've come to see her.'

'I can't bear the thought of her being this ill. Tell me

Carol, wasn't there a new man in her life and has he been around to support her?'

'No, that was merely a quick fling that lasted a few weeks. Come on let's go upstairs as she will be wondering where I have got to.'

Nothing prepared him for seeing Joan as he gazed at her withered, sunken face. She looked so fragile and he carefully hugged her. The croaky voice was difficult to understand and he had to concentrate to make sense of what she was saying. As weak as she was, she still gripped his hand and he spotted a solitary tear run down her cheek. Her headscarf lay at an angle revealing a totally bald scalp. It was pitiful seeing her lying so still on the bed and just raising her head occasionally from the pillow. He prayed her passing would be painless and preferably in her sleep.

When her friend went to the kitchen to make some lunch, it started to dawn that this could possibly be the last time he would ever see her again. He established she had carers assisting with getting her up in the morning and to bed last thing at night; any chores or shopping were handled by friends. The special nurses who Joan said were so kind visited once a day. She revealed that the cancer had spread around her body and it wouldn't be long before she would be admitted to a hospice.

Joan made William promise he wouldn't come to her funeral as she didn't want him getting low again. Instead of him making contact with her again she asked that he spoke with her friend Carol. All of this came as a terrible shock as he really felt he wanted to be there for her.

After four long hours of sitting with Joan he left the flat feeling desperately sorry for her. Questioning the unfairness of this cruel twist, the reminder of yet another chapter of his life was closing, stung fiercely in his mind.

He was going to miss Joan.

The rest of the day was a blur with an early return to the hotel. Later he phoned Sarah to relay the sad news. He also mentioned that Martin and Scooter had invited him for a meal that evening.

* * * *

Seated on the plush sofa in Scooter's expensive London pad, William took in the modern furniture and large TV that was secured to the wall. No expense had been spared on this luxurious home.

The two men soon became concerned when they caught sight of William's face. They were upset to learn how ill Joan had become and offered their help. He thanked them saying there was nothing anyone could do.

Sipping his gin and tonic, William got Scooter's attention. 'Sarah and I can't thank you enough for setting up that visit to meet your parents in New York. We had a great time and they were wonderful hosts.'

Scooter's boyish face lit up. 'It was a pleasure and I've since heard from them that they enjoyed your company.'

'You said you loved Brooklyn and I remember you telling me about that pen…'

Scooter's face was beaming with excitement as he interrupted. 'Yeah, the pen Billy Joel gave me. I was downtown, it was snowing and I entered this diner. The place was busy and I sat opposite him. I knew it was him straight away and he…'

Martin quickly mouthed, 'Boring, yes. Do we have to hear that story again?'

William, pretending to be interested in a singer that he had hardly heard of offered, 'No, it's not boring; I was impressed that you actually met him. Now, going back to your parents, I was wondering if you could give me their telephone number. I want to ring and thank them properly.'

'Awesome, that's what I like about you English guys, always so polite. They will be thrilled; shall I give it to you now?'

William passed over his mobile. 'I'm no good with entering contact numbers, do you mind helping?'

When he handed back the phone, Scooter's face was beaming with excitement. It was obvious there was something he wanted to show him. He crossed the room to extract a small padded envelope from his desk drawer. Handing it to William he emptied the contents carefully onto his hand. Out slipped the slim silver pen along with a signed photo of the singer that read, *Good luck with your writing Scooter.*

* * * *

Shortly before lunch William packed his bag in preparation for leaving for the airport. Before checking out of the hotel, he used his mobile to ring New York, having first checked the time difference. It took a while for the call to be connected and, on hearing Mr Martinella cough, it painted a picture of him standing in the hallway of his Brooklyn apartment puffing on a cigarette.

'What was that you said fella? Speak up, I can't hear you.'

'Hello, sir, it's William from the UK. You kindly gave us tea when we visited.'

There was a sudden high-pitched sound that was obviously him adjusting his hearing aid. 'Who's there?'

William repeated his name and was relieved to hear a

voice in the background say, 'Salvatore, it's thosa guys from London, Scooter's friends.'

William now had Mr Martinella's attention. 'Oh yes, it was awesome seeing you. You really made our day and next time you are in town you drop and see us again.'

The wheezy cough returned. 'Scooter rang the day after you came and he was singing your praises.'

Gripping the phone William decided to go for it. 'I wanted you to know that on getting back home, I bought a lottery ticket. I took the number of your apartment block, then my age and came up with a winner.'

'That's swell. You treat that good lady of yours to a smack up dinner.'

'That's why I'm ringing, sir. I want to share some of my winnings with you.'

William heard the man gasp and his wife came on the line. 'We don'ta do charity mister, but thanks for the kinda offer.'

'No, you don't understand. It's not a fortune as I have won one thousand pounds – that's all.'

'That's stilla a gooda win.'

'I've plenty of money and have decided to share it with our friends. We loved meeting you and want you to have five hundred dollars. Spend it on whatever you want. Please say you will accept, as it would make us very happy. You really are a great couple.'

Mrs Martinella sounded excited. 'Are youa for real? We hardly know you. Are you really surea you wanta give us this money?'

'Yes. I've already posted a cheque to your apartment. Just one thing.

Please don't tell Scooter as this matter is just between us. I really must go now. Take care Mrs Martinella.'

* * * *

As William climbed into the taxi to take him to Heathrow airport, he was happy to know that his gift would help these kind people. Keeping their son out of the equation was essential as there would be fireworks if he got wind of what had occurred. Equally he'd not mention it to Sarah just yet, in case she worried about him upsetting her agent.

As for winning the lottery, yes, he had won with the numbers he'd gleaned from his trip to America. If the truth be known, the amount was actually just ten pounds, but his plan was to finance the balance from his savings.

* * * *

Within two weeks of returning home, William got the call that Joan been admitted to a local hospice. Saddened by this news, his dilemma was should he break his promise to attend her funeral when the time came. The thought of losing her was unbearable and he wanted to pay his respects.

When he confided in Sarah, her opinion was that he should attend the service. Deep down he knew even in death he should be there for Joan.

****

Four weeks later William stood around in the car park of the South London crematorium. The afternoon sun was beating down on the small group of mourners as they waited for the funeral car to make its way up the driveway to the church. As it drew close, the nervous chatter ceased and the sound of planes overhead still continued. A young man walked in front of the hearse.

He held his black velvet top hat at chest height and carried a cane. On reaching the doorway the simple pine coffin came into sight with two floral tributes balanced on the lid.

William felt every muscle in his body tense as he heard the casket slide along the runners of the hearse floor. Four men in dark suits carried Joan into the church with the mourners following behind. There were no more than thirty people present, mostly family and friends.

He chose to sit in the front of the church and stared at the coffin. He had to force his mind away from imagining her lying in the darkness of the wooden box. He wondered if she was dressed in a white shroud or had a friend taken in clothes for her to be dressed in. He felt terribly sad that it was now her turn to join their son who had died all those years ago. He looked down to his wrist to Steven's watch that he wore every single day and sighed.

There were tributes from two of her friends that were moving reminders of her life. The brief address was by the vicar, a woman who spoke with a Yorkshire accent. Her account of Joan's immense kindness to others and contribution to the local community was moving. William acknowledged there was probably so much more he didn't know about her years without him.

After the singing of two hymns and prayers, the curtains enveloped the coffin and a protracted hush followed. William remained seated whilst the others made their way out of the church. Clutching the service pamphlet with the unflattering picture of Joan, he finally stood up to leave.

Outside it had clouded over. Another service was about to take place making him feel he should ring for a taxi, but first he felt it was necessary to chat with the family. He gazed at the floral tributes and addressed Joan's sister.

'Hello Liz, how are you?'

The woman in the black sack of a dress was surprised to see him. 'Is that really you William. I would never have recognised you if you hadn't come over. You look so thin; even your face looks different. Joan said you lived in Spain. Are you living back here now?'

'No, I've put roots down over there. Look, more importantly, how are you coping after losing Joan? I can't believe we are not going to see her again.'

Liz was clearly having problems keeping control of her feelings and started to sob. 'I miss her so much. I was with her when she passed. Fortunately, she was drowsy with all those drugs.'

'I wish I'd been there to support her. I'm not sure if you know, but she didn't want me at the funeral. I had to come. Despite us going our separate ways, I believe we never truly stopped loving each other.'

'Yes, she was still fond of you. I know she has included you in her will. I'm pleased about that. Before we go home I must take your e-mail to advise the solicitor.'

William looked stunned. 'No, that can't be. I have no right expecting her to think of me in that way. It's best just the close family are included in her affairs.'

'It was her wish. Now, you are coming to the reception to celebrate my sister's life, aren't you?'

'Sorry, but no, you'll have to excuse me on this occasion. If you don't mind, I'll give the refreshments and tea a miss. I'm sure I still have your telephone number, so I promise I'll keep in touch. You asked for my e-mail, do you want it now?'

From her handbag she pulled out a notebook and

copied down the details.

Before anything more could be said other relatives joined them who now remembered who he was. Everyone was terribly kind and it felt good being part of the family again. There followed much catching up with questions from both sides. William even swapped addresses with a couple of them.

Whilst it had been a sad day, something was definitely changing in William. At long last he was seeing life through clear eyes. There was no longer the fear of being back in his old hometown and meeting up with acquaintances. From now on, he was going to face up to the past.

Meeting up with the couple who had lived next door to them in Croydon also brought back many happy memories. They insisted on giving him a lift to the station. Rather than take them out of their way, he asked to be dropped off on the outskirts of Croydon. There was something he had to do.

* * * *

Entering the Goose and Bear pub, William took in the old Victorian building that now looked smarter than he remembered. Inside the modern interior, a new wooden counter ran along a side wall with an illuminated sign that flashed relentlessly advertising the burger bar. The smell of food being served made William hungry. Fortunately, pie and chips were still on the menu and he went up to place his order.

Settling down with a pint of bitter, he looked around the almost empty pub hoping to see James, but he wasn't there.

He toyed with the idea of leaving but as he had paid

for his meal he remained seated. His mind dwelt on his short walk along the familiar streets. On seeing the new townhouses where his business once stood, surprisingly, it didn't distress him. Coming to terms with a number of things felt good. Surely this was the turning point he'd waited so long for? Soon he'd be returning to Sarah to tell her his news on how well he had coped.

Tucking into his meal, it was then he noticed a man standing at the bar who was anxious to attract the attention of the staff to refill his glass. Seeing this drinker reminded him of the fine line of slipping into addiction. He immediately thought of Sarah. It was late afternoon back home and she'd have finished with her typing. Would tonight see her having too much to drink?

Then publican James appeared. He was drying glasses and storing them below the bar. William stood up from the table to wave at him. Surprised to see him, it wasn't long before the two men were chatting away like old friends with James texting his wife to join them. Struggling to hear his friend he shouted over to a member of staff to lower the volume on the music.

When Marleen joined them, she kissed William on both cheeks. Soon her joyous welcome was to change as she learnt that Joan had died. They both said how sorry they were to hear his news asking if they could offer any assistance. William thanked them saying the family had everything under control.

Eventually James' wife left to help out at the bar. William talked freely about the old days, even answering questions on the events that led up to the closure of his business.

'Tell me, how did you let things slip so badly? The press had a field day with the story about the wrong body you buried. I thought you guys had all sorts of checks to prevent this happening.'

William lent back in his chair before answering. The moment had arrived to tell someone what actually occurred.

'It wasn't quite as it seemed. I lost the plot and was having an affair with a girl young enough to be my daughter. Away from work on so many occasions, I left Steven to run the place, something I will always regret. Fortunately for us there weren't any repercussions on the legal front, but my son lost his life.'

'That was terrible. He was good lad. Tell me what made you close your firm?'

'I couldn't live with the shame. The Institute of Funeral directors demanded a meeting which I never showed up for. With Joan demanding we divorce my life was a real mess. I shut up shop and sold the land for a lot of money. You met my friend Martin at the festival and it was him who literally saved me from ending it all. With his help I managed to settle in Spain. Worst of all was losing Steven and I will never come to terms with that.'

James drew breath. 'God rest the poor lad. What a tragedy that was for you in the middle of all that work chaos. He'd worked with you for long enough, surely he was more than capable of looking after things? I would have expected Steven to cope even if you weren't around.'

Fingering Steven's watch he was determined to reveal the real story. 'I had no idea how much pressure he was under and the mistake with the body was his, not mine. I've covered up the truth for all these years. I told the police it was my error.'

James momentarily closed his eyes then touched William on the arm. 'Shit, you have been through a hard time. Why didn't you just put the record straight; you could have avoided all this heartache?'

'Because I was a cheating sod who ignored his wife and son and let's not forget it was my name over the door. If I'd spotted the signs of Steven's illness, he might still be alive now.'

'Oh, come on, you can't blame yourself.'

'Yes I can. Just after all the problems at work, it was there in the office that he died. It's what sent me off the rails resulting in that breakdown.'

James was clearly shocked with the revelation. 'Am I the first person you have told about all of this?'

'Yes, I just had to get it off my chest. I've bottled up this madness for far too long. I think it was attending Joan's funeral this morning that made me see sense.'

'Well, that's a positive step and keep remembering that despite all of the grief you have been through, you landed on your feet meeting Sarah. She really is a beautiful woman and you are getting married soon. You have another chance William. I take it she's too young to have retired, what does she do?'

Telling him about her success as an author seemed to impress James who was already swiping the screen on his smart phone to search for her books.

When it was time to leave they shook hands and William keenly said, 'Please let me know when you are next in Spain.'

'As it happens, we should be over in a few months' time. We could take the bus over to you. How about we treat you and Sarah to a meal?'

William warmed to the idea and immediately nodded his head. 'Yeah, let's go for it. You mail me and we'll check the diaries.'

Then panic struck in William's head as he anxiously said, 'I haven't got around to telling Sarah what really occurred. Whatever you do, don't say anything.'

'Sure thing. I get the message. You can trust me not to spill the beans.'

* * * *

Despite being desperately sad at losing Joan, there was no denying William had finally seen the light. He was determined to stop beating himself up with the shame and guilt he had carried for too long. With so much to look forward to, his mind was now on his wedding that would soon come around.

The pressing issue was to put his apartment up for sale and search for a larger place to live. Life suddenly felt real again with the chance of regaining his confidence and dignity. Winning the girl of his dreams remained the icing on the cake and this time he wasn't going to let her down. There was nothing he wouldn't do for her. He needed to stop all the nonsense about her carrying a torch for her old flame in Finland. She still had to work and any help in climbing the ladder to enhance her career should be viewed as beneficial.

****

The flight back to Girona and bus ride home went smoothly. By mid-afternoon he'd already showered and was drying himself when the phone rang. Dropping the towel on the floor he left wet footprints all the way through to the lounge. Grasping his mobile he was thrilled to take a call from Sarah.

'You got back alright then. I missed you something terrible.'

'Me too; I hate us being apart.'

Having already filled her in with the details of the funeral, he mentioned his publican friend James.

'You really surprised me with you going into his pub. I distinctly remember your aversion to having anything to do with him. You called him a creep.'

'And I was wrong as per usual. Catching up was fun and he and his wife are coming over soon. They've invited us out to lunch.'

'Well, there you are with your clouded viewpoint and now things don't look so bad, do they?'

'That's right, and I'm going to make a big effort to get on with things. Can we meet up later?'

He heard Sarah giggle and then she uttered her classic line that was always so tempting. 'Why don't you pop over now?'

* * * *

William let himself into the villa and called out that he'd arrived.

'No need to shout, I'm in the garden room.'

His eyes lit up on seeing Sarah who was wearing shorts and a white bra that left little to the imagination. Lounging in a comfy chair, her legs crossed, he noticed her discarded tee shirt on the tiled floor. Today, for the first time, seeing the tattoo on her arm with his initial meant a great deal to him. It really did confirm their commitment to each other.

He leant down to kiss her lips.

She patted his arm. 'You've been away a few days and it seems like ages. I think we have some making up to do.'

Feeling excited with the prospect of making love, he stood behind her running fingers over her neck that gradually strayed further down. He heard her groan as he kissed her bare shoulders. She was wearing the same

215

perfume as last time they were together.

Encouraging her to rise from the chair he led her through the lounge and it was then they heard a tap on the window. They both sank to the floor for fear of being seen in their state of undress. Craning his neck William caught sight of Martin who was standing close to the glass. The knocking started again.

'God, it's Martin. Ruddy bad timing. What does he want?'

Sarah laughed nervously and held both arms to her chest. 'Do you think he saw us? I'm practically naked. Why doesn't he ring the doorbell like everyone else?'

'Not sure. You slip into the bedroom and I'll get rid of him.'

When he was happy Sarah was safely out of sight, he buttoned up his shirt and made his way to the hall. The sound of the bell made him jump. Taking a deep breath and trying to look calm he opened the front door.

'Sorry I couldn't get the button to work, so I banged on the window.'

William snapped, 'Well it worked just now when you rang it.'

'Oh, who got out of bed the wrong way? I have a parcel for Sarah that was delivered by mistake to my place. Can I have a word with her?'

'She's in the shower washing her hair. Thanks for bringing that around and I'll pass it on. I really must get on with cooking dinner, so how about we catch up tomorrow.'

Sarah appeared in the hallway.

Handing her the parcel Martin giggled. 'You must have an awesome dryer as its dried your hair really quickly. Sorry to have disturbed you from your shower.'

Confused and struggling to comprehend what he was

going on about, Sarah thanked him for his help.

Having said goodbye to him, they closed the door and broke into fits of laughter.

Leading William by the hand into the bedroom Sarah first yanked the blinds shut before pushing him onto her enormous bed. As she pulled off her clothes he studied her beautiful body in the half light and begged her to hurry up.

Chapter 19

Catching up with Martin the following day it was apparent he had something on his mind. His friend asked how the funeral went and expressed his condolences. He then switched to how much he loved Scooter.

'When you came to see us in London, I don't know if it was obvious, but we'd just had our first row. I was worried you might have felt uncomfortable with us practically ignoring each other.'

He paused to sip his coffee and then greedily loaded his plate with three biscuits.

William frowned. 'No, I didn't notice anything untoward. Don't be too concerned as we all fall out occasionally. If anything, it strengthens the relationship. What were you disagreeing on?'

'Oh, this and that. He's so ruddy strict about tidiness and keeps picking me up on leaving things around. You wouldn't say I'm an untidy person, would you?'

William drew breath. 'Well actually, yes.'

'Really!'

Martin then launched into the reason for his visit. 'The other thing was with you going to New York and saying what an incredible place it was, I asked Scooter if we could visit. He was so negative about taking me. He became all hissy with me and that night I slept in the spare bedroom.'

'Oh, I see.'

'His reaction made me think he really hated the idea of going back. I got to wondering if he'd been in prison or something like that which he wanted to hide. Am I being silly?'

'Oh, come on, that's crazy talk. For heaven's sake

what made you even think he might have been a criminal?'

'I don't know.'

'Your imagination does run away with you sometimes. Let me assure you there will be a perfectly normal explanation for him not wanting to go back home.'

William chose not to expand on the real reason, let alone mention the money he'd sent abroad. If he intruded any more, there was a chance he may bring grief to his friend's relationship. Instead he said, 'My guess is he probably made a clean break from America. Just give him time and he'll tell you all about it when he feels ready.'

'That's what I like about you, your cool, calm head.'

William coughed. 'I wasn't always this calm, was I?'

'No, I suppose not. The other thing I wanted to say was I won't forget the advice you gave me about finding my son.'

'I should hope not.'

'Staying with Scooter in London gave me the opportunity to do the rounds with my relatives who seemed pleased to see me. When I asked about my lad I got quite a shock. Discovering what he had been up to frightened me.'

Martin helped himself to another of the chocolate biscuits managing to drop crumbs all over William's immaculately clean floor.

'What hurts is nobody bothered to tell me what was going on. Then again, I suppose it was my fault for avoiding them all for so long. It seems he's a heroin addict and has moved away from the area. He could even be dead for all I know. What am I going to do? If there's a chance he's still alive, I need to see him. Have you got any ideas?'

'Drugs you say, that's really bad. You could try contacting the Salvation Army as well as the hostels. Sometimes they can get a message to people, but it will be his choice whether to reply. I can't promise anything but I'll rack my brains for a solution.'

* * * *

The first William heard about his share of inheritance from Joan's estate was through a solicitor calling from London. After completing the security checks and returning the forms, he was shocked with the news that he had been left one hundred thousand pounds. This was the remainder of her monies from the sale of their old business. The flat and her treasured Mini car had been left to her sister. Overwhelmed by her kindness, he planned to put the funds towards purchasing the new property in Spain.

He recalled his last afternoon with Joan when she told him his future lay in making a new life with Sarah. He was not to repeat the same mistakes he'd made with her. Her words still resonated with him and now it was really time to take back control.

* * * *

Anxious to share his news with Sarah about the money he had inherited, he set off for the villa. On letting himself in there was a strong smell of disinfectant in the hall and lounge. Many of the windows were wide open. He asked her if she'd been doing a deep clean and overdone things, but she offered no reply.

Switching the subject away from the overpowering stench of cleaning materials, he mentioned his windfall, which seemed to please her. She rebuked him saying he must have been mad cheating on this wonderful woman and that it was evident she loved him right up to the day she died. William hung his head low and said nothing.

The bombshell that Sarah was about to drop was to change the course of their lives and he never saw it coming. She reached for his hand and in a nervous voice whispered,

'There's something I need to tell you.'

Breaking into a sweat William's words tumbled out. 'Oh my God, you're not ill, are you?'

'No, nothing like that, I've just seen the light and am going to put a change in place.'

He was convinced she was ending their relationship and was about to hand him back the engagement ring. He moved away from her and placed a hand on the sofa to steady himself. Feeling giddy he waited for her to speak.

'I have a confession. When you were away at the funeral, I got really off my head on booze.'

'Oh bugger, I told you to go easy. Where were you?'

William wanted to move forward to comfort her but remained perfectly still.

'Here in the villa but it got out of hand. It was midday and I hadn't written a word. Another ruddy writer's block and I nearly threw the laptop in the bin. I'd got an e-mail from Scooter who needed an update on how I was getting on. It was a pleasant enough message but I noticed something at the bottom of the text. He'd inadvertently included a communication from the publisher urging him to put pressure on me. I saw red and reached for the wine and for the first time in my life drank from the bottle.'

William was shaking wondering what else she was going to tell him. 'How much did you drink?'

She looked ashamed and covered her eyes with both hands and muttered. 'More than enough. I was staggering around knocking over things and then was violently sick on the bed. It took me a while to sober up and all I could think of was how I'd let you down. Cleaning up was horrendous and I ended up throwing away my new quilt. I'm sorry about the smell.'

Now at her side, he drew her into his body. 'It was just a slip darling.' He paused as he was about to say they could sort this out, but he wasn't that sure it would help.

'You kept saying I should see the doctor for advice on finding a self-help group and I am definitely ready to do that.'

Encouraging her to sit on the sofa he told her she'd taken the first step asking for help.

'It hurts me to see you struggling with this problem and as for your writing, surely your mental health is more important.'

'I'm with you on that one. Before you came over I rang the medical centre. I've got an appointment at four this afternoon with a woman doctor. Will you come with me?'

Glancing at his watch there were a few hours before they needed to go. 'Of course I will. Let's pop out and get some air freshener, but first I want you to tell me if there is any more alcohol in the villa. It needs to all go down the sink.'

'I didn't think of that. I think we should box up anything here and take them over to Martin. He'll be thrilled with getting a few bottles.'

'Forget gifting Martin with the booze as it is all going to be destroyed.'

* * * *

The medical centre was situated in a new building close to the bus station. The glass-fronted single storey building had an enormous poster in the window advertising for new patients.

Inside they were greeted by a slip of a girl with bright blue hair and a tattoo of a spider's web that crept down her neck and possibly further. She looked flustered as she attempted to deal with the influx of visitors. Seated on the comfy leather chairs, William observed the other patients, who were mostly ex-pats who had swapped the rain for the sun. There were two doctors in the practice and the wait seemed never ending. With every person that went in to be seen it seemed to take ages before the next patient had their names called out.

Sarah sat nervously crossing and uncrossing her legs. Flicking through a property magazine it was clear her mind was working overtime. When her turn eventually arrived, William accompanied her into the modern room with grey furniture. A bright red examination couch lined one of the walls with rolls of paper sheets stored on a shelf. Doctor Medley spoke with a welcoming Birmingham accent and asked how she could be of help. Sarah first looked at William, then back to the woman with the trim figure and short skirt that barely covered her tanned legs.

'This is embarrassing for me. I'm not an alcoholic, but I'm worried as recently I have been drinking more. I just wanted some advice.'

'I'm sorry to hear that. I have to ask you – when was the last time you had a drink?'

William was shocked to hear her say after breakfast.

The doctor quickly typed some notes into the screen and leant back in her chair. 'As this is your first visit to the practice, you will appreciate I don't have any records on you. I will need to know what medication you are on. Tell me about why you drink and the number of units a week you consume.'

She glanced back to her notes in an effort to recall her patient's name quickly added, 'Sarah.'

'Probably in the region of about fifteen in a normal week but sometimes more.' She quietly added, 'Large glasses.'

Leaning forward the doctor gently shook her head. 'Well Sarah, that's well above the recommended guidelines. Do you get depressed or are you under any pressure at work? Sorry, but I have to ask have you ever self-harmed or had any thoughts of...'

'No, I haven't. 'I put myself under too much strain with work and get low, but that's all.'

'And, are you able to modify what you do or possibly switch careers? What do you actually do?'

Sarah, in a dismissive voice replied, 'Oh just a bit of writing.'

Her mood suddenly changed. 'What's my job got to do with all this? Maybe coming here today wasn't such a good idea after all. I think I'll just leave.'

William tapped her on the arm. 'Calm down, the doctor is trying to help.'

'Just back off, won't you?'

Interrupting, the doctor was determined to be heard and raised her voice. 'The danger is you may be tinkering on the edge by consuming too much alcohol. Are you eating enough and do you suffer from hangovers after drinking?'

'Yes, to both questions and I don't want to take any tablets.'

'Well, this is just a suggestion. Every Wednesday, at

seven in the evening, a Mr Sullivan holds a meeting at the back of this surgery.'

Sarah gasped, 'You mean alcoholics anonymous! I don't think I'm anywhere near that stage.'

'No, I'm hoping that is not the case. There are a few people with serious problems who attend, but some like you who are seeking advice on how to avoid slipping further. I think you should go along.'

Looking to William for reassurance she then nodded at the doctor.

'Great, now I need to check your vitals for the records and you can tell me what tablets you take.'

In a quiet voice that began to grow Sarah sadly said, 'I just want to get on with my life without all this going on.'

'Well done, Sarah, none of this can have been easy for you. Just one thing, please try to have a rest from having a drink. There are some excellent non-alcoholic beers and wines that are really quite like the real thing. Your husband will be with you all the way.'

William blushed with pride hearing the reference to him being Sarah's spouse. Somehow, they were going to get her back on the right track and enjoy the rest of their lives together.

* * * *

The following morning, William arrived at the villa in time for breakfast and, as agreed, he made the call to Scooter at the publishing company.

'It's like this, Scooter; Sarah is poorly with stress. We've been to the doctor who says she needs total rest. She must take things easy so won't be doing any work for a while.'

Over the speaker on his mobile they listened to her agent sigh as he took in the news. 'Can I talk to her please?'

'Sorry, she doesn't want to speak to anyone at the moment. I'm sure you wouldn't want to put her under any more pressure than necessary. I promise we will be in touch next week. Thanks for being so understanding.'

* * * *

On Wednesday evening after an early meal, William accompanied Sarah to the door by the side of the medical centre. It took an age before anyone let her in. A youngish looking man with a bushy beard wearing shorts and flip flops introduced himself as Bob Sullivan. William left her and went across the road to a bar for coffee and hoped she wouldn't be too distressed attending the group.

Entering the small meeting room, Sarah weighed up the other people who were chatting away. She had expected to see a large number of alcoholics at the meeting, but this was not the case. The people here, if in another location, could all quite easily have been attending a beginner's course in Spanish. Bob, the man in charge, put her at her ease by offering tea and biscuits, which she declined. The woman next to her leant over to introduce herself, prompting others to raise their hands in the air as a welcome.

When the session commenced, it soon became clear that three of those present had a serious issue with drink. Similar to what Sarah had seen in soaps on television, everyone was encouraged to tell their story. The heavy drinkers clearly accepted that by having just one more glass of alcohol they would slip off the wagon again. In contrast, others feared crossing that line. Their common ground was that they all worried about the grief they brought to their friends and families. An older man, who kept repeating that he had lost his wife to cancer, admitted he could no longer cope and had turned to the bottle.

When it was Sarah's turn to stand up and address the others, she briefly mentioned the stresses of being an author and how alcohol helped her to unwind. She also quickly pointed out that there were periods of time when she never had a drink.

There was a round of applause and one member patted her on the shoulder saying it couldn't have been easy telling them about her experiences.

There was much conversation about spotting the signs of excessive drinking and controlling the urge with the various substitute drinks on the market. Sarah hung onto their every word telling herself this was a wakeup call. She hadn't reached rock bottom and still had a chance. Agreeing to come back for the next session, she left the building feeling pleased with herself, but in reality, knew she wasn't out of the woods yet.

* * * *

Over the remainder of the month, Sarah attended all the sessions. Accepting there was no magic answer or quick fix, she was determined to give it her best shot. She developed a taste for the imitation wines, but curbing her addiction was not all plain sailing. There were days when the temptation was at its peak and she didn't know what to do. On these occasions, the wine consumed certainly didn't fall into the category of non-alcoholic. Unbeknown to William, on more than one occasion, she visited a local bar on her own.

* * * *

Having had the break from writing, Sarah now felt ready to work again. Her publisher gently swayed her into agreeing dates for the Finland trip as well as book signings in the UK. Understandably, William was apprehensive about her overdoing things again, but hung back from giving advice.

Once again she started to think about her group that had been temporarily disbanded. There had been so many messages bouncing into her inbox asking when new classes would resume. A decision was made to review this at a later point. There were sure to be a few peeved writers who were fed up with the interruptions to their lessons.

Top of their list of priorities was their wedding. They had chosen a local hotel to handle the ceremony and lunch. Martin had engaged the services of a photographer, someone he knew from the new housing development on the outskirts of the town. With a guest list of thirty, some travelling from the UK, it had been tricky securing accommodation, but gradually things were falling into place.

One bit of news that pleased William was that his publican friend James and his wife were flying out at the end of the week. The arrangement was for them to come to the villa for drinks then visit a restaurant for a meal.

William reflected on the last few months wondering just how they'd coped. At times it felt like the world was crumbling under their feet, then suddenly he was in a state of heavenly bliss. The wedding vows would strengthen their commitment to care for each other.

Adjusting to the curved balls that life was throwing at them certainly hadn't been easy.

Chapter 20

On the morning James and his wife were due to visit, Sarah took a call from William. He was concerned that he wouldn't arrive in time to welcome their guests and would she mind seeing them in. He hurriedly explained that at the last moment he had been persuaded to help out in the English library. He promised not to be more than half an hour late. Before ending the call, she reminded him she loved him and kissed the picture of his face on her mobile phone screen. Her thoughts were on the strain she had caused him and how tired he looked these days. She hoped that today he would smarten himself up and shave before coming over.

Just lately she thought he was just a shadow of his former self and pondered on whether he may be unwell. He was no longer a young man and all the recent stress couldn't have been good for his health.

James and his wife Marleen arrived early having taken the bus from Lloret de Mar. Despite William's worries that they would struggle to locate the villa, the couple had no trouble in finding them. Holding a bottle of champagne, James was keen to pass over their present. Sarah felt disappointed that she wouldn't be able to enjoy a drink with everyone. She allowed herself a moment to imagine the taste of the sparkling wine that she loved to mix with fresh orange juice. Possibly just one glass would be okay if she sipped it slowly. The thought was immediately dismissed.

She tried not to stare at James' stomach; she was sure it looked even larger than when they last met. Dressed in jeans with a tee shirt that advertised the name of his pub, he looked a mess.

In contrast, Marleen looked stunning in her miniscule white skirt and slender legs. Her more than ample bosom was straining against the expensive designer shirt. The voice was as annoying as ever and, like her husband, her choice of drink was beer.

Surprisingly, for this time of year, it was a sultry morning and Sarah suggested they sit in the garden whilst she fetched their drinks. From the kitchen window, she watched James waving his hands in the air. If she wasn't mistaken, he looked cross. Were they having a disagreement?

She was concerned that William had not yet sent a text to say he would be there soon and was disappointed at having to look after his friends for a long time on her own. She wished he'd hurry up so they could open the champagne. Her mind was on sneaking a glass and pretending it was non-alcoholic wine.

Carrying a tray into the garden, she was pleased when James rose from his chair to help her. 'Let me have that and you sit down. Let's hope your fiancé arrives soon as we want to celebrate something with you, hence the champagne.'

'I'm sure he'll be here any moment. He's always helping someone out; today he's putting up shelves in the library. Tell me, what are you celebrating?'

James excitedly said, 'We've sold our apartment and hope to find a bigger property, possibly a house in the hills near Tossa. We may even become neighbours.'

Trying to sound pleased Sarah forced a smile, 'That's ace.'

'Just what I was saying to Marleen on the bus. We'll be able to meet up more often,' said James loudly.

Looking around the garden and to the house he quickly added, 'I wonder if we could afford this place.'

Aware that her brother was desperate to sell as there had been no recent enquiries, she hoped he wouldn't do a deal with these people. Changing the subject to William, she enquired about their friendship back in Croydon.

She could see he was thinking about his answer and waited patiently for him to speak.

'Well, your other half and I go back a long way. I first met him was in a garden centre, or should I say car park. I was just walking away from my car and heard this almighty bang. William had reversed into my vehicle. I lost my temper and called him an idiot.'

'Oh my God,' said Sarah as she tried to suppress her laughter.

'Our next meeting was some years later when I was running the pub. There was a commotion outside. Quite a few of our customers had gone out into the street to take a look. I followed and saw your William. There had been a car accident.'

'William was involved in a car crash, was he hurt?'

'No, he was first on the scene and was administering first aid to a woman with a nasty injury to her head. As we all stood around, he kept talking to the woman saying she'd be okay. Right from that moment I knew he was a decent bloke, someone who really cared about others.'

In a proud voice Sarah responded, 'That sounds like William.'

'After that, for many years he came in for a drink at the end of the day. I used to pull his leg about where he worked. I don't think he liked being an undertaker.'

James took a mouthful of beer and wiped his lips with the back of his hand. 'I don't know how anyone could work in that trade. My heart still goes out to William for losing his son and all that business over the mix up at his funeral parlour. That was the last straw that broke him.'

Confused and interested to learn more Sarah turned to James. 'What exactly do you mean by mix up?'

'Surely, William has told you all about this already.'

'No!'

'You know, when the wrong man was buried. It must have been terrible for the relatives thinking they had laid their loved one to rest then to discover the blunder. If my memory serves me right, the man in question should have been cremated. The press practically crucified William and he went to pieces. That's when young Steven died and his firm closed down. Joan and he split up not long after.'

With a look of horror on her face Sarah whispered, 'Oh my God, no this can't be right!'

The penny had dropped and she ran into the villa shouting that she felt ill. Her visitors looked on helplessly and waited for her to return.

Locking herself in the downstairs cloakroom she was violently sick. Grasping the sticky rim of the toilet bowl she howled out as if in pain. She was the woman who had gone through that terrible ordeal of viewing the incorrect body.

What a cruel trick of fate it was in learning the truth from these people. There was no doubt in her mind that it was her partner that William had mistakenly buried all those years ago. He was the funeral director who had torn her heart in two with his unforgivable mistake. All this time they had been lovers, she couldn't believe she'd been sleeping with a man who chose not to tell her his deepest secret.

She was convinced that, just like her, he had never realised their earlier connection when they first met in Spain. The likelihood of meeting someone new and then discovering they'd crossed paths before was beyond the realms of coincidence.

No wonder she had not remembered him from their brief encounter in the undertaker's office. He had lost so much weight, changed his appearance, shaved head and now had a much thinner face. The chances of falling in love with a man who in truth had brought her so much unhappiness was hard to comprehend. She vowed never to forgive him.

Moving away from the smelly toilet, she glanced in the mirror at her clothes that were covered in sick. Her fingers came into contact with the sparkling engagement ring. In anger she scraped it against the side of the sink with the intention damaging the diamond. It was then that she heard William's voice as he let himself into the villa and then out to the garden.

William greeted his guests but was alarmed by their obvious distress. They mentioned Sarah had rushed into the villa and they had heard her crying out as if in pain.

Aware that something awful must had happened, he encouraged them to leave straightaway. Returning to the house he discovered that Sarah was in the cloakroom and she was refusing to come out. She kept yelling, 'Get out of my house.'

He leant against the doorframe and spoke softly, 'Darling, what has happened? Open the door please. I've got rid of our visitors.'

It was a long wait until Sarah finally came out and she looked terrible. Clutching her soiled tee shirt, she dropped it on the floor. The smell was so overpowering that he had to step back. With a hand held in front of his mouth he said, 'Are you all right? Have you eaten something that's upset your stomach?'

'Get out of my way, I need to take a shower. I want

you to go.'

'For heaven's sake tell me what's up. Have you been drinking?'

Her eyes shot up to the ceiling in disgust with his suggestion.

'It would be entirely your fault if I had,' she spat out.

She stood in the hallway studying every imperfection of his face. Her eyes traced the lips that she once loved to kiss and now hated. This was the face of the man who'd held a funeral for John, despite her instructions to cremate him. Not only had he interred him, but the wrong family had been under the impression that he was their loved one. All of this was down to William.

Thinking back to when she eventually learnt about the nature of his career, for some reason she had been able to cope reasonably well with his news. She had glossed over the fact that he worked in South London, but how could she have failed to put two and two together? It was William at the time who had comforted her and yet now the wretched man looked so different. Whatever he offered in his defence, there could be no exoneration.

'I can't stand to look at your face. You are a liar and have deceived me.'

'Now hold on – what's all this about? We love each other and are getting married. You still haven't told me why you are so upset. Is it something I've said or done?'

'Let's get one thing clear – there is no you and me any more, we are history.'

'Please don't say that. When I spoke to you this morning and there wasn't a problem. What's been happening that I need to know about?'

'Does the name John Johnson ring any bells?'

William shuddered involuntarily. He stuttered, 'Jo…

Jo… Johnson! Was it James who mentioned this name to you?'

Sarah nodded and unleashed her temper on him. 'I was the woman whose partner's name was Johnson. I trusted you with John's body and you broke my heart. Now I know it was you, I hate you with every last breath of my body. I should have sued you, finished you off altogether!'

William steadied himself against a wall. The shock of learning his fiancée was the woman from his past was clearly having a profound effect on his body and mind. He was shaking badly and kept blinking as he formed his words of reply.

'Oh, my God, you were the lady in the chapel of rest. Believe me I had no idea it was you when we met all these years later. I've hated myself for the grief I brought to everyone. What I can't get my head around is how is it possible that life has brought the two of us together without either one of us working out the connection. I'm begging you to forgive me.'

'I'll never forgive you, I just want you out of my life.'

'No, please don't say that. Surely, I've paid the price for my mistake. I had a breakdown that nearly finished me off…'

Interrupting him, she repeated the word breakdown and laughed. She was determined to make him suffer. In her mind she felt like the girl in her Finnish novel who sought revenge and that was just what she intended to bring about.

With tears streaming down her cheeks her voice raised to screaming point, 'Can you even begin to understand how I felt about his body having to be exhumed? It was like something out of a Frankenstein movie. A good enough reason for me to have started drinking, don't you think? This is all your doing.'

Sarah was unconcerned by the sudden change in his face that was now bright red. His mouth was quivering with fear and he was clutching his arm. It was obvious he was processing everything she had said, but all she wanted to do was hurt him.

'For me, I can't bear the thought of you coming anywhere near me. You make my skin crawl when I think of what you did. The wedding is cancelled. I need to shower and you know where the door is. Give me your key.'

William watched in disbelief as Sarah raised her hand to pull off the engagement ring and thrust it in his direction. It landed on the floor by his feet and with a look of immense sadness he closed his eyes.

Staring at the tattoo on her arm of the sunflower with the first initial of his name, Sarah slapped her skin so hard that it made a cracking sound that made him jump. 'Bloody hell, I should have listened to you and not had this done.'

As she marshalled him to the door, she sarcastically said, 'Your mate James kindly brought us a bottle of champagne. As soon as I'm all cleaned up, I'm going to celebrate our splitting up.'

Chapter 21

Unable to accept that their relationship had ended so abruptly, over the next few weeks William hardly left his apartment. It was Martin's intervention that once again gave him a lifeline. Seeing his friend in such a state must have been heartbreaking. William had broken his glasses so now had one of the arms crudely taped on. He was unshaven and had been in his dressing gown all week and was bare foot.

Martin had guessed that things weren't right between him and Sarah, but had hung back for fear of upsetting him. And now he had the full story.

The two men sat in the untidy lounge with remnants of food on the sofa and floor. The smell of unlaundered clothes was unpleasant, inciting Martin to scoop up the garments for placing in the washing machine.

'Sit down, you are doing my head in,' said William grumpily.

'What a fool you have been getting into this state. We don't want Sarah learning you can't cope. What am I going to do with you?'

'Give up on me like she has. I've blown any chance of winning her back. This must be the coincidence of all times: meeting and falling in love with the very woman I had faced at the worst moment in her life. It was bad enough for Sarah losing her partner, but we put her through so much more pain. I can't blame her for hating me; I hate myself.'

Martin sucked in breath. 'It all comes down to couples not keeping secrets from each other. I can though understand your reluctance to be upfront as it wasn't exactly a pretty story to reveal. The thing is, you now have to move forward; first though, you need a shower and a shave. You look like something the cat's dragged in.'

'I can't cope without her, it's like my life is over.'

'I'm not offering you any more sympathy, just a helping hand. I won't be seeing Scooter for a while as he's really busy, so how about you and I spend more time together like the old days?'

Suddenly, a little of William's spark came back as he joked that there better not be any of his funny business. Martin shot back with, 'I'm sure I don't know what you are suggesting.'

William in an anxious voice then whispered, 'How am I going to cope with her still living here? In a small town like this I'm bound to bump into her. If I'm going to have any chance of getting her back I can't be seen to be hassling her. I'm worried about her drinking.'

'I'm sorry but with all due respect, that's her problem for the moment. You have to let go.'

Martin looked deep in thought. 'It's awkward for me living next door to her as she blanked me yesterday. The last I heard was her brother is so desperate to sell the villa that he's reduced it to a silly price. Someone will snap it up for sure then there is every chance she will return to the UK. You won't be able to stop her.'

'No, she can't do that. I have to make amends.'

* * * *

Informing William's guests that the wedding was off was never going to be easy. He avoided going into too much detail saying the relationship had broken down.

It brought back the reality that Sarah would not feature in the rest of his life. He kept thinking that if he'd levelled with her from the start, things might have been different. At this precise moment living in this wonderful part of Spain meant nothing to him without her. As far as he was concerned he may as well be back in London breathing in the foul air with a backdrop of high-rise buildings and crime at unprecedented levels.

Strangely, he bore no ill feelings towards James for spilling the beans. When he eventually got around to ringing him, the news of the breakup came as a great surprise to them.

William recalled Sarah saying James had brought a gift of some champagne and her threat to finish off the bottle. Her words about celebrating the end of their relationship echoed in his head. She had said she knew relatively little about him; wasn't it the same with her? They were both shadows lost in this sea of lies and confusion.

* * * *

Two painful weeks passed with the occasional sighting of Sarah as she walked through the town. On one such occasion William attempted to talk to her, but she totally ignored him. She was wearing the shortest of skirts that she had to keep smoothing down as it lifted in the warm breeze. Despite the strained look on her face, he thought she looked incredibly beautiful. What he'd do to hold her in his arms again and kiss those warm lips. It was hard to believe that a few short weeks ago they were so close and planning a future together. Just a few days ago he posted a note through the villa door about collecting her clothes from his apartment, but she never contacted him. As he watched her slowly disappear into the crowds of holidaymakers, it felt like the curtain was coming down for the very last time. Standing in the doorway of a shoe shop, he raised the fabric on the sleeve of his shirt to look at the tattoo. He cursed the fact that her name was there to be seen every time he took a shower or changed his top.

* * * *

The day that Martin announced there was a sold sign on the villa, William went out on his balcony to gaze in the direction of where she lived. There was a lot of activity down on the shore with holidaymakers and sun umbrellas covering much of the stony beach. Noisy motor boats tore into the waves and fishing boats returned with their morning catch. The temperature was up in the eighties with a forecast for even warmer weather by early afternoon.

Martin appeared carrying two tiny cups of coffee that he placed on the tiled table and commented on how lucky they were living there.

'Depends on your take as to how you rate lucky. Tossa holds no magic for me any longer. I'm dreading Sarah moving away.'

Downing his coffee in one go, Martin explained that he had seen Sarah and her brother loading boxes into a van. It was merely a matter of time before the new owners moved in.

'Oh, bugger, that's just what I didn't want to hear. Do me a favour, ring Scooter, he'll know if she is writing again. He might also say if she's moving back to London.'

'I'm two steps ahead of you on that one. When I spoke to him last night he said she'd be in touch and given a new address in Tossa. Now don't get upset as I'm just the messenger. She's also planning that trip to

Finland to work on her book.'

William saw red and kicked the balcony iron railing. 'And it's a no brainer who's behind all this. Bloody Pavvii.'

☐

Chapter 22

The man in the sauna with the super thin body looked over to Sarah and urged her to remove the towel that was tightly wrapped around her body. Pavvii had always been a control freak and his tactics for persuading his old girlfriend to return to Helsinki, had finally been fruitful.

'Loosen up won't you. Us Finns don't worry about things like that. It's not as if it's anything I haven't seen before.'

Sarah, reluctantly let the towel slip onto the pine bench. She felt his eyes scan her body through the steam and swivelled her legs away from the coals that were throwing out so much heat. The sweat was pouring from her skin bringing about a feeling of giddiness. Her mind was on their earlier lovemaking in the hotel bedroom. If truth be known, the real reason she let this man back into her life was to hurt William.

Pavvii leant forward to switch off the stove and wiped the sweat from his brow, 'I've been thinking about that old guy in Spain you hooked up with. You are never to see him again; do I make myself clear?'

'I'm not seeing him.'

'You should live in this country and keep me company. Write books from here. I can keep an eye on you, just like before.'

Aware of how it used to be with him telling her what to do all the time, she now wished she hadn't taken the first flight out to be with him. He was so demanding. Yes, the sex was good, but he never seemed satisfied to just talk to her. It was all about Pavvii and what he thought she should do. Casting her mind back to when she lived there, the memories were still raw. There was the time he stole her address book from her handbag. His explanation was he'd found it on the floor. Later she discovered he had copied down most of the contacts into his notepad. On asking for an explanation he shrugged it off saying she should thank him for making a copy. His insistence that she had to tell him everything about her life and work was disconcerting. It appeared he was calling all the shots deciding on who she could have as friends.

There was also the incident when she was recovering from a hangover and was struggling to get dressed. He said he was pretending to take a photograph on his camera and in her drunken state she foolishly posed for him. A week later he took delight in showing her a saucy black and white picture. There was an almighty row with him saying he didn't know what all the fuss was about. She did get him to destroy the negative, but deep down she knew a further copy would surely exist somewhere.

For some unknown reason, she still felt drawn to him to the extent of forgiving the monitoring and cruel intrusion of her life. When they last met he was so professional with his work on that article and never laid a finger on her, but he was now back to his old tricks.

As Sarah stood up to leave the sauna she held the towel in front of her body. He jumped off the wooden bench to touch one of her legs. She frowned and eased his hand away.

Pavvii still managed to fondle her breast. His pummelling of her skin went on for a couple of seconds before she screamed, 'You are really hurting me, let go!'

This time he yanked his hand away. 'What's up with you?'

'Stop it. I'm not happy with you coming on to me in here. This is a hotel sauna, anyone might come in.'

'I've locked the door so nobody is going to come in, are they?'

'You've done what – unlock it at once!'

This time he raised his eyebrows and smirked. 'Just relax, it's just you and me in here.'

'When I rang you from Spain, I told you I needed company and someone to talk to. All you seem to be interested in is one thing. Anyway, won't your wife get suspicious with me on the scene?'

Pavvii yawned and in a dismissive voice said, 'Don't worry about her, she rarely comes to the apartment. I tend to go home at weekends. She's hardly going to come to this hotel, is she? It means we can spend more time together, just like the old days.'

She shuddered as she recalled how controlling a boyfriend he had been. Even in the relatively short time since she arrived back in Helsinki, he was attempting to manipulate her life again. The business of him having to know her every movement was irritating. She had chosen to take up with him and the underlying reason was purely to get back at William.

'Are you even listening to me? I just said we could spend more time together. You could stay over at my apartment.'

'No, I need to be on my own to concentrate on the research for the sequel. I'll continue to stay with my friend, if that's all right with you.'

'Mmm, I don't know enough about this woman you are staying with, do I? I think you should tell her that you no longer need a bed at her place, or for that matter wish to see her again.'

Horrified by the return to his old ways telling her who she could see, she stood up to leave.

'Not so fast. It's rude to walk away like that.'

She turned around to face him. She felt frightened as he pointed at her arm. He stubbed a finger hard into the tattoo on her arm and moved closer to inspect the image with the single letter.

'What the hell is this?'

Desperately trying to process her reply, it came out as a nervous stutter. 'Th… th… that's just something I had done years ago.'

'What does the initial stand for?

'My old pet. The dog's name was Wallace.'

'I remember you saying you didn't like dogs. Oh, whatever, I still think it looks stupid. Tell me, have you got any more tattoos on your body?'

Before she had a chance to speak he once again made a grab for her. Standing naked in front of him she froze on the spot as his eyes scanned every inch of her body.

'That's enough I'm going back upstairs to get dressed. I have a train to catch so I will be off shortly.'

'Take a later train. You can't go yet as I've paid for the hotel room and it's still early.'

'How dare you say that! I'm not some call girl you picked up in town.'

He thumped his hand on the doorframe. 'You owe me for that article that helped to promote your books.'

Disgusted with his outburst she bravely faced him. 'I owe you nothing. It was a lucky break for me getting that publicity, but it wasn't a lifetime passport for you to do what you want with me. What you said about getting value for the hotel room, it really disgusts me.'

His face now changed to one of worry as he said, 'Oh, I have really upset you. Forgive me and I promise there will be no more pressure from now on.'

This was the first time she had ever heard him back

down on anything. Could she really trust him again? After that remark about getting value for the hotel room and holding her to ransom for his professional services, the answer was obviously no. She simply said, 'I meant what I said about having to get the train.'

He crossed over to her placing both hands around her shoulders and kissed her gently. His wandering hands still managed to stray to the tops of her thighs leaving her fuming with anger.

'Don't do that!'

'You've changed your tune; normally you can't get enough of me. Okay, you said you wanted to go, so once I've got rid of the room I will walk you to the station. Tomorrow I'll ring you.'

Pulling on her bathrobe, her mind was spinning. Once again, she had catapulted herself into his quirky and complicated life. He was so demanding and always got his own way. She would have to be careful she didn't accept any of those tablets that he used to give her that messed with her head.

Back in the changing room, as she pulled on her shirt, the tattoo came into sight reminding her of William. Whilst she wanted nothing more to do with him, she knew that he would never have treated her the way Pavvii did. Her mind was made up to end the relationship with the horrible man and cut short her stay. The publisher wouldn't be pleased with this further interruption to her work, but what the hell. She would thank Pavvii for the invitation to stay with him, but say she had to return to Spain. By pretending to be friendly it would give her the opportunity to collect some files she had left behind in his apartment. Then would she extract herself from his weird life.

On calling Pavvii the next morning to say she would see him later that evening, he excitedly told her to wear the red skirt he had given her. It was much shorter than anything she normally wore. It was too revealing, verging on a pelmet and she had no intention of wearing it. Along with the photo he'd given her of him when she arrived back in Finland, the skirt was going in the bin.

On ending the call, she sighed as she acknowledged what a fool she had been. With all the heartache of the breakup with William, she had jumped headfirst into a trap with her old boyfriend. It was another reminder of how chaotic her life had become with much of the agony having been self-inflicted.

She nearly jumped out of skin when her mobile vibrated followed by the horrendous new call tune Pavvii had installed. What if it was him ringing her again? The caller display brought up William's name and number. She cursed herself for not deleting his contact details. Disconnecting the call, she shouted at the screen, 'And you can get lost. Leave me alone.'

* * * *

It was gone eight o'clock when Sarah entered Pavvii's apartment. Surprisingly, despite him being happy to see her, he didn't immediately insist they retire to the bedroom, like so many times before.

She was relieved he hadn't told her off for not wearing the skirt. Instead he couldn't wait to tell her his news about his promotion.

'I've got a huge hike in salary. This is going to help with the divorce settlement. It also means you and I can

248

set up home. Aren't you thrilled?'

'Hold on there. You never said anything about divorce. It's been fun, but I'm leaving Finland in the next few days. My publisher is insisting I cut things short at this end. I just need those research files I showed you.'

Pavvii practically exploded as his voice rose to an ear-piercing scream. 'You aren't going anywhere.'

He reached for a glass and poured a drink for Sarah. 'You are saying crazy things. Calm down and have a drink of this incredible wine.'

'No, you know I want to stop drinking, so stop trying to persuade me.'

'One glass is hardly going to hurt you. I've got some pills that may make you feel good and they are non-addictive. Shall I fetch you one?'

Feeling like this man was once again in charge, the sensible thing to do was leave immediately. Knowing how strong he was, her worry was he could force her to stay.

Not caring about any of her possessions, the moment he left the room she managed to run to the door and open it. Trying not to trip on the staircase, she was soon down on the ground floor. There was no sign of Pavvii who was still back upstairs. It was odd he hadn't chased after her. Hopefully, his obsession with the English woman was finally over, but there would always be another victim waiting in the wings.

☐

Chapter 23

It was always hotter around lunchtime in Tossa and William and Martin settled down in an air-conditioned bar that was busy with holidaymakers all wanting something to eat. This year there had been an influx of German tourists mainly due to the airport taking in extra flights from the economy airlines. The place was so noisy and it was difficult to get served.

Martin managed to get the attention of a waiter who took their order. He then placed both elbows on the table, it was obvious he had some news to convey.

'Look, I don't want you throwing a wobbly and making a scene, but she's back.'

William felt like his heart was going to stop as he whispered, 'No, it can't be true. The villa's been sold and you said Scooter told you she was in Helsinki doing her research.'

'I know, but I've seen her a few times going into a scruffy apartment block off the bus station road. All I can think is she must be renting for a while. I'd have thought Spain was the last place she'd want to live, now the villa has gone.'

They were interrupted by the arrival of the drinks. Martin grabbed his beer and downed it in one go. 'Cor, that was good, I fancy another one.'

All William could think about was the possibility Sarah had returned and had forgiven him. It was a crazy hypothesis, especially in view of the strength of her feelings last time they spoke. Still he pondered with the thought that she might be waiting for him to make contact. He stared at the many couples who all looked happy, then back to Martin who was shaking his head.

'I can tell when you are thinking crazy thoughts. I was hopeful you were getting over her, but now I'm not so sure. My guess is she is between homes waiting to move back permanently to the UK.'

Staring into his half empty glass, William frowned. 'Yeah, I know all about that, but why would she choose to even come back here and live in that dreary part of town?'

'I don't know. Best to let go or you're going to add to the pain you already feel.'

What happened next surprised Martin as he watched his friend rise from the table and leave without any explanation. William was on a mission to find Sarah and sort out their differences. He knew exactly where those apartments were located and, even if he had to knock on every single door, he needed to speak with her.

Dodging through the crowds of people in the main square he clutched his mobile and glanced at the home screen to Sarah's picture. In the bright sunlight it was too dim to view, but he still sought shelter in a doorway to look at her. It was the photo he took on the balcony the day they got engaged.

Walking past the tacky souvenir shops and the new Indian restaurant that was full of people wanting curry despite the crazy heat, he went over what he planned to say to her. He scanned briefly the tree-lined street with the enormous roundabout carpeted with brightly coloured flowers. Ahead was the bus station with numerous coaches parked up and masses of people queuing to board.

The wooden frontage of the apartment block came into sight and it was apparent that it was in dire need of repair. Seeing the peeling paint and so many of the missing red, faded pantiles from the pitched roof this was unquestionably one of the worst apartment blocks in town. Being so close to a petrol station, this property wouldn't have been William's choice of place to live. What was Sarah thinking of ending up in this dump? Had she run out of money or was it just a bolthole until she left for good?

Hesitating in front of the many doorbells that came into sight, his deliberations were disturbed by a screech of tyres. He turned to see a moped that had come to a stop in the middle of the road. A woman had stepped off the pavement and thankfully she appeared unhurt. Her shopping lay littered on the cobblestones with packets of food and a smashed wine bottle covering a large area. She was apologising profusely to the young girl in the bright orange crash helmet who kept swearing in Spanish.

Rushing over to the unfortunate lady who was attempting to scoop up her purchases into two plastic carrier bags, William first checked she was alright. Conversing with the scooter driver in Spanish he also wanted to know if the young girl needed any help.

Attempting to pick up broken glass from the wine bottle he nicked his finger. Wrapping tissues around the wound, it was then he heard a voice behind him. A voice he knew could only be Sarah's.

'William, I saw what you did back there. That cut looks bad.'

His spirit lifted, as this was the first time in ages that she had spoken kindly to him.

William was elated to see her. 'It's nothing, just a scratch. I was on my way over to catch up with you.'

The magic faded abruptly with a return to Sarah's angry voice. 'I don't remember inviting you.'

'I know, but I have something to tell you.'

Her aloof expression worried him. 'I'm not

interested. That was a good thing you did back there, but I stopped to see if I could offer help like you did. Let's get one thing clear, I want you to leave me alone.'

Her outburst left William dumbfounded. He watched her march off swinging her bag like a soldier on parade. Turning his attention back to the spilt red wine on the road it brought back memories of Sarah's drinking. He made sure the remainder of the woman's shopping was safely stowed in her bags and bid her farewell.

* * * *

A surprise visit from Scooter left William wondering just what he wanted. There was no sign of Martin which was strange as they were normally inseparable. Carrying a bottle of wine, the tall man with the New York accent looked so smart in his expensive jeans and blue shirt. He ran his fingers through his long brown hair that today hung loose around his shoulders. William invited him into the apartment.

'I thought you were in London. Where's Martin?'

With a gentle wave of his hand he smiled. 'I arrived yesterday, I'll be here for three days. A whistle stop visit as you British say. It was you I wanted to see.'

Feeling uneasy with the thought that his friend's lover was possibly showing too much interest in him, in a feeble voice he muttered, 'Oh yes.'

Trying to think of an excuse to get rid of Scooter he still gestured for him to sit down. 'Can I offer you a coffee? The thing is I have to go out in about twenty minutes. What is it you want with me?'

Still clutching the wine bottle, Scooter grinned from ear to ear. 'No nothing to drink for me, thanks. I won't keep you long, but you and I have some unfinished business to attend to. Just what have you been up to?'

'Oh, what do you mean? I haven't upset you, have I?'

'I want to talk to you about that visit to my parents. I think you know what I'm on about. I'm referring to that money you gave them.'

Relieved that Scooter wasn't coming on to him, there was still the possibility the man sitting opposite might get nasty. Thinking back to his intervention in his parent's affairs, it may not have been the brightest thing to have done.

'Martin is aware of my visit and wanted to come along but I said no. This one is between you and me. He's now in one of his moods. I'm sure you have experienced the sulking that goes on forever. He's a real drama queen at times.'

William laughed nervously. 'Yep, he has his moments.'

Scooter then handed over the bottle. 'This is a gift for you for making my folks' day.'

William smiled with relief. 'It was a small gesture as they had been so kind to us. I shouldn't have gone behind your back though.'

'At first I was furious that you had interfered. I had no idea my folks were in such a mess and I intend to put things right. Your generosity has touched my heart.'

Relieved to hear this William nodded his head. 'I don't know what to say.'

'My mother said you had won the lottery and shared that money with them. Well, I don't believe for one moment you had a winning ticket. You didn't win, did you?'

'Actually, I did. It was ten pounds.'

Scooter laughed loudly. 'Darling, that's just awesome. Martin said you were an incredible guy and I gotta agree with him.'

'Oh, I don't know about incredible.'

'You have to understand, William, that I never went back to the States as the memories of losing my partner in that car smash were so raw.'

'I can appreciate that, only your parents love you so much.'

'And me them. I now regret not having kept a better eye on Mom and Dad. It was a couple of weeks ago that they rang and mentioned what you had done for them. I got to thinking you must had seen something about the way they were living. I insisted they tell me the truth.'

'Yes, Sarah and I were shocked to see them scraping by like that.'

'Me too. I gotta tell you that last week I jumped on the first plane and took a ride back to Brooklyn and was shocked by what I discovered. The place sucks. I hope they are a lot more comfortable now I have put a few things in place. I just wish I had enough bucks to find them somewhere else to start over again.'

'Good on you.'

'I've sorted out their financial worries and plan to go over at least once a year. You'll meet them again when Martin and I tie the knot. I'll be sure to get them over for our special day. Now, back to that money you gave my folks, I'll credit it back to your bank account. I can do it online.'

'Hold on there, that's not necessary. I just did what I thought best; so don't go insulting me please. That's the end of the matter.'

'Are you kidding mister? Are you for real?'

'No, I meant what I said.'

Scooter shook his head. 'I can see I will upset you if I insist. I can't thank you enough. You are a top guy.'

He then looked at his watch, 'I'd better be off or you'll miss your meeting. You said twenty minutes and I've been here at least that long.'

When Scooter stood up to leave he moved close to William and said, 'Come here. I know you don't normally go for men hugs, but you sure did a good thing back there in New York.'

* * * *

Feeling pleased with himself William acknowledged that for the first time since losing Sarah, there was light at the end of the tunnel. He had good friends and lived in a wonderful place, it was up to him to make the rest of his life work. He was pleased to have given up on his writing as the inclination to create stories had long since vanished. He had unceremoniously dumped his unfinished manuscript in one of the rubbish skips on the edge of town. That chapter had finally come to a close.

One bit of good news was the transfer of the money from Joan's estate. He had intended putting it towards their new marital home, but that was never going to happen now. Instead, part of the funds would be invested in a bond to cover living expenses for the future. The balance was going to charity.

* * * *

On one boiling hot morning, the air was sticky and hot and William went for a dip in the sea whilst Martin sunbathed on the stony strip of beach at the water's edge. The sea was not particularly warm but invigorating and he swam out further than he would normally venture. Martin became concerned his friend was in trouble and hobbled along the sharp stones down to where the shore dropped steeply away. The choppy waves crashed around his feet and threw up fine stones around his legs. Waving madly, he called out to William but got no answer. Being a non-swimmer, his next action was to call out to one of the lifeguards who was chatting to a pretty woman on the beach. The next thing William knew was the hunky young man was heading towards him like he had a propeller driving his body at great speed.

After an embarrassing few moments, the rescue was called off and William swam unaided back to shore.

Shivering, he vigorously shook his towel that someone had managed to tread sand into. It made a cracking sound that disturbed a family close by.

Blinking in the strong sunlight Martin feebly said, 'I was worried you'd got into trouble. Didn't you see me waving?'

'No.'

'You must have seen me waving. I was wearing my hat.'

William stared around the crowded beach to the multitude of men many of whom were wearing similar hats and sarcastically replied, 'You must have on a new one I've not seen before. Thanks for rescuing me though.'

Martin pulled out two cola drinks from his cool box.

'I don't like to drink fizzy drinks. I thought you were bringing my water. You are really annoying me today,' snapped William.

Martin sitting cross-legged on his towel he continued to read his much-crumpled copy of a magazine for British expats. He studied the article that related to a local social group that held evening functions. He whistled tunelessly and stabbed a finger at the page.

'Here we are, this looks right up our street. They have dances, quizzes and walking trips, it sounds okay to me. We could go along if you like. I bet we'd have fun with some great people. They have an Abba tribute band playing on one of the nights.'

Much to William's embarrassment he went on to sing loudly one of the songs and got most of the words wrong.

'Shut up won't you; everyone's listening. If you think a man of my age is going to dance away the night to that music, you have another thing coming.'

'You need to let your hair down and have some fun.'

Of course, he was right, it would do him good to meet new people and take a more active role in the community.

'Okay, you win; but remember, this was your idea and not mine.'

Chapter 24

Despite acknowledging that life had to go on without Sarah, William still experienced moments of sheer unhappiness. Someone and no one was how he thought of himself. He summed up his life as having stepped off a stage for the last time. It may have been better all those years ago, if Martin hadn't dragged him away from that railway track, then there would have been no relationship with Sarah. Telling lies had not been the best way to escape the nightmare. After all, how many times could you dust yourself off and start over again. The comforting thought was that there no longer existed the necessity to bend the truth.

The evening William chose to drown his sorrows in a bar on the outskirts of town was possibly the final straw. Just when he thought nothing else could go wrong, to his horror he spotted Sarah with another man. Judging by the way they were knocking back the drinks it was clear she was well out of it. The scruffy looking Spaniard was kissing the side of her face and she was staring vacantly into space.

Their table was littered with empty glasses with a pool of beer that was dripping onto the floor. Alarmingly, people were staring at the amorous advances of Sarah's companion. William gazed at her hair that looked unwashed and much-crumpled clothes. She could easily have been mistaken for an alcoholic. Above the noise of the crowd her voice could be heard as she shouted out with all her might for another drink.

Here was the woman he loved more than anything in the world and this animal was pawing her in a public place. He glanced around the dingy surroundings of the bar that was obviously a serious drinkers' den and sighed. It was noisy and the place smelt of stale beer. Observing the faces of the customers, it was apparent this was their regular haunt as their raised voices filled the old Spanish building. He'd come here himself to have a few drinks and now wished he hadn't.

His eyes strayed to the pathetic woman sprawled over the table in the corner. Sarah's fingers were scraping back long strands of hair from her face. The red handbag he'd given her after they got engaged had been dropped on the way to her seat; someone had probably kicked it, as it lay wedged between the skirting board and a table leg.

William made his way over to where the bag lay to retrieve it and clasped it to his chest. As he caressed the stitched leather he craned his neck to look at Sarah's face, but this time he was really scared, he didn't know if he could take any more. His dilemma was should he stay and help her or take the selfish action and run away?

He ground his teeth and bit hard on his lip. The pain was excruciating. He made no attempt to stem the warm trickle of blood that ran from his mouth.

There was no more room for indecision; he knew what he had to do.

Aware that his interference may lead to him getting hurt, he positioned himself in front of Sarah as he attempted to encourage her to leave with him. The Spaniard who spoke perfect English removed his hand from her shoulder and angrily told him to back off. Clenching his fist, he waved it close to William's face. He then sat down heavily and smiled before turning his attention back to his companion.

William was at his wit's end seeing her so drunk. He kept an eye on the man who may well have had a knife in the pockets of his coat and raised his voice. 'Sarah, you are to come with me.'

Looking blankly at him, he knew she did not even recognise him. Her reply was difficult to decipher, it was something along the lines of her mother telling her not to talk to strangers.

'It's William and I'm taking you home.'

There was no response. He watched her hand desperately reaching for more wine.

It was at this point her partner shoved William onto the floor. People stood back expecting a fight to break out. Fortunately, the bar owner intervened and demanded Sarah and the man leave. He then turned to William who had hurt his arm in the scuffle to check if he was all right. William then scooped up the handbag and left the building.

Following Sarah and the man who were stumbling around on the pavement and knocking into parked cars, he watched them disappear around a corner. He hung back from getting too close as unquestionably there would be trouble. His concern was for Sarah's safety and, after a short rest to catch his breath, he once again set off after them.

Had they entered a building, or God forbid gone behind some houses? He wondered if this was his wake-up call to walk away from her forever. She'd made it perfectly clear she didn't love him anymore. Surely, there had to be a limit to how many times he could look out for her. The woman was on a mission of self-destruction and the more he helped, the worse matters escalated.

Who was he trying to kid? This woman had got under his skin and he was never going to give up hope. In her vulnerable state anything could happen and he had to be there to pick up the pieces.

The streets were quiet and deserted but he pressed on. Under a streetlight he stopped and held the handbag up to the light. He recalled the look on her face when she unwrapped his gift. He'd bought the designer handbag online and now, seeing its sorry state, it summed up their tired and battered relationship. He set off again in an attempt to find them, but there was no sign of Sarah or the man. A church clock in the distance was striking midnight and there was no silver carriage in sight to take home his princess.

* * * *

Throughout the early hours of the morning, William's agonizing recurring dream featured the man in the bar dragging Sarah to his bed. Her head hung limply from the edge of the mattress with eyes that pleaded for the ordeal to end. He pictured himself gazing up to the apartment window unable to help her. Frozen to the spot he heard the church clock strike. Twelve heavy thuds to the gigantic bell signified a further wedge had been placed between Sarah and himself. Was there no end to the misery of this nightmare that was gathering speed all the time?

* * * *

Struggling to cope with all this added anxiety, like many times before, he turned to Martin for help. Looking dishevelled in the clothes he had worn the previous evening the sight that greeted his friend must have been disturbing. Martin noticed a small cut to William's lip and the badly bruised arm.

'God, you look rough. You haven't been fighting

have you?'

This time it was William who demanded a hug. He cried so loudly and at first refused to discuss the previous evening. When they both sat down on the sofa, the story that was eventually relayed was shocking to hear.

'She's a mess and out of her head. I got into a fight when I saw this guy touching her. My worry is he may have had his evil way with her. She had no idea what was going on.'

Martin drew breath. 'I don't want to upset you, but it could have been a new boyfriend. With you two no longer an item you can't go meddling in her affairs. As lovely as she is, she's a total train wreck.'

'I know all that, but I feel responsible for her and I'm not giving up. I don't expect you to understand how I can still love a woman with so many problems, but I do.'

'Behave, won't you. You have carried a torch for this woman and been the perfect gentlemen. What you have been through this year losing your ex-wife and now all this, it's no wonder you feel so low.'

'It's payback time for me.'

'You are your own worst enemy looking out for her. My concern is a man of your age shouldn't be picking fights. I read the other day that someone got knifed in Lloret de Mar; you need to take care.'

Holding back the tears, a small voice rang out. 'I can't let her go. I'm stuck in no man's land. Right now, I feel like I'm finished.'

With a pained expression building on his face, Martin spoke loudly. 'I can't bear seeing you torment yourself in this way. We have to remember Sarah has demons that probably can only be sorted by her and not you.'

William sighed. 'That's if she doesn't end up dead. I just wish deep down I didn't still love her, but I do.'

Martin looked agitated as he nervously rubbed his chin. 'There's something else you should know.'

'I don't think I can take much more of this. It's not about you and Scooter, is it?'

'No, it is something he said to me yesterday when he rang. He confided in me saying that the publisher was running out of patience with Sarah. They've practically had no work out of her and what they have had has been of a poor quality.'

William closed both his eyes and muttered, 'If she doesn't buck her ideas up, her career as an author will soon be over.'

* * * *

A week can be a terribly long time when you are worrying about someone. The last few days saw William writing a letter and delivering it to Sarah's apartment block. Unaware of the actual door number, he asked a young woman on the first-floor landing for clarification. Posting his note through the designated post slot, he wondered if she would even read it. A further envelope was left on the following day. Sadly, neither of his notes would reach Sarah, as the woman had given him the wrong mailbox number.

The days dragged with him spending time walking the town. On more than one occasion he sat on a bench at the Villa Vella area staring at the statue of Pandora. The wonderful bronze lady with the pigeon droppings and ribbons from weddings stood firm and erect as she guarded the town. He observed the tourists on the steep road taking photos of the sculpture. Someone even asked him to assist with a picture of their group. In holiday mode their smiles and excited voices resonated with him.

Not so long ago, he had been a happy individual but now the sun may have been shining, but not for him. All he could think about was his own Pandora wondering if he should try again to contact her.

* * * *

One bit of news that pleased William was from a friend back home who got in touch on Facebook. Having worked in the police force for many years, the advice he gave him for tracing a lost person would be invaluable. His promise to Martin to find his son Billy was still something he planned to undertake. The first step was to gather as much information as he could on the missing man then use social media to assist in tracking him down.

The obvious sites to search were Facebook and the Salvation Army. There were plenty of avenues to check out on the internet. There was a stark warning from his friend that the person may not want to be found or may even be dead.

Martin managed to find some old photos and the description he gave was useful for filling out the online forms for search agencies. It had been such a long time since the father and son had seen each after years of disagreements. His son had turned his back on his parents and friends. Despite the initial searches, no one had discovered anything new about Billy. Back then, the police got involved and the trail ran cold, but this time with William's help, Martin was keen to find his son. Surely it was better to ascertain if Billy was still alive and then there was at least a chance of a reunion.

Fortunately, Martin remembered some of the names of his son's friends to try and contact. His suggestion that they call the family again was also worth a try, but he wouldn't bother with his ex-wife.

Holding his mobile tightly to his face Martin was shaking with fear as the call connected with an old family friend.

The gravelly voice on the phone sounded surprised. 'Ruddy hell, is that really you, Martin. I wasn't sure if you were still alive. Didn't you go to live in France?'

'Yeah, it's me but it's Spain where I live. How are you Simon?'

'More to the point, how are you? You went off the radar.'

'It's a long story, but the reason I'm ringing is I haven't spoken to my son Billy for many years. My wife, or should I say ex-wife, and I spent ages trying to track him down and now I'm having another go.'

There was a pause, then a nervous cough. 'Well I might be able to help you there as he got in touch about three years ago and lives in London. You will remember he always got on well with our Kevin and I think they meet up every so often. I would have thought your wife would have told you all this already.'

Switching off the speaker function on his phone, Martin turned swiftly to William. He was seething with anger. 'Bloody woman hates me. She knew how upset I was losing Billy and yet still couldn't be bothered to tell me he was okay.'

'Hello, are you still there?'

'Sorry, the signal here is bad. I can't thank you enough for telling me he's safe, more than the rest of my family thought to do. Have you got his address?'

'Sorry, no, but I can give you my son' e-mail. I think he's also probably on Facebook. You have heard of Facebook?'

'Not sure about that one, but no sweat, my mate here

is a dab hand with all things electronic. I must go now and thanks.'

'Hold on a moment, I need your e-mail address to send you the details. I'll let Kevin know to expect something from you.'

There was a frantic struggle as Martin couldn't remember his user name. It was William who came to his rescue as he checked his own phone for the details. When the call ended Martin pocketed his mobile and put both arms in the air. 'At least I know he's alive, no thanks to those guys back home. The next step is to find out where he lives and hope he will agree to a visit.'

William was overjoyed with the result. 'Sounds like a good plan. What do think about the two of us taking a flight back home and staying for three days? With a fair wind we'll track down Billy.'

'Sounds like a plan to me.'

'Even if the two of you don't meet up you can draw a line under the past knowing he is safe. And, I can pay my respects to my son Steven again.'

'Thanks a million, I owe you one.'

'It's the least I can do after all you've done for me.'

Martin excitedly started to open the plastic shopping bag he had dropped on the floor. 'I nearly forgot that I have a present for you.'

'It's not my birthday until September.'

William stared at the festive wrapping paper with the images of Christmas trees and smiled. Once opened, a chunky set of gold cufflinks fell onto his hand. He was overjoyed with his friend's generosity but wondered if he would ever wear them. The last time he wore a long-sleeved shirt was with his suit for Joan's funeral.

* * * *

The business of finding Billy was fairly straight forward as Martin's old friend's son came up trumps with an address. The plan was to take a chance on arriving unannounced.

Staying in a budget hotel off Old Street in North London, nothing was right for Martin as he complained his room was cramped and noisy with the lift directly outside his door. The cooked breakfast was also disappointing with just two slices of bacon. If the truth be known, he may have been having second thoughts about being there. It was a balancing act for William keeping him positive. On their first morning, Martin spoke rudely to him, which was rather upsetting. It was a callous remark about him not knowing how it felt to lose a son. Determined to keep things on an even keel, he tried a different tactic.

'I may need your help. I know you are nervous about seeing Billy again. Would you mind visiting the cemetery with me? I understand from the family they planted a rose bush for Joan there. I'm not sure I can handle all this grief having now lost Joan and Steven.'

A more confident Martin was there for him saying it would be a pleasure.

* * * *

North London was where Billy lived in a small terraced house within walking distance of King's Cross Station. William was banking on the fact that providing the man was not on holiday or working shifts there was a chance of a meeting. He questioned whether, with the family history, he would even want to see his father again? A missing piece of information that Martin revealed over breakfast in the hotel was the wayward lad also had a drink problem. An account followed of him stealing from his parents. All of this had occurred at the time of Martin's announcement that he was coming out and planned to live with his lover. Billy struck his father so hard that he needed stitches to his head. The young man panicked and fled from the house to effectively disappear off the map.

When the prodigal son returned to the fold, Martin's ex-wife had chosen not to tell her husband. It was possible she never forgave him for divorcing her. The opportunity was there to keep him in the loop as she was aware of his address in Spain. This resulted in years of sadness for Martin as he punished himself for not being a good father.

Hanging about at the end of the street for hours on end Martin hoped to catch a glimpse of his lad. He was beginning to give up hope of seeing him. It must have been a matter for concern for other the residents with a stranger watching their every move. It was fortunate that nobody had called the police.

He kept his eye on the sorry-looking Victorian two-bedroomed house with three wheelie bins placed in front of the bay window. A broken, wooden gate lay in the long grass of the small garden with rubbish piled high against the brickwork of the house. He spied a much-dented paint tin without a lid that sat on the windowsill. Someone had started to decorate the front of the property but had given up at about the height of ten feet. This house was definitely the worst maintained home in the entire street.

The only person to come out of the property was a youngish looking woman dressed in tight jeans and a jacket. She wheeled a young child in a pushchair; a boy, about two years old, with a runny nose and clutching a teddy bear. His mother walked straight past Martin not giving him a second glance. What was going through his mind was whether or not the child was his grandson. Where was Billy though? Perhaps he should have knocked on the door rather than sneaking about in the tree-lined street.

An almighty sound of the front door being yanked open made Martin jump. A man in torn jeans and long hair ran out onto the pavement. To all intents and purposes, he could have been a leftover hippy from the seventies. His voice boomed out as he shouted at the woman who was hurrying away from the house.

The South London tone startled Martin. 'Lisa, come back 'ere.'

She ignored him and continued to make her way down the street.

Billy was about to return indoors when he caught sight of his father standing beside a white van.

As if unable to believe his eyes he stood rigidly still and shouted, 'Shit, Dad is that you?'

Nervously moving away from the vehicle, Martin struggled to form his words. 'Y… y… yes… it's me son. Don't be alarmed, I'm not here to cause trouble.'

'You nearly gave me a heart attack creeping up like that. I thought you lived in Spain.'

'I still do. We need to chat; I won't stop long. I've got something to say that has waited too long already.'

The aggressive looking man with the face piercings that included a ring through his upper lip suddenly appeared friendlier. He gestured for his father to enter his home. Shamefacedly, Martin followed observing the poorly decorated interior that smelt of stale tobacco. In the sparsely furnished lounge there was just one area to sit. The much-stained sofa was littered with baby clothes and toys. A large TV was showing a football match, which Billy switched off. There was the smell of burnt toast and bottles of beer were scattered around with ashtrays over spilling with cigarette butts. Martin stared at the cat litter tray in the kitchen that looked like it hadn't been cleaned out recently. He was aware of a dripping tap that was making a sloshing sound in the washing-up bowl full of dishes.

Lighting a cigarette, Billy blew a cloud of smoke into the room. 'What the hell are you doing here?'

'I found out last week you were okay and I wanted to see you. All the time you were missing, I didn't know what to think. Your mum didn't care to tell me where to find you.'

'You look older and fatter Dad. You haven't left your husband waiting in the street, have you?'

Martin frowned. 'Sarcasm doesn't suit you. Yes, I'm still gay if you really want to know. I'm here to make sure you are okay. How are you?'

Scratching his bare arm, Billy raised his eyes to the ceiling. It was obvious with the marks on his skin that taking drugs was still the path he was treading.

'Me, I'm just ace. My partner is threatening to take my son and live with her mother. The bitch!'

'Oh God, that's terrible. Your little boy, what's his name and is he my grandson?'

'I don't want you anywhere near Drake. Look, there is no future for you and me. You weren't exactly good to me as a teenager and I'll never forget the way you treated me. You told me to sod off and that's exactly what I did. Leaving you and Mum was the best thing I ever did.'

'And I'm sorry. I've never forgiven myself.'

Remembering back to the unhappy years with his wife and the times he took out his frustration on Billy, he

271

was right, it had been unforgivable taking it out on the boy. Their relationship had been at rock bottom and coping with parenting was difficult, especially with their son experimenting with drugs.

'I was the worst father on the planet, that was me. I've regretted being so awful to you. I just want to say sorry.'

Billy's next statement annoyed him as he instinctively knew what was coming.

'You could start by giving me some money.'

'That's not the answer, is it. You will buy more drugs like before.'

'Then you can get the hell out of my pad.'

Martin attempted to say goodbye but the scream telling him to go confirmed there was no chance of reconciliation. His earlier plan to hand over some cash would have been inappropriate with the lifestyle that Billy had adopted.

Outside in the street he heard the door slam shut behind him. There was every probability that the two of them would never meet up again.

However badly the lad had turned out, he was content to have seen him this one last time. It hadn't been the outcome that he had wished for, but at least now he could draw a line under the matter.

* * * *

The following morning was all about honouring two very special people in William's life. Within the cemetery grounds the garden of remembrance was peaceful to walk through. Six enormous flowerbeds with individual rosebushes celebrated so many lost lives. The pleasing thing was the beds were beautifully kept with neatly

272

trimmed grass. On viewing Joan's inscription plate, William kissed the tips of two of his fingers and touched the shiny brass surface. He whispered that he missed her. Laying a single rose on the soil between the bushes, he then extracted a tissue from his pocket to polish the nameplate.

Moving on to Steven's grave the area was immaculate with the trimmed grass neatly licking the sides of the concrete plinth. Someone had obviously recently visited as there was an attractive plant in a pot that brightened up the plot. Martin hung his head down low as he heard his friend sigh. William inspected the stone for signs of wear and leant down to place another rose on the base. The last thing he did before leaving was to glance at Steven's watch that was visible on his arm. How he wished he could see him again, be it for just one short moment, to tell him he was sorry.

* * * *

Later that evening, their meal in a hamburger restaurant in central London saw Martin enjoying his treat with an extra portion of thick cut fries and plenty of tomato sauce. Both men were talkative but steered clear of the sadder moments of their trip. They spoke of the future and their plans to start afresh. There was Martin's wedding on the horizon and the surprise announcement of his wish to have his closest friend as his best man.

They were interrupted by the pinging sound of an e-mail arriving on Martin's mobile. Excited to discover it was Scooter messaging him, the happy face soon turned to a long one.

'He says he called Sarah on the phone on the day we left and she was saying strange things. Now he can't get hold of her and is worried she may have done something stupid.'

William's heart sank on hearing this. Was there no end to the misery? The trip had brought about a certain degree of acceptance of the necessity to start over again, with or without her. Now, a new calamity had suddenly kicked off. They would now have to go and check on Sarah when they returned home. Fearing she'd been drinking to excess again, he considered just what awaited them on their return? Had she had a fall and couldn't get to the phone or worse.

Chapter 25

In the sweltering sun, wheeling their cases at speed to Sarah's apartment proved to be hard work. There had been no time to go home to freshen up and on arriving William led the way up the staircase. He hammered on the front door. To their amazement an old woman in a long, black dress opened the door. The smell of cooking wafted into their faces. It was an unpleasant aroma that reminded William of his mother's attempt to cook liver and bacon.

'Is Sarah alright?' asked William anxiously in his near perfect Spanish.

The mostly toothless woman leaned on her stick and was clearly puzzled.

This time he mentioned the lady in question was English and her name was Sarah Barney.

This brought an immediate reaction as she informed him that the woman lived on the top floor at number eleven. Suddenly William knew the letters he had popped through the wrong post box had not reached Sarah.

Leaving their cases outside the apartment they dashed up the stairs to reach the next grim-looking landing. With crumbling plaster hanging precariously from the walls it was hard to believe they were still in the picturesque town of Tossa de Mar. The distinct smell of cat's pee was ignored as they reached the correct apartment.

'Sarah, it's me. Let me in please.'

There was no reply and Martin, being the heavier of the two men, took a run at the door that sprang open sending splinters of the wooden frame around the stairwell.

'You idiot you've ruined the door!' shouted William.

Entering the small apartment, the prospect of finding her in a terrible state was daunting. Once inside there was no sign of Sarah.

Martin whistled as he went back to inspect the broken woodwork. 'Sod it. I just bashed her door in and she's not even here. Do you think she will understand that we were concerned?'

'I really wish you hadn't done that. Why you don't think before doing things is a mystery. Knowing Sarah, she will hit the roof when she sees the damage you have done. I wonder if we can get it repaired before she returns.'

Pulling out his mobile Martin swiped the screen to view his contacts list. 'Possibly Dave down at the club can help. He's an ace carpenter.'

Thankfully the tradesman answered the call with a promise to arrive within the hour. In the meantime, a decision was made to visit the pizza store opposite the apartment building. They would sit on the wall and eat their late lunch while keeping an eye out for the repairman.

After just two slices of the twelve-inch Margarita with extra chorizo topping, both men panicked when they caught site of Sarah approaching. She was dressed in a beautiful blue summer dress with a leather handbag swinging on her shoulder.

With a worried look on her face she angrily confronted them. 'What are you two doing here? Why don't you eat your disgusting food elsewhere?'

William launched in, 'We've had an accident.'

Laughing Sarah replied, 'Judging by the pizza on your face I can see that.'

'No, you don't understand. It was your door.'

'My door!'

'Yes, Martin bashed it in to see if you were alright.'

'Bloody hell, what possessed you to do such a thing?'

'We got a message from Scooter saying he couldn't get hold of you and we thought you might be in trouble.'

She shrugged her shoulders. 'Oh, not him again. He was saying all sorts about discontinuing my contract so I just ignored his messages and phone calls. I don't like being threatened. I imagine you thought I was drunk or dead.'

Martin chipped in, 'Well what were we to think? I've got my mate in town coming to fix everything so I'll leave you in William's capable hands while I go and chase him up.'

Off he went dragging his purple case muttering something on the lines of he could do without all this hassle.

Sarah gazed down at William's luggage. 'Are you off somewhere?'

'No, just back from London and we got the call from Scooter who was concerned for your welfare.'

'I just wish people would stop interfering and that includes you.'

She pointed to Martin's half eaten pizza that he had dropped on the wall and raised her eyes to the sky. 'What a mess. Can't you teach him some manners?'

Scooping up the discarded food into the torn box William mumbled a gentle apology.

'Come on then, you need to show me just what you've done upstairs, but first dump that muck in the bin over there. I expect you to mend my door properly. You can bring your bag into the lobby if you want.'

'Thanks. I give you my word the damage will be repaired as good as new. I really am sorry.'

'Not as much as the landlord will be if he gets wind of this and he will if it needs a new lock. My short-term lease ends soon and then I'm off to London for good. Hopefully, William, you and I will never meet again.'

Unhappy to hear her say this, he remained silent as they climbed the staircase.

On catching sight of the damage, she slapped her hand hard against the wall. 'Oh, for God's sake, are you two mental, or what?'

He was amazed that she invited him into her apartment. As they entered the clean and tidy lounge his eyes scanned for signs of any bottles, but there were none to be seen. Earlier he had been convinced they would find her on the floor in a pool of sick, or they may have arrived too late to help.

He gazed at the tired-looking apartment with poorly painted walls with splashes of white on the tiled floor edges. The cheap, modern furniture did nothing for the room, or the hideous pictures of Spanish dancers that hung crookedly on the walls. Whilst he didn't look out of the window, he knew the view would not be of the wonderful sea but of the approach road to the bus station.

Having calmed down, Sarah volunteered information on her imminent return to London and the inevitable showdown with her publisher. William wished her luck, but she suddenly became irritable again saying she didn't know why she had let him come into her apartment. She stressed that, as Martin was sorting out the repair, he should now go.

On the way down the staircase he remembered to collect his case from the ground floor. Outside in the street it was noisy with coaches pulling into the tired depot. He texted Martin to chase up the repair. A reply swiftly shot back: *The guy is going to be another thirty minutes. It's going to cost an arm and a leg to fix – could murder a beer.*

* * * *

Over the next week, William must have seen Sarah at least four times in the town as she went about her business shopping and going for walks. Each time he attempted to talk to her she gave him short shrift. On one occasion he told her that he'd written to her and posted the letters through what he thought was her post box.

'What did you write to me for. What part of back off don't you understand?'

'I thought you deserved a proper explanation of what happened in the past.'

Sarah gritted her teeth. 'I think I have all the details already. You cocked up big time. Nothing you could say holds any interest for me. It's hardly going to change what you did, is it?'

'Why don't you ask that lady on the floor below if she kept the letters I put in her box?'

'No William, even if she gives them to me I wouldn't read them.'

Annoyed and momentarily not caring if he made things worse between them, William snapped, 'You never know a person properly until the shit hits the fan. I still care about you. When are you going to give me a break?'

Turning on her heels Sarah stormed off. He watched her walk swiftly away from him. She stopped briefly to talk to a woman in the doorway of a shop. Cemented to the spot, William watched her kiss the woman on both cheeks before saying goodbye. Just before she set off again she turned to look back to where he was standing. This time she smiled, only it was a hard smile. How he wished he could get the old Sarah back, but knew he couldn't.

* * * *

Over the following days William busied himself with helping down at the English library in an effort to take his mind off Sarah. He played with the idea that with a bit of luck her meeting in London would be successful and she may even decide to return to Spain to live. He just had to find a way to tell her the truth about his son's mistake and hopefully she would stop blaming him. Until then he would remain like a shadow with nowhere to fall.

☐

Chapter 26

The night the Abba tribute band was due to perform there was an almighty thunderstorm and torrential rain. This was crazy weather after such a glorious day and the tourists anxiously dodged the puddles as they sought out restaurants for their evening meal. Martin and William ate early before braving the elements to walk to the hall where the performance was due to begin at nine o'clock. Sheltering under Martin's huge golf umbrella they arrived at the bar to discover the place was heaving with people, many of whom appeared to be their age were dancing to seventies disco music. The venue was larger than the exterior suggested with a small stage and restaurant area to the rear of the premises. The aroma of fried chicken and fries filled the air prompting Martin to say he was hungry again.

William frowned when he saw the queue for the bar and insisted Martin got the drinks. As he stood close to the dance floor, he spotted a woman and instinctively knew there was something familiar about her. Dressed in denim shorts and blue bikini top, she was gyrating her trim body to the music of Van Morrison belting out Brown Eyed Girl. He caught a glimpse of her freckled face and tiny nose. She couldn't have been more than five feet tall and was in good shape for her age, which he gauged to be similar to his own.

Captivated by her long brown hair which was being thrown from side to side with her enthusiasm for dancing, she reminded him of his first girlfriend. As a youngster at the Glastonbury festival he had first met Carol. Similar to today's appalling weather conditions he recalled standing around for hours in soaked clothes pretending it was all worthwhile. He wouldn't have attended if it hadn't been for the incredible bands that were due to play and his friends making arrangements to get there.

Back in those days he enjoyed listening to pop music in the privacy of his bedroom but finding himself at this enormous show left him feeling uneasy. On the downside there were the vast crowds, camping and having to endure disgusting toilets; the plus side was unquestionably meeting this incredible lively girl. The whirlwind relationship that followed with Carol saw William lose his virginity.

And now, here on this evening in Spain, this woman could easily be his Carol from the past. She had been the girlfriend who quickly became bored with his old-fashioned ways. She soon moved on to date someone more exiting, but it had been good while it lasted.

Today here in this Spanish bar, this older woman who reminded him of his old flame from forty plus years back, was holding his attention. When the song finished she stood perfectly still and it was then that their eyes met over the crowded dance floor. She crossed the room and stood by William who could now see the crow's-feet around her eyes and the abundance of makeup that was plastered on her face.

She was the first to speak. 'Hello I'm Lisa; are you here on your own?'

'Oh hello, I'm here with a friend. I'm William. Are you local to Tossa?'

'Me, yes. My husband and I moved here when he was made redundant.'

'Husband?' said William as he looked nervously around the bar for a man of his age that may well disapprove of his wife chatting him up.

'My other half and I have separated. He's already gone back to the UK.'

'Oh, I'm sorry to hear that. I was admiring your dancing. It took me back to when I was young.'

Then what happened unsettled him as she linked arms with him. He pulled sharply away. He certainly wasn't in the mood for striking up a new relationship with this girl or anyone else, especially with someone who was in the process of a divorce. Just for a moment seeing her dance brought back his younger and carefree days. On reflection he wasn't interested her. What was he playing at encouraging her? His heart belonged to Sarah and always would.

It was at this point Martin finally arrived with the drinks and William introduced Lisa. Determined to be rid of her, over the sound of the disco, and not caring if she heard, he spoke loudly, 'Help me get shot of her please.'

Then to his astonishment Martin reached out to hold his hand and informed the woman that the two of them were an item. She left without saying a further word.

'I can't get over what you just did Martin. God knows what she thinks now. Don't ever hold my hand again.'

'You told me to get rid of her and that's what I did. Wasn't she your type?'

'Definitely not. She was coming on to me and I already have a partner, don't I?'

'Yep and now this disco woman thinks it's me,' said Martin looking pleased with himself.

'Thanks a bunch, fancy telling her that.'

'My guess is she won't even remember you in the morning. Anyway, I was pleased to see you making an attempt to talk to other women. How many times lately have I told you there is life after Sarah.'

William decided to ignore the remark and noticed the Abba tribute band setting up. He roared with laughter when he spotted one of the female singers already dressed in her costume. At her age she looked ridiculous in huge white flares and a skimpy, shiny top. Missing today for this unfortunate performer were the platform heels as she had a broken leg and hobbled onto the stage with the aid of crutches.

Both men were now falling about in hysterics and spilling lager on the floor.

'I never thought I'd see a one-legged Abba singer,' joked Martin.

'Yeah, but just look at the guy on the organ with the tombstone teeth and bald head. He bears no image to Benny who wrote the songs.'

Despite the appearance of the members of the group, when they launched into Dancing Queen the place rocked. They were professionals with voices that could well have been those of the real band. The flashing disco lights lit up the bar and people sang along to the songs. William even joined in with his awkward dancing much to the amusement of the people around them.

The performance proved to be a great success that transported many people back to the seventies. Fortunately, the enigmatic dancer Lisa was nowhere to be seen. She had disappeared just like William's old girlfriend Carol had done as soon as she grew tired of him.

When it was time to go they shuffled out into the street. The rain had stopped and along with others they joined in with singing tunes that still meant so much to them. Martin said goodnight then set off for his house and no doubt for something to eat. His rendition of the Abba hits made William laugh. He never could remember the words of pop songs so made up his own.

Coming out tonight and joining in with the fun felt good. It showed that he could enjoy himself without fretting over what Sarah was up to.

With all the grief of recent months nothing had made him laugh more than witnessing that girl singer shuffling around on the stage. Balancing on her crutches, he had to admit she still managed to deliver a good evening's entertainment.

And now he was almost home and still feeling bright was determined as ever to hang on in there for Sarah. If it took the rest of his life, then so be it. Somehow, she would have to come to terms with the past. He would find a way to forgive her crazy ways and addiction to alcohol. It was just a waiting game to be endured until they got back together again.

Chapter 27

The following day Martin had begrudgingly agreed to his partner's request to drive Sarah to the airport. He had deliberately chosen not to tell William. A meeting had been arranged in London to see her publisher whom she had upset by not keeping to the terms of her contract. She told Martin that she hadn't written a thing in months and was going to have to promise to get her act together.

Holding her passport in her hand, she nervously said, 'I can't see that my chat with them will go well as I'm way behind with the rewrites. They warned me if I didn't turn up to this meeting they would wash their hands of me.'

Martin had already had the story first-hand from his partner Scooter. He feared that she had blown any chance of recovering ground as a writer with her time about to be called. Severing their agreement would effectively leave her without representation. It was essential she convince them she was prepared to honour her commitments.

Driving along the dual carriageway, the rain suddenly started to fall. Heavy storms were not unknown even in mid-summer on the Costa Brava. The sunroof, that always leaked, had a small towel wedged around the rubber seal. Martin had failed to clean off patches of white mould on the leather interior from previous downpours. The smell of petrol in this old car was particularly bad today. This was the vehicle that he had purchased on arriving in Spain all those years ago. The engine reliability had recently become an issue. Then again owning a relic from the mid-nineties had its problems with many expensive repairs. Most of the time the car was garaged and started first time, but it was definitely costing too much to maintain.

The thumping of rain on the windscreen and roof of the car was so loud they both had to shout to be heard. Slowing down due to poor visibility and the build-up of traffic, Martin glanced at his watch and frowned. As was his way, he never left enough time to reach the airport, but today it would be touch and go for Sarah to check in.

'We may be running a bit late with this rain, but I'll do my best.'

He changed the subject away from the appalling weather to her luggage. 'I see you only brought one suitcase, does this mean you are coming back to Tossa?'

'No, that's me done with the sunshine. The bulk of my stuff was shipped last month and is stored at my brother's place back home. I plan to live with him and his family for a month and then rent. Everything is so expensive there, not like here in Spain.'

Martin chanced what he said next. 'I'm sad you guys split up.'

'I'm not. I'm much happier right now.'

'I hope you don't mind me asking, but is there no chance you can make up with William? You don't sound so cross about things just lately.'

Stretching her legs further into the footwell of the old Ford she quickly replied, 'Nope, we've gone too far along the path for any reconciliation. You are right though, I'm not as angry with him as in the past, but he slipped up big time not levelling with me. I assume you know about what he did all those years ago and how it affected me.'

'Yes, he confided in me and I can assure you that you have it all wrong. He's the kindest person I've ever come across. What you are not aware of is the money he gifted to Scooter's parents. They really were in such a mess financially and hid the fact from their son. The outcome is Scooter has already visited New York and is now helping them. This is all down to my friend's wonderful intervention.'

'Oh my God, he did that? He didn't tell me.'

'That's him, never looking for thanks. He also encouraged me to find my son who I'd lost touch with. Again, without his help this would never have come about. You also need to know the horrific mistake at the undertakers wasn't his fault.'

Sarah let out a startled gasp. She closed her eyes and gripped tightly the edge of her seat. 'Let me have that one again, he wasn't responsible?'

'Yeah, it was his son who got it wrong, not him. Steven, unbeknown to his father, was suffering from stress and made a number of poor decisions. William's mistake was in being absent from work so often and leaving Steven to cope on his own. He still blames himself for neglecting the business and letting his son down so badly. Tragically a few days after your terrible experience at the undertakers, Steven died of a heart attack on the premises. William first lost his son, business, then his wife and almost gave up on his own life.'

Holding a hand to her face, Sarah's mind was literally doing somersaults as she struggled to process the news.

'So you see, he covered up Steven's errors saying he was responsible for the mix-up. He just had to protect his son's reputation.'

'I had no idea.'

'Yeah, and three months later, I met my friend whilst he was suffering from a breakdown. I helped him to believe in himself again. I have so much respect for that man and all he does for everyone.'

Felling desperately sad Sarah said, 'If only I'd known.'

'Would it have made a difference?'

'Well, possibly yes. It's too late now as there is too much water under the bridge. I have to start my life again and it won't be with William. It's imperative I get to London to convince the publisher I'm serious this time.'

With a mixture of annoyance and sarcasm in his voice Martin momentarily took his hands off the steering wheel. 'Forgive me for thinking love is more important than your work. So, you are going to walk away from the most caring and wonderful man in the world.'

'Stop it Martin, you are making me cry.'

'You must know he worships you and I suspect you still care for him. What about everything he did for you? Let's not forget about your drinking – He tried his best to be there for you.'

She closed her eyes and above the sound of the noisy engine yelled, 'Even if I thought we had a future together, I'm not sure he'd want me.'

Martin shook his head. 'Of course, he wants you. Any fool can see he is mad about you.'

'Well for a start, who would want an alcoholic like me?'

'So, you can finally admit it. Did something happen in Finland?'

'You could say that. There was a guy who kept trying to get me to have a drink and I slipped up big time. When I got back to Spain I hit the booze bars around Tossa. My hangover was so bad that I can honestly say I can't recall what occurred the previous evening. I was convinced that nobody would care if I lived or died.'

Martin banged the dashboard hard with his hand which frightened Sarah. 'That's not true and you know it!'

'I wasn't thinking straight and just saw William as a threat. I was starting to get my act together again but shut myself away in the apartment for a while. Then you guys came to my aid and broke my door.'

'Ah, yes, the dreaded door. Tell me, how long is it since you had a drink?'

'Nearly a month and I've attended a few meetings with alcoholics anonymous again. It's early days but I'm determined to beat this affliction.'

'Wow, that's the best news ever. William will be over the moon to hear that.'

'Yeah, but much of what I've gone through could have been avoided.'

'What do you mean?'

'Like, I ignored the doctor's advice on my medication. Taking alcohol with the tablets was stupid and yet I did it again and again. It's no wonder I got into such a state. Depression does silly things to your mind and somehow being merry from the booze just takes over.'

Martin was furious. 'So, all the worrying my best friend has been doing was down to you ignoring medical advice on not mixing drink with medication.'

She paused and then added, 'I'm not going back to William.'

'I'm beginning to think you going back to the UK is probably the best solution for us all.'

Sarah lent back in her seat and said not another word for the rest of the journey.

Despite the rainstorm they made good time and Martin dropped her off and helped with her suitcase. She hugged him briefly and he told her to take care. Before he climbed back into the car he watched her walk to the entrance and must have been wondering if that was the last time he would ever see her.

* * * *

Walking through the busy departure terminal Sarah headed for the baggage drop. So many questions must have been shooting around her mind. How different things may have been if the truth had been known from the outset.

As she queued to hand over her case, her attention was drawn to an elderly man who dropped his shoulder bag on the floor. He was frantically trying to retrieve coins and travel documents. She could tell he was distressed as he scrambled to pick up his belongings. The scene reminded her of William's kindness on the day the scooter driver and the woman had their altercation. He'd made sure both parties were unhurt before setting to work on collecting up the scattered shopping. He even cut his finger but made light of the injury as he helped everyone to get on their way. This is what William did; he was the perfect gentleman.

It irked her that nobody around the proximity of the desks was helping this man. She quickly wheeled her suitcase to one side before going to his aid. He was so grateful to her as she helped scoop up the last of his possessions. On saying goodbye, the anxious traveller touched her arm and kindly said, 'There aren't many kind-hearted people like you around. I hope someone touches your heart like you have done mine today.'

His words were the catalyst for kickstarting her life again. She glanced back at her luggage, which she decided not to retrieve, and walked away in the direction of the exit. Just like the case she had just discarded, the important meeting in London suddenly bore no importance. The writing dream had finally come to an end with more important matters to attend to.

Outside the rain had stopped falling but the puddles were still there as the cars pulled up in front of the terminal building. A shaft of bright sunlight and comforting warm air made her feel happy to be alive. The feeling of calmness was overwhelming. A glorious sun overhead signified not just the immense heat but reassurance that in an instant her life could finally be back on track.

When she climbed into a shiny yellow taxi, the driver asked where she was going.

With a smile on her face Sarah replied, 'Home to my fiancé... Sorry, I mean Tossa de Mar please.'